EXSANGUINATED

THE BOOK OF MALADIES VOLUME 7

D.K. HOLMBERG

ASH
PUBLISHING

PREPARATIONS BEGIN

A lec moved a stack of papers on the desk, not content with how they were organized. There was nothing about this room that felt quite right, but mostly because it was far larger than any he had ever had before. Now that he had been moved to the masters' quarters, promoted within the university to a position where he still didn't know that he belonged, he was given a suite of rooms, far more than he thought he deserved.

The room was practically empty. Alec didn't have enough belongings to fill it. Whatever sparse belongings he once had destroyed in the fire that consumed his father's original apothecary shop, burned down when the Thelns first attacked the city. Everything he had could fit within the satchel that he carried with him, the notes and references he had made since coming to the university all he prized any longer.

A knock came at the door, and Alec turned. Beckah poked her head in.

Her eyes were tight, and she frowned, the perpetual smile she once had long since faded. Ever since the attack, and Master Helen's attempt to kill her, Beckah no longer smiled quite as easily.

"You don't have to stay at the door," Alec said.

"I wasn't sure," she said.

He stared at her. There was an uncertainty in Beckah that had never been there before, and he felt it his responsibility to see if he could help eliminate that. What happened to her was his fault. Master Helen had attacked Beckah because of him. "You're welcome to come in. I would be happy to have you here."

He didn't have too many visitors. Since his promotion to master physicker, he was still trying to come to grips with his role at the university. It wasn't that reaching the master physicker level wasn't what he wanted. Ever since reaching the university, becoming a master physicker had been the dream, though it had been one he thought unlikely, at least for him to obtain it in such a short period of time. Alec had only been at the university for barely more than a year. In that time, he had been promoted quickly—far more quickly than anyone else ever had. Part of that was out of necessity, but part of it was because of the training preparation his father had given him long before he had ever attempted to come to the university.

"How are you settling in?" she asked.

"I'm settling in about as well as I can. It doesn't take too long, but mostly that's because I don't have much to do."

Beckah looked around the room. "There's so much space here."

"You'll have more space after your testing."

"I don't know that I'm ready," she said. She stared down at her hands, fidgeting.

"What do you mean? You were ready months ago."

She looked up at him, and her eyes remained haunted. What exactly had Master Helen done to her? Beckah hadn't shared, and when they had found her, she was tired and sickly, but not poisoned, not the way that Alec had been. He wished she would speak of it, if only for him to understand what she'd gone through so he could help her better.

"I might have been ready months ago, but not anymore."

"Beckah—"

She took a deep breath, forcing a smile. "When I'm ready, maybe it'll be easier with you there. You *will* be there, won't you?"

"There aren't that many master physickers remaining," Alec said.

Far too many had left the university. Master Helen had forced them out, taking them with her, and there had been no sign of where they went. That troubled Alec more than it troubled others.

"You didn't answer," she said.

Alec smiled. "I will be there."

"That might make it easier."

There was a knock at the door, which Beckah had left slightly ajar, and Alec looked over and saw Jalen. He wore a long physicker jacket that came to his knees. It was the jacket of a full physicker. He'd tested for that but still had not yet achieved the master physicker level, not the way Alec had. His own testing had been straightforward, though time-consuming. It had consisted of a week of questions given to him by each of the master physickers, spending hour after hour sharing his knowledge, but it seemed that his creation of the easar paper had been the most convincing. It was almost as if he had proven himself with the discovery. Alec felt a little guilty about the fact that he hadn't really discovered anything. He had simply followed instructions in a book his mother had left long ago, and it had been the prince—now the king—who had discovered the svethwuud to be the key.

"I didn't know you had company," Jalen said.

Beckah got to her feet and bowed deeply.

Jalen glanced from Alec to Beckah, shaking his head. "That's not necessary here. "Here, I am a physicker, the same as you… Well, the same as you will be."

Beckah flushed and lowered her eyes.

Jalen glanced over to Alec, frowning.

"She's not certain she wants to be tested," Alec said.

"Why?"

"After everything that happened, she's…" Alec shrugged. He didn't fully understand what she was feeling, but he was determined to find out, if only to better understand what Master Helen had done to her. It had turned her into a cautious person who had lost all the self-confidence she'd once shown. Alec would see that she was restored to the woman he knew.

"We need good physickers," Jalen said.

"I understand, Sire. It's just that I—"

Jalen stepped forward and shook his head. He touched

her on the arm, and she looked up, meeting his eyes. "Here, we are all physickers."

"It's just... It's just that I don't know whether I can continue to do this," she said.

"I know that you can do it," Alec told her. "If it's simply a matter of gaining confidence, then use the people who care about you. Use your friends." She looked at him, and he could see a brief glimmer of hope in her eyes. "And if you need a mentor, then use me."

She eyed him for a moment, and finally nodded slowly. Alec felt a little guilty about offering himself in that way, knowing that now, not only did he offer his friendship, but because he'd been promoted to master physicker, she as a student wasn't in a position to refuse his offer, even if she were to want to. Then again, Alec was determined to help her, even if she didn't want to help herself.

"How about I meet you at the hospital ward in a few minutes after I speak with Jalen?" He made a point of using the king's first name, though he still felt awkward with it. It didn't feel quite right for him to be so informal with someone so important, but for Beckah, he needed to show her there was something almost normal about having the king wandering the halls of the university.

She took a deep breath and left the room. When she was gone, Jalen turned away from the door and looked at Alec. "I would pay much to know what Helen did to her during her captivity."

"I would too," Alec said. "She's not the same person she was before."

"Do you think she has turned against us?"

"Beckah? I don't see how that would be possible."

"You saw the documents. You know what Helen was working on."

Alec's gaze drifted to the table set along one wall of his sitting room. On that table was a stack of easar paper, and written on the easar paper were Master Helen's notes detailing her attempt to turn the Kavers who had been working with them against the rest of the Anders family. She had been successful—far more successful than she should have been. Alec was still trying to work through exactly what it was she had done. It was difficult because her method of documentation was somehow different from that of the physickers and from how his father had trained him.

"I know what she was working on, but that doesn't mean that she used Beckah that way. Beckah hasn't turned against us. It's more that she's uncertain. Her confidence is gone."

"You care about her?"

"She's been my friend since I came to the university."

"It's unfortunate what happened," Jalen said.

"Even more unfortunate would be was not finding a way to bring her back," Alec said. "She's incredibly smart, and with as many physickers as we lost, we need to help her as much as we can."

Jalen watched Alec for a long moment. "And what about you? How are you feeling?"

"Other than overwhelmed? I was still struggling with serving as a full physicker when I was promoted to master physicker."

"That's not what I mean. How are you *feeling*?"

Alec sighed. "I feel about the same as I have for the last month. I'm coming to terms with what it means for me to tire easily, and I am still not fond of the taste of the eel meat, but I appreciate the fact that it helps."

"I have given some thought to whether there could be any long-term complications to you consuming it. I have not yet come up with an answer."

"You have given some thought?" Alec smiled at him. "Is that because you have been eating it?"

"It wouldn't be much of a test for us to be ignorant of the effects that the eel meat has on someone else, now would it?"

Alec chuckled. "I think you enjoy the way it makes you feel."

"Perhaps, which is why I recognize the danger. If I'm enjoying it, then I need to be careful. I begin to see why it had been forbidden."

"I still think it needs to be forbidden, or at least strongly monitor its use. We can't let others know the way it can be used."

"No. I don't think we can reveal the truth of eel meat to many. It seems there are already too many people who know."

"They are all master physickers."

"Other than your father. Bastan. Your Kaver."

"I get your point."

"That's not the point. The point is that I worry for you —about what might happen if we fail to harvest more. What happens if our supply of the eel meat dwindles?"

Alec had given some thought to it, but he tried not to spend too much time, knowing that it wasn't a problem he could easily solve. They didn't know how to breed eels, so there wasn't an easy way for him to create a supply for himself. It meant that he had something else to study, but he didn't know if studying the eels was going to be helpful. He and Sam had tried, but they hadn't come up with any more insight to them.

"At least the supply hasn't diminished yet," Alec said. He looked over at Jalen. "Is that the whole reason you came?"

Jalen flashed a smile. There were times when Alec still couldn't believe he had befriended Jalen. It must have been the same way Sam felt when she first went to the palace to live and train. This was different, but mostly because Jalen had come to the university to live and train. Whereas Sam had been somewhat the prisoner under Elaine and Lyasanna's control. Now, the palace was essentially abandoned. The Anders, represented solely by Jalen at this point, and the university united for the first time.

"It's not the entire reason I came, but I do worry about you. Probably the same way you worry about your friend."

"I appreciate that you do."

"It's not entirely a selfless act."

"What isn't?"

"My worries. It's just that, if something happens to you, I fear the ruling council of the university will be disrupted."

"I'm sure you will find a way to restore it."

"I'm sure that we will, as well. But it would mean more change. Change I fear we aren't strong enough to navigate. I'd rather not have to replace any council members so soon. And you have identified my concern—there really aren't that many master physickers remaining. Besides you and Eckerd and Carl…"

"There are a few others," Alec said.

"There are others, but none of them are Scribes, and though they are skilled healers, they don't understand the intricacies of what we have been doing. They don't understand the challenges we face."

Alec met Jalen's eyes. "I don't know that I fully understand the intricacies and challenges you speak of."

"We have rogue Scribes who may or may not be in the city. We have Kavers who have been placed under their control. Eventually, Helen will attempt to lead this rebellion, and from there, she will attempt to lead something more."

"You think she would lead a rebellion instead of rescuing your sister?"

Jalen's face clouded. "My sister. I still don't know what to do with her."

"I don't know how long she can be held effectively," Alec said. "If Helen has a supply of easar paper"—and with what she'd removed from the palace, he knew she did, more than what they had managed to accumulate, even considering what they found stored in the palace—"then it's possible she will eventually find some way to spring her."

"That's my fear, as well. If she gets my sister out and has her allegiance, she would have the potential to gain support within the city. I know you dislike the idea of the class system, but if she were to gain the support of the highborns, there would be great difficulty in the city."

"Bastan has control of the outer sections."

"Yes. The outer sections, but there are more people in the inner sections, and unfortunately, there is more wealth. If Helen manages to free my sister, I fear we will be facing a civil war in the city."

"Then we just have to keep your sister confined."

"As you said, that might not be possible."

"There might be something we could do."

Jalen arched a brow. "What are you suggesting?"

"Well, we don't have to leave your sister fully equipped to do harm should she escape."

"Do you mean to poison her?"

The idea disgusted Alec, but with what the princess had done, and the way she had abused her power, and the threat that she posed, did it make sense?

"I don't know that we poison her, but perhaps we find some way to mitigate her Scribe ability."

"It would have to be something Helen wouldn't know about."

"It would. And… I think I know who I could ask."

Jalen took a deep breath before letting it out in a heavy sigh. "I don't like it, but I think you're right. I think we need to make sure my sister doesn't pose too much of a threat to the rest of us. If she managed to get free, we would have more than a rogue Scribe on our hands."

Jalen set a jar on Alec's table. Alec knew what was in it, and looked up, smiling. "You don't have to leave that. I have a supply of my own."

"I think I need to stop consuming it. It's not beneficial, and it only puts me at risk of becoming dependent upon it."

"I doubt that you could become dependent on it."

"You don't know what it's like. It helps you; it gives you a boost of energy that makes a difference since you're weakened, but for me, not weakened at all, it does more than that. It provides clarity of thought, and it makes me more alert, almost feeling as if I'm more alive." Jalen stared at the jar on Alec's table. "I shouldn't allow myself to continue to rely on it. I never had before, and I don't know that I should now."

Alec closed his eyes. What must that feel like? The constant fatigue he'd endured ever since he was poisoned made every day a challenge. What would it be like to feel that energy again? That clarity of the mind? He was grateful that the eel meat gave him a little boost and let him at least function, but would his constant need become a dependency, as Jalen feared himself? Would he ever return to normal and not need it any longer? And, worse, was consuming the meat dangerous for him in any way?

"Maybe, for now, you keep it," Alec said. "I have enough of a supply, and with Bastan able to harvest it, I don't think I'll run out, at least not anytime soon. Besides, we might need you to have such clarity of thought. We might need you to be able to come up with answers."

Jalen studied the jar for a long moment, and the knit of his brow hinted at a debate warring in his mind. "I don't love the idea, but you might be right."

He took the jar and slipped it back into his jacket pocket.

"There's another reason you should have it," Alec said.

"And what is that?"

"You have to be tested soon. You might need it to help make sure you pass the promotion."

Jalen frowned. "You don't think I could pass without it?"

"I don't know. I hear one of the people who will be testing you will be quite rigorous in the questions he will ask."

"Maybe that person would be interested in offering me a hint as to the questions that will be posed."

"Maybe, but probably not."

Jalen flashed a smile. "I've been spending most of my time in the library here, reading practically everything I can."

"I think you're going to be fine. From what Master Carl says, you are the brightest student he's ever worked with."

"Only because he refused to work with you."

Alec shrugged. "He and I have never been on the best of terms. I don't think he particularly cares for my father."

"You need to get past that," Jalen said.

"We can work together. You don't need to worry about that."

"That's good. I wouldn't want to think that you would let your irritation with each other prevent you from helping to lead the university."

Alec smiled. "It's not so much me that you need to worry about."

"Don't worry. I had the same conversation with Carl." Jalen glanced toward the door. "You intend to go to the ward and work with your friend?"

"I told her I would mentor her."

"Would you want company?"

Alec looked at Jalen suspiciously. "Why?"

He flushed slightly. "It's not like that. I just thought that with as busy as the hospital has been lately you might want another set of hands."

"I won't turn down help, and I'm sure that Beckah would enjoy having you there as well."

Jalen pulled the jar out from his pocket and opened it, pulling out a piece of meat. He handed one to Alec and then took one for himself and popped it in his mouth. As Alec chewed the meat, he wondered if he would ever get used to the bitter taste. He hoped he wasn't reliant on it for long enough to find out. But with as much as they had to do, with as much danger as there was with Helen and the other Scribes still on the loose, he needed every bit of clarity he could summon. And if that meant consuming eel meat, that's what he would do. For now.

But maybe there was another way. Maybe he could find the cure, but to do so, he needed to find Helen and have her tell him what she had added to the easar paper mixture that day.

If he couldn't, then he might just have to accept that this was how he would always feel. He would have to accept that he would be forever reliant on the eel meat, and he would have to hope that there would not be any long-term complications to his consumption of it.

Jalen watched him, and Alec tried to smile and appear confident, not wanting his friend to worry about him, but he doubted he was successful. At least Sam didn't seem quite as concerned, though maybe she wasn't showing her concern. Knowing Sam, she worried about him as much as he worried about her. With what she planned, he feared for her safety.

Alec shook himself. The eel meat had given him a boost of strength, and he grabbed his jacket from a hook behind the door and headed out of his quarters with Jalen alongside, making certain to close—and lock—his door as he left.

As they made their way down the back stairs to the hospital ward, neither of them said anything. When he stepped inside, the air had the familiar strong medicinal smell, but there was something else mixed in it, an odor of filth and rot that had not been present the last time Alec had been here.

Something new had come to the university.

Alec took a deep breath. "It's time to get to work."

2

SEARCH FOR A SCRIBE

The hospital ward was busier than it had been in a long time. Nearly fifty more cots had been brought down, crammed into the existing space, and people on them were in various states of alertness. He paused at the wide double doors, resisting the urge to look over to Jalen, and looked for where he could be of most use.

"This is your fault, you know," Jalen said.

"That we're here?"

"That it's so busy."

Alec smiled. "Good. When I was first studying here, there were times when the hospital ward was almost slow," Alec said.

"You won't make nearly as much money."

"I'm not sure that the wealth generated by the university was always well spent."

"No? How else could they buy easar paper?" he asked with a smile.

It wasn't until recently that Alec understood that was the purpose of the funds generated by the university. If he could truly find an alternative source of easar paper, if he could make it himself, then there would be multiple advantages, not the least of which being that there would be less of a need to charge exorbitant fees for healing. How many people in the city would be benefited? Quite a few more than were now.

"Think of all the things the physickers missed seeing because they refused to treat them," Alec said.

"I didn't get to treat anything," Jalen said softly.

Alec glanced over. "That was your choice."

"I had to hide the fact that I was a Scribe. My family... we were all Kavers. My sister was the first Scribe, and she was never going to rule. There had to be continuity for the city."

"Are you so certain that you and Lyasanna were the first Scribes descended from your family?"

"There were no others."

"That you know of."

Jalen shrugged. "It's possible others preceded my sister and me. If they did, they kept it concealed the same way I did."

"I don't understand why you would conceal it. Especially since the university council has as much influence as it does."

"It's for that very reason that I didn't want to reveal what I was. I didn't want to complicate the structure in the city. As far as anyone knows, it is the Anders family that rules, not the university council. And for the most part, the Anders family does rule. It's only when it comes to certain things that the university has the authority."

"As far as you know," Alec said.

"As far as I know," he said. "It is complicated."

"It doesn't have to be," Alec said.

"I didn't think you wanted to get involved in politics."

"I never did. I was content spending my time at the university, and before that, at my father's apothecary, doing everything I could to heal."

"And look at you now," Jalen said.

"What is that supposed to mean?"

"It means you are drawn into what you will be drawn into. Sometimes, you get to choose how you get involved, and other times, it's chosen for you. I know you didn't necessarily want this, but it suits you."

"Master physicker?"

"Master physicker. University council. Chief Scribe."

Alec shook his head. "I can't be the last."

"I know you want Eckerd to do it, and likely he will, but you haven't been corrupted by the university system the same way the others have been. You have been apart from it, and I begin to think that might be beneficial."

Alec breathed out, wishing he didn't have to be asked to be Chief Scribe, but maybe it did make sense for him to get involved.

He saw Beckah working along a row of cots and made his way toward her. She had the record of one of the patients in hand and was skimming the page.

"What can you tell me about him?" Alec asked, looking down at the man lying on the cot. He did a brief survey, identifying him as a person in his mid-thirties, with sun-darkened skin suggesting that he worked outdoors, and based on the dirt under his nails, perhaps near the steam fields. It suggested to him that this man was from the outer sections, which meant he was someone who had only recently been allowed to come to the university. He breathed regularly, though every so often, his breathing paused. A grimace came to his face, though he said nothing.

Beckah looked up from the records. "It says that he was brought here after suffering from some sort of ingestion. He was found along the outer canals, practically near the steam fields," she said, wrinkling up her nose as she said it.

Alec was surprised she would still feel that way, especially since she had gone with him to Caster, and she knew he didn't feel quite the same way about people that others felt were lowborn, especially not after spending as much time with Sam as he had.

"He moans at times but hasn't really been awake."

"Could he have inhaled too much of the steam?" Jalen asked.

Alec pulled down the man's jaw and looked in his mouth. There was no sign of scalding at the back of his throat that he would've expected with the steam. He looked up his nose, searching for any other signs that it might be steam toxicity, but could find nothing. He checked the man's pulse, and it was regular. He lifted him, rolling him so that he could examine his back, then looked at the skin on his arms and legs and stomach but found nothing there, either.

"It's possible," Alec said.

"I don't know much about steam inhalation, not from the steam fields. But I did read something a while back that reminds me of this."

"I doubt that anyone knows much about it," Alec said. "The university never allowed people like that to come here to be studied."

"If it is simply an inhalation, won't it resolve in time?" Beckah asked.

"It's possible, but if there are any strange substances in the steam that his body has now absorbed, it might not. It might be more than what he can tolerate, and it might be that he needs something more than simply supportive care."

"You could try a combination of enbar fruit and boiled jissom oil," Jalen suggested.

Alec glanced over, smiling. "That might be effective. It would certainly sooth his tissues, especially if they are inflamed from the steam." He looked over to Beckah. "Beckah, do you think you could help Jalen find the necessary items?"

Her eyes widened slightly, and she glanced at Jalen before nodding quickly.

When they left, heading back to the supply room, Alec made a few notes on the record. He moved on, joining a group of junior physickers, and looked at the patient they were working on. The patient was clearly sick, with pale skin and sunken eyes.

"What happened here?" Alec asked.

"Master Stross, you don't need to focus on this one. She is beyond our help."

Alec frowned. "Beyond our help? Why would that be?"

"She has nearly been exsanguinated. She was discovered in the Loran section and had lost quite a bit of blood by the time she reached us," said Thed, a junior physicker.

Loran was a merchant section. It surprised Alec that they would come across someone who appeared to be lowborn in that section. Crime wasn't common in sections like that, but it did happen.

"How much blood was estimated to have been lost?"

"We don't know."

"What about the person who brought her?"

"They didn't say," Thed said.

"Did they comment on how much blood they saw where they found her?"

The junior physicker shuffled his feet. "I guess... I guess I didn't think to ask."

"It's helpful to know how much blood loss there has been. If you have a sense of the amount of blood loss, you can determine whether there's anything that you can do." He checked the woman's pulse and found that it was thready but intact. "And she still has an adequate pulse. With appropriate supplementation and hydration, it's possible she can recover."

"Even with significant blood loss?"

"I have seen people who have lost quite a bit of blood come back with appropriate care. Most of the time, it needs to be only supportive."

"Is there anything that can be done if they've lost more blood than that?"

Alec looked over at Thed. "There are rumors of

physickers who have tried blood donation, but that was only tried in extremis. Supposedly, they were trying to save one of the Anders and were willing to do anything they could to do so."

The recollection made him wonder whether he would do the same thing for Jalen if it were to come to that. He had never considered blood donation as a viable option and had often felt the same way as Thed, that there wasn't much that could be done, especially when someone was as far gone as this patient.

"What was the mechanism of injury?"

Thed pulled her arm out from underneath the blanket, and Alec saw a sutured laceration across her forearm. "Whatever was used to injure her cut through one of the main veins."

Alec examined the arm. A wound like that would have to be either very lucky—or unlucky—or intentional.

Alec turned his attention back to the woman. He had seen another person exsanguinated recently, and with what was taking place with the missing Scribes, as well as the Kavers that Helen commanded, he worried that maybe there was a connection. Could it be that Helen had found another Kaver and had taken her blood to continue with whatever she had planned?

"Why don't you see if you can learn anything more about this woman. Find out who she is, who she knows, and anything else that you can learn."

"Master Stross?"

Alec nodded.

"What will that do?"

He sighed. He didn't want to worry the junior physickers, and as far as he knew, none of them had trained as Scribes, something they wouldn't discover about themselves until they were farther along in the university. There was a testing, though if they were to discover more Kavers, maybe that testing would need to be expedited. Rather than worrying Thed, Alec decided to try a different approach.

"There is often much that can be understood about a patient when you see where they come from."

"See? You want me to go out to the Loran section?"

Alec shrugged. "There were several times when I would leave the university to discover what I could about patients." He smiled at Thed. "It would be the kind of initiative that might gain you more recognition."

Thed nodded and then made a few notes on the woman's record before turning away.

Alec continued on through the hospital ward. There was something good about spending his time there. It was something that felt right, reaching out and seeing who he could help and who he could make a difference with. It had been too long since he had spent any amount of time at the university, and it had been too long since he had felt as if he could be useful as something other than the person who had discovered easar paper. In the ward, he felt a sense of purpose.

That was why he had struggled with doing anything other than working as an apothecary, or now as a physicker. Even though he had a connection to Sam as her Scribe, he felt a calling to heal.

He stopped and saw a few more patients, looking at

the notes and making a few of his own, offering suggestions for treatment. But as a master physicker, there was an expectation that he wouldn't complete the treatment himself, short of any sort of surgery, and even in that, he didn't have the necessary skill to be allowed to operate. He wasn't sure that he wanted to, anyway. He enjoyed his time working with Master Eckerd and learning how to operate, but he found it much more rewarding to use his knowledge differently.

He made a circuit of the ward, nodding to some of the junior physickers he knew, surprised that there were fewer students than he expected, before catching up with Jalen and Beckah near the back of the ward. They were talking quietly, mixing the berries and the oil, and bringing it to a boil. Alec watched, standing off to the side and not wanting to interfere. Beckah needed to do this, and maybe she needed the time with someone other than him to help guide her.

And maybe there was something else he needed to do.

He left the hospital ward with something of a heavy heart. It was different coming here now as a master physicker. When he'd been promoted to full physicker, he still continued to help others, having essentially skipped the level of junior physicker, which was when physickers spent the most time on the ward. Time on the ward, understanding just what could be done for the patients, was what drove him. It was where he felt he had the most purpose. During his first months at the university, if he wasn't in the library studying, he'd been in the ward, and though he had been viewed strangely, people understood. If he were to do that now as a master physicker, there would be a different perception because master physickers weren't supposed to be as hands-on.

Alec tried to shake his melancholy as he made his way to the library. There was one place that he hadn't explored since his latest promotion. The library had a room devoted to master physickers, a place only those with a certain rank were allowed to access. Alec had been so busy of late that the idea of exploring that hallowed room hadn't even entered his mind. But with the wards in order and having to wait for his latest batch of easar paper to dry, he figured it was a good time for him to go.

He passed through the library, nodding to a few of the librarians. They were both full physickers and incredibly skilled researchers. When he reached the door to the masters' section of the library, he paused with his hand on the doorknob and took a deep breath before stepping inside.

Alec had been inside only one other time, but not by invitation. That time, he'd found Master Eckerd leaning over a book on a large table in the center of the room. He thought of that book as he entered, wondering if he'd find it there still.

A pair of lanterns provided light. The massive ornate table he remembered took up most of the room, and rows of shelves lined the walls. Alec immediately turned his attention to the shelves. These were the books he'd never had access to before, but Master Helen would have. Would there be anything here he could learn from, anything that would help him understand what knowledge she might've been concealing?

Alec made his way along the shelves, his gaze skimming the names of the books. There was nothing obvious. All of these works were old, some of them centuries old, but nothing here was clearly what he was looking for. It was possible that something useful was right in front of him, but it would take him a long time to discover whatever it was.

What he needed was someone who had spent time here before. He thought about Master Carl, but he was difficult at the best of times. Master Eckerd might help, but Alec had the sense from him that he still wasn't certain about his role in any of this. Not that Alec could blame him. Master Eckerd was a Scribe, and he had sided with the university council until recently. It would be difficult for him with everything else that had happened.

In the absence of anyone who might help, he needed to find time to do it himself. Since he didn't intend to join Sam on her journey to find Tray, he now had more time to devote to it, but he couldn't lose sight of the urgency of the situation. Master Helen wasn't done with whatever she had planned. Time was of the essence, but he felt overwhelmed.

"Is this your first official visit? I haven't seen you here since your promotion to master physicker," Master Eckerd said as he entered behind Alec.

Alec turned and smiled at him, looking a bit abashed at Master Eckerd's reference to his unwelcome intrusion all those months ago. "With everything that's been going on, I haven't had the time. I probably should have, especially since whatever knowledge Helen has would likely have come from something here."

"I don't think there's anything here that would help you with whatever she has planned."

"Probably not," Alec said. "Is there anything you can think of that might be helpful? Is there anything here that might relate to Scribes?"

"That information is kept out of even this section. Not all the masters were Scribes, Alec. Only the council would have access to such information."

They had searched Master Helen's rooms and had found nothing. Alec believed there was something, if only he could find it.

"Where would that information be kept?"

Master Eckerd shook his head. "Helen was the keeper of such information, and I don't know where she kept it. She has been secretive about allowing others to access it."

"And that didn't raise any concerns for you?"

"What was I to do?"

"You're a master physicker. You don't think you should have a greater responsibility because of that?"

Master Eckerd approached the large center table and gripped the edge of the highly polished surface with both hands. "I may be a master physicker, but when it comes to being in any sort of command here, I don't have any position of authority. Not as Master Helen did. She was the one who was in charge of the university. She was the one who commanded the Scribes. Even if I wanted to mitigate her influence, there would've been little that I could have done without sitting on the council."

"And now that you do sit on the council?"

Master Eckerd straightened and took a deep breath. "Now that I do, I would like to better understand what it is that we are. I would like to better understand the role that the Scribes play in the city. I would like to better understand just what it is that we do."

"I would like that, as well."

"Unfortunately, I fear that for us to fully understand what we are, we may have to journey beyond the borders of the city," Master Eckerd said.

"I have heard from several people that those who go to the Theln lands don't return. They warned me that the Scribes who venture beyond our borders stay away. Why is that?"

"There is a danger to leaving the city, at least from what I've been told. Why the Scribes that have attempted to leave don't return, I can't say."

"There has to be some reason for it that we have yet to discover."

"There likely is some reason," Eckerd said. "But none are willing to risk going without knowing exactly what it is that happens to Scribes when they leave our lands."

Alec stared at the rows of books. If he couldn't find anything here, and if there were no answers in Master Helen's rooms, and if they could not come up with what she had done with the records that related to the Scribes when they managed to capture her, did it mean that he would have to risk going to the Theln lands?

Someone would.

For them to fully understand what it meant to be a Scribe, someone would have to risk themselves, and Alec wasn't opposed to it being him, especially if Sam was going to go there anyway. If they went together, they might finally have answers to all of their questions.

"What happens if we don't find her?" Eckerd asked.

"We have to find her," Alec said. "We can't allow her to be the reason the city falls."

He just hoped Sam was ready, and that nothing happened to her while she was searching for the missing Scribes.

3

WITHIN THE SWAMP

The strange trees jutted out of the water, twisting in the darkness. There was a hint of a breeze, something that was unusual for the swamp, and it carried the foulness of the air to Sam's nostrils. She pushed on the pole, guiding the barge toward the trees, using a hint of an augmentation to do so. Had she trusted anyone else to make this journey, she wouldn't have been the one to come, but Alec needed her.

"How close to I need to get to them?" she asked.

"Close enough for you to go underwater to the roots," Alec said.

"And Jalen did this?" She couldn't imagine the prince—well, now the king—going underwater, especially in the swamp. He wasn't a Kaver, which meant that he didn't have the same ability to place augmentations, though he had pretended to be a Kaver for a long time.

"He went, but then again, remember he had armor on."

Sam fingered the fabric of her cloak. It wasn't thick

enough to avoid the biting jaws of the eels, so she doubted it would be all that effective at keeping her safe were she to fall in. What kind of armor would Jalen have used? She had never seen him wearing armor, though to hear Alec tell of it, he had it on at all times, and it must have been thin enough that Alec wouldn't even have known he wore it. Armor like that would create the appearance of an augmentation.

"I hope we can find some way to find this elsewhere," Sam said. "Otherwise, we're going to have to keep coming into the swamp to harvest the roots of the trees."

"It's not only the roots I need," Alec said. He stared at the trees, and he had a darkness to his eyes that went even deeper than the depths of the night.

Ever since he had been poisoned, Alec had retreated. How much of that was because of the illness and how much was in his head? Sam didn't know. Some of the fatigue probably was real, but she suspected that not all of it was. She suspected he wasn't nearly as sick as he believed himself to be. Then again, what did *she* know? She wasn't the one who had been poisoned. She wasn't the one who relied on eating eel meat to to stay strong.

"You want me to grab a few eels on my way back up?"

Sam didn't like the idea of grabbing one of the slimy eels, but for Alec, she would. She would do pretty much anything for him.

"You don't need to. Bastan has his men coming in here often enough to harvest that I don't need to worry."

Bastan. Now that the palace had fallen, and now that authority in the city had shifted, however subtly, Bastan was more open with his intentions to gain power. It wasn't even about power; it was about consolidation of his influence. He remained in the outer sections, preferring to stay in Caster. She suspected he would be able to move toward the highborn sections, though Bastan had no interest in that.

She was thankful for his willingness to continue to provide eel meat for Alec. Without Bastan, someone else would have to harvest them, and while she was willing to do it, it would take considerable time away from other things that she needed to do.

They reached a cluster of trees, and Sam slowed the barge.

It was a small barge, not quite as large as the ones used by the merchants to transport goods throughout the city, navigating the canals. This one was used for other reasons, little more than a way of maneuvering to and from the larger barges, though she rarely saw it used like that. Then again, maybe it was used in sections she didn't frequent. Bastan had little trouble finding the barge and had little difficulty arranging for her to have access to it. If it was meant to be something more secretive, it seemed to her he would have hesitated to give her access to it.

Sam grabbed some of the branches of the tree, holding on to them to slow the barge. When it came to a complete stop, Alec stood and looked at the tree, though she couldn't tell what he saw when he stared at it.

"You need a section of root?"

Alec nodded. "Only a small section."

"Wouldn't a larger section allow you to make more easar paper?" They needed to make as much as possible, especially since she suspected Helen and the others with her had a significant supply.

"I want to perfect the recipe and determine exactly how much to use, so as not to waste what we harvest. I don't want to damage the trees any more than is necessary."

Sam sighed. She didn't either, but she wanted to have an adequate supply of easar paper, mainly since it would be their best way to combat Helen. She had to trust him on this and not get too controlling.

"Hold the pole," she said.

Alec took the pole, and she took a deep breath, readying herself. While she did, she focused on the augmentations needed when she went underwater. She needed to make her skin impervious, not wanting to be bitten by the stupid eels, and she needed to have enhanced eyesight in the darkness. She didn't necessarily need strength, though it might help her tear free a section of the root.

Alec could help—with the small supply of easar paper that they now had, he could use that to place some augmentations on her—but she needed the practice. When the time came that she would confront other Kavers, Sam needed to be ready; she needed to be able to overpower them, even without augmentations gifted to her by Alec.

She felt her augmentations washed over her, starting deep within her and moving up through her body before rolling through her chest. When they set, she jumped.

The water was warm, almost unpleasantly so. She sank to the bottom and tried not to think about what other creatures might be in the water with her. Sam didn't know everything about the swamp and had never ventured in this far until recently.

But if Jalen had been able to do this, she was determined to do the same. She wouldn't allow the king to be more daring than she was, especially not in front of Alec. He already thought quite highly of the man, though she couldn't blame him. He was impressive, especially given that he was primarily a Scribe, and soon would be testing for master physicker level.

The trees jutted out of the bottom of the water. The ground around them was mushy, and small weeds grouped around the roots. They were propped up on something like stilts, and she reached for the root of the nearest tree.

When she did, something slithered against her hand.

Sam jerked her hand back, knowing she didn't need to. The augmentation she placed would protect her, and she didn't need to fear the eels, but she couldn't help it. The stupid things could bite, and she didn't want to have one of them latch on, even if it couldn't puncture her skin, thanks to her augmentation.

Was it an eel?

Even with her enhanced sight, the water was dark, practically murky. She tried not to think about what else was in it, or what made it quite as murky as it was, thinking only of the need to grab the root. She reached for it again, wrapping her hand around the slimy wood, and pulled.

It came free easily.

That surprised her. It shouldn't come free quite that easily, should it?

With the root in hand, she swam toward the surface. This time, she was sure something slithered against her. She grabbed the edge of the barge and quickly threw herself up onto it. She set the section of root down next to Alec and then squeezed the water out of her clothing.

"That was… disgusting."

"We might have to come up with a different way of harvesting it," Alec said.

"Anything we can do where I don't have to go under-water like that would be better."

"I could bring Jalen."

"Could you?" she asked. "Do you think the king wants to come out in the swamp and jump into the water again?"

"He's already done it once."

"I was kidding," Sam said. "Besides, if you bring him instead of me, how will you and I be able to spend time together?"

Alec glanced down to the root before sliding over and grabbing her hands. "I'd rather have a different time with you than this."

"I'm not sure, not anymore. It seems the only time we get together is when something has to be done."

"Sam—"

Sam shrugged. "I don't blame you. I know you have your responsibilities, especially now, but I keep thinking things will slow down, and we will be able to have…"

But have what? What did she want? It was difficult for

her to admit her feelings, let alone to accept what it was that she wanted out of the time she had with Alec.

"I guess all I want is for us to have more."

"I want that too."

They stood in silence, Alec holding her hands, and her covered in the filthy water of the swamp. Sam shook her head, feeling ridiculous at what she had said and the way that she felt. "We should head back. I'm sure you have other things you need to be doing."

"You wanted me to see if I could make more easar paper," he reminded.

"I think we need to have as much of a supply as we can collect," she said. "Especially if Helen has a supply of it."

They didn't know how much Helen had taken from the palace when she escaped. Considering that she would have known more about the palace's supply, she likely would've taken everything she could. And they had been distracted, focused on what had happened to the king, so they hadn't even known to go looking for Helen. They hadn't known what they were missing out on.

"It's a slow process," Alec said. "I'm trying to expedite it, but that doesn't change how long it takes to make even a single sheet."

"There has to be a way to make it more quickly. The Thelns seem to have that down."

"Without going to the Theln lands—"

"You're not going to the Theln lands," Sam snapped.

"You intend to go, but you don't want me to go?"

"I intend to go so that I can bring back Tray." She kept telling herself that, but the longer it took for everything to settle down in the city, the more she began to wonder whether she would ever go to get Tray. The longer that she avoided it—or was kept from it—the less likely it was that Tray would even listen when she went for him. He was her brother, but did he view himself the same way?

She no longer knew.

Sam took a deep breath. Rather than saying anything more, she began to push the barge back toward the city. It had taken nearly an hour to make their way to these trees, and it would've taken longer had she not known the direction, but she had traveled out into the swamp enough times now that she had a pretty good sense of direction. For those who hadn't been out in the swamp, they could get lost and easily struggle finding their way back. It protected the swamp in some ways, keeping out those who might otherwise learn its secrets.

The city came into view. From the water, there was something almost peaceful about it, especially at night. Candles glowed in windows, and none of the sections appeared any different from any others. There was no class system, not at night, not in the darkness. Everyone was the same.

Alec slipped his arm around her, and he stood next to her, saying nothing as she continued to push them toward the city. She moved with less intensity, no longer motivated to pole them quickly to their destination. She wanted to have another moment or two with Alec, even if they were borrowed moments that she wasn't sure she deserved.

When the barge ultimately reached the city, they started into the canals leading between the sections, and tension settled back into her. It started slowly, but it built, making her shoulders ache from it. There was just so much to do.

They remained silent as she pulled up next to the university. Alec hesitated, taking her hands for a moment and squeezing. "You could come in. You could see how the easar paper is made, and we could…"

Sam smiled sadly and shook her head. "You have your responsibilities, and I have things that I need to do."

Alec stepped off the barge, and she watched him until he made his way into the university. He paused at the door and looked out, though she doubted he could see much in the darkness.

She poled the barge over toward the palace. There was a time when she would never have even dreamt of visiting the palace, and a time only a short while ago when she wouldn't have imagined coming so openly on a barge like this, but since the attack, much had changed.

Sam tied the barge up on the palace side of the canal and jumped off. She headed across the lawn and was greeted at the door by a pair of now-familiar soldiers who barely nodded as she entered.

When she made her way inside, Marin stopped her in the hallway. "Samara. I've been looking for you."

"Why?"

"Where have you been?" Marin looked at her, seeming to notice her wet clothing.

Sam turned around to see if she'd left a trail as she came in, apparently not having dried all the way. She was soaked to the skin and wanted nothing more than to strip off her swampy, smelly clothes and get into something clean and dry.

"With Alec. He wants to try to make more easar paper."

"That's good. I think we're going to need quite a bit more." Marin glided down the halls of the palace, having quickly adjusted to her return. It had been a decade or more since Marin had walked these halls, a decade during which she had spent time hiding in the outer sections, staying away from anyone who might recognize her, yet staying within the city.

"What is it?" Sam asked.

"I don't know. Maybe some good news. Maybe not."

"About what?"

"Helen."

"You found her?" They had been looking ever since she had disappeared but had found no sign of her.

"We haven't found her, but you need to see this."

Marin guided her down the stairs, taking them two at a time, and Sam realized where they were heading. There was only one place in this part of the palace where she could be going. "Has she escaped?"

Marin glanced over. "No, but…"

They reached the cells, and Marin glanced at the two men standing guard. They stepped off to the side, and Marin pulled the door open, stepping into the room. Sam followed.

She scanned the cells and was reassured when she saw that the princess remained confined. Her fear was that Lyasanna would manage to escape. If she did, it would create difficulty for many. Though Sam wasn't as well versed as Bastan about the politics of the city and how it would impact things, she believed him when he said the princess getting free could cause problems that would make life in the city difficult.

Lyasanna sat in her cell and looked over at them when they approached. A dark sneer parted her lips, the same as it always did, and she glanced from Sam to Marin.

"Have you come to taunt me again? I would think you'd prefer to make these visits earlier in the day, but maybe you enjoy doing things like this at night."

Sam ignored Lyasanna and followed Marin to the end of the row of cells. Marin nodded to the wall, and her gaze was fixed on it, staring at the stone.

Sam frowned and turned her attention to the stone. "What is it?"

"Look," Marin said.

Sam took a moment to realize what it was that Marin wanted her to see.

There were markings in the stone. They were symbols, though they didn't mean much to her. Sam had seen symbols like this once before, back when she had been captured and held in prison.

"Is that—"

Marin nodded. "An augmentation." She spoke softly, her voice barely more than a whisper. "It wasn't there before. I searched to be sure before we left Lyasanna here."

"What's the point of the augmentation?"

"It's designed to break her free."

Kyza. If they had some way of getting Lyasanna out of here… "You can read it?"

"I can't read it, but I have seen something like it before."

Sam suppressed the urge to comment on Marin continuing to be evasive, even after everything they had gone through. Didn't Sam deserve more information now? But holding on to her anger with Marin didn't help her. She had to find a way to let that go. "How could it have been placed here? Lyasanna is in the cell, so it can't be her."

"I don't think she put it here. And I don't think they are placing it directly."

"I don't understand."

"Helen is the most skilled Scribe in the city. I think she is placing an augmentation from a distance. If she succeeds, she will be able to break in and free the princess. And if that happens…"

"Then we need to counter the augmentation."

"We will, but I wanted you to be aware of it."

"Is there any way for us to use it to our advantage?"

Marin frowned. "How would you propose we do that?"

Sam looked at the cells. "If they think they have placed an augmentation that we haven't discovered, maybe we could create a wall here that would trap them inside, at least until we had a chance to capture them."

"I don't know that it will work. Once someone breaks in, a wall won't be able to hold them."

"It will if we place our own augmentations on it. We need to find Helen, Marin. If she's going to continue to threaten us, we need to capture her and get her under control. Otherwise we will always be worried about what she might try next."

Marin smiled tightly. "That's actually a reasonable plan."

"But?"

Marin glanced at her. "I didn't say anything."

"Marin, I grew up around you. I know when there's something that's bothering you. You're not convinced that even if we do this, it will be enough."

Marin turned toward the cells. Her brow furrowed, and one hand rested on her disassembled canal staff hooked to her belt. She was troubled and looked more bothered than Sam had seen her in quite some time.

"We're outnumbered, Samara. That's what bothers me. If they try something, they will likely succeed. Helen has more Kavers than we do. She has more skilled Scribes than we do. We are outnumbered, and I think we're lucky that she's turned her attention to securing the princess, because if she were to do anything different, if she were to change her focus of attack and go after the Thelns, there wouldn't be anything you or I could do to prevent it."

"Then we have to stop her before she succeeds."

"I'm trying, Samara. And I know you're trying. But Helen… There's a reason I never returned to the palace. She is incredibly bright. And she has years of experience. And…"

"And what?"

Marin looked over at her. "And she is the only one who has ever been to the Theln lands as a Scribe and returned."

4

BACK HOME

The tray of food in front of her smelled delicious, but Sam didn't have much of an appetite. How could she when her mind was racing, leaving her feeling nauseated? Maybe the nausea wasn't only about her mind racing. Perhaps it was just as much about the fact that Alec was off at the university working on making easar paper, and working with Jalen and Beckah and others, while she was trying to find Helen, having only Marin—and Bastan—to help.

The tavern was mostly empty, only a few people at tables, most in quiet conversation. A fire crackled in the hearth, but no minstrel sang tonight. The absence left a void in the tavern.

"You need to eat," Kevin said, taking a seat across from her.

Sam looked up at him, and she smiled. Kevin was one of her oldest friends, though they had a strange sort of friendship. It was built on one common factor: they both served Bastan. Kevin was the one who always ensured that she had enough food to eat, and for that, she was eternally grateful.

"I'm trying," she said. "It would help if the food wasn't so terrible here. It's almost as if whoever is cooking it barely knows what he's doing."

Kevin grabbed her tray and started to pull it across the table. "You don't have to be mean about it," he said. "If you're not hungry, you don't have to eat. You're not going to hurt my feelings."

"I'm going to eat," Sam said, dragging the tray back toward her. "And you know you're the best cook in the section."

Kevin arched a brow. "Just in the section?"

Sam shrugged, forcing herself to take a bite of the stew. "I can't speak of how your cooking compares in the other sections." She smiled, and Kevin glared at her slightly. "But I'll give it to you that you have better food than in most sections?"

"I'll take it," he said. Kevin looked around the tavern before his gaze settled back on Sam. "If you're looking for Bastan—"

"Is he gone again?"

"Ever since the attack, he has not been here quite as much. I think he feels he needs to be visible in other places. You know how Bastan can be."

"Yes. I know how Bastan can be."

As she picked at her food, the door to the tavern opened and Bastan entered. He was wearing a navy cloak, and it was better made than most he'd worn until recently. Ever since the attack on the palace, Bastan no longer bothered to hide his wealth. He had begun to openly carry his sword, and there was a certain determination in his step.

He glanced around the tavern and noticed Sam sitting with Kevin and walked over to join them.

"Samara. I didn't expect to see you here, but when you weren't at the palace—"

"You went to the palace to look for me?"

Bastan nodded.

"You're going to have to be careful, Bastan. You might start to lose your reputation as a terrifying crime lord."

"I don't think I ever had a reputation as a terrifying anything," Bastan said.

"You might be surprised," Kevin said.

Bastan shot him a look. Kevin shrugged and stood and made his way back to the kitchen, tipping his head to the tray as a signal for Sam to keep eating.

"With everything that has changed, I almost thought that you might decide to move to one of the highborn sections," she said to Bastan.

"Not so much has changed that it would keep me from my home," Bastan said.

"You don't have to stay here. I think Jalen would let you stay in the palace. The gods know he's not staying there."

Bastan frowned at her, staring at her for a moment. "You say that almost as if it bothers you."

"I guess it bothers me that Alec has gotten so friendly with the king. I guess it bothers me that it turns out the king is a Scribe. It bothers me that—"

Bastan shook his head. "It bothers you that you have

responsibilities and you can't spend all the time you would like with your friend."

"That bothers me," Sam said, shoveling another bite into her mouth. It did nothing to settle the nausea in her stomach, but she forced herself to chew and then to swallow.

"There are advantages to remaining in the outer sections," Bastan said. "Especially with the issue we have in the city."

"The issue?" Sam looked up and paused before sticking a lump of bread in her mouth and chewing.

"The entire outer rim of sections is under my observation," Bastan said. "Everyone who lives in any of the outer sections will report to me or people who work on my behalf."

"The Shuver now works on your behalf?"

"I have provided him with certain freedom he didn't have before."

"You don't care about his violence?"

"A certain level of violence is required with what we do, Samara. You have seen that. And Chester is no more violent than any others who have operated in these outer sections."

"You're not that violent."

"No. I have never needed to be."

Sam stared at him, considering. "You're keeping an eye on him. That's why you don't worry about what he might do."

Bastan merely shrugged. "I wouldn't let someone operate in the city that I didn't have complete faith in. And I don't have complete faith in Chester, at least not to do as I think is necessary. This way, I am simply ensuring that he doesn't attempt anything that I feel would be overly ambitious."

"How?" Sam set down the piece of bread she'd been eating. She couldn't force anything more into her stomach.

"I have men observing him. It takes little more than that. And he knows I have men observing him. If he wants to remain in power, even in the Oldansh section and those adjoining it, then he will abide by my expectations."

"And this is how you will find out what Helen is up to?"

"I suspect Helen has money and connections that will allow her a different type of access," Bastan said.

"By that, you mean she will be in the highborn section."

"Either highborn or merchant. I don't know, but I have people searching."

Sam breathed out, controlling the frustration she felt. She had to trust Bastan, and she did. If anyone would find what Helen had done, or where she had gone, it would be Bastan. Having eyes literally in every section, it was unlikely she could leave the city. In essence, she was trapped, even if she didn't know it. That meant they had only to find where she had gone.

But the city was enormous. Even with Bastan's people searching, Sam knew his access in the inner sections of the city was limited. If Helen had access to the merchant and highborn sections, it would be difficult to find her. There were just too many places for her to hide.

"She's up to something," she said.

"And by something, I presume that you mean the markings that Marin showed me."

"Marin showed you?"

"She thought I should be aware. She wanted me to keep an eye out for anyone who might be making those markings."

"Why?"

"You would understand this better than I would, but she believes we will find them on the paper. And when we do, that's how we will know. Marin wanted me to be aware so that we would recognize them if we came across them."

It was a good plan, but it didn't make it any easier. Knowing about the markings didn't mean they would be able to find them, and even if they did, it wouldn't stop Helen and the others working with her from making others. It did nothing to prevent them from continuing to attempt to break free.

"I don't think we'll be able to stop her."

"If you think that, then we won't."

Sam shot him a look.

Bastan only shrugged. "If you believe that you will fail, then you already have. If you believe you will succeed, then the likelihood is high that you will."

Sam lifted the bread and took a quick bite. "Every time I think I know you, you say something that surprises me."

"Why would that surprise you?"

"It surprises me that you sound like you've become a philosopher. I bet you would fit in well at the university."

"They would never accept me there."

Sam laughed, thinking that Bastan was making a joke,

but he didn't laugh along with her. "You wouldn't want to go to the university."

"I have never wanted to be a physicker, but that doesn't mean I wouldn't pursue knowledge, especially at a place like that."

"I don't know. Now that Alec has been promoted to master physicker, you might be able to spend more time there than you realize."

Bastan grinned at her. "What makes you think that I haven't?"

She waited for him to laugh, and when he didn't, she stuck her tongue out at him. He was taunting her. She was sure of it.

"What are you doing to find Helen?"

"I'm doing what I can. As I said, my connections in the inner portion of the city are not quite as robust as what they are elsewhere. There are limitations to who and where I can reach."

"We need to find her as quickly as we can," Sam said.

"No, you want to find her as quickly as you can so that you can go after Tray. You don't have to wait to do that. No one will fault you for choosing to leave."

"Choosing to leave? I don't intend to leave. I'm just saying—"

"You're just saying that you want to go after Tray. You have made that clear over the last few months, Samara. Your friend would understand."

Sam watched Bastan for a moment, and then she sighed. "Alec might understand, but others won't."

"What others?"

"You."

Bastan smiled at her. "Do you suddenly care so much what I think?"

"It's not suddenly, but…" Now that Bastan had shown his true colors, how could she feel anything but affection for him? "I do care. I don't want you to think I'm abandoning you too. I know what you've done for me."

"Ah, now you're going to make me blush. You don't have to worry about what I think of your decision, Samara. I want for you what I've always wanted."

"And what is that?"

"I want your happiness. If that involves you going after Tray, then so be it. I understand the importance of your brother to you."

"You don't think I should leave well enough alone since he's not really my brother?"

"Why is he not really your brother? Because you don't share parents? Plenty of people don't share parents yet have a connection that would only be described as sibling-like. I think Tray is as much your brother as anyone can be. You care about him the same way any sister would care about her brother, and you would do anything for him." Bastan smiled. "Is that not what you thought I would say?"

Sam took a deep breath. "I… I don't know."

"If you think that you need to remain because others expect it of you, I want you to know that is unnecessary. As I have tried to tell you, you need to do what is best for you and what you feel is right."

Sam pushed the tray away from her, sliding it across the table. She hadn't felt hungry to begin with, and now she watched Bastan, trying to decide what she would say to him.

The door to the tavern opened, and a man Sam had not seen before walked in. He had a balding head and a thick beard and was well dressed—far better dressed than anyone in Caster tended to be. He hesitated for a moment, looking around the tavern before his gaze settled on Bastan. The man hurried over to the table. "Bastan. There is something you need to see."

"Edward, it's not wise for you to come here."

"I understand that it's not wise, but as I said, there is something you need to see."

Bastan got up, and Edward turned toward the door, heading out of the tavern. Sam grabbed another bite of bread and hurried after them. When they were on the street, Bastan glanced back at her, shaking his head. "No, Samara. This is not for you."

"I get to decide what's for me."

Bastan glared at her for a long moment before taking a deep breath. "I suppose that you do."

Edward guided them out of Caster and across the bridge into one of the neighboring sections. Sam nodded at the two men guarding the bridge, smiling to herself when she realized they were both Bastan's men. He had never openly set his men on the bridge before. He'd always bribed them, buying their service, but had never been quite so flagrant about who he had stationed around the city. Was it like that everywhere now? Sam hadn't taken the time to wander the various sections to determine if Bastan had placed his men so openly everywhere, but she wouldn't be surprised if he had.

They crossed a few more sections, heading into a merchant section. The streetscape changed as they transitioned from the outer sections of lowborns and into one of the merchant sections. Barges lined the canals along the merchant section. Most were tied up for the night, secured with heavy ropes, and the barge poles had been stowed, hidden away so they wouldn't be stolen. Sam had a hard enough time navigating the narrow barge on her own, and she couldn't imagine how the captains managed the enormous transport barges. Many of the sections like this had warehouses lining the canals, best for moving shipments in and out, and storing goods in between transports. Sam had broken into those warehouses before, but they were difficult to maneuver, and often they were guarded, making thieving from them challenging.

Edward hurried along the streets with a sense of purpose and familiarity—as if he belonged.

Was he a merchant?

Or could he be highborn?

Sam started to consider his clothing. It was difficult to tell, but with the cut of his cloak, he could very well be highborn. There were stripes of color within the cloak, though it was subtle. It was a detail few merchants bothered with, as the cost was prohibitive. And none from the outer sections bothered with color. If they wore a cloak, it was typically black or gray, something more utilitarian. Sam's cloak was something of an exception, but hers was borrowed from Marin, and that was only because of the properties it bestowed.

They crossed into another section, this still a merchant section, though mostly storefronts. It reminded her of Arrend, Alec's section, with the way the shops lined the street, most with bright letters and fresh paint. Shops in Caster were more run down, and half the time you had to know what you were looking for when you entered, otherwise it was easy to overlook what you wanted.

Edward stopped at a building, and he nodded to it. "This one."

Sam glanced at the sign. It looked to be a metalsmith based on the sign depicting jewelry. There were three letters on the sign, though she didn't know whether they were the initials of the store owner or whether they had some other significance for metalsmiths.

Bastan frowned as he studied the sign. "Are you sure?"

Edward nodded. "You told me to keep an eye out, and I've been watching this for the last week. I'm certain."

"Thank you. You should return before anyone sees you here."

Edward nodded and hurried along the street, disappearing into the darkness.

"Who is he?" Sam asked.

"One of my contacts."

"I gathered that, especially considering he came after you, but why did you have him looking here?"

"I have my contacts looking everywhere, Samara." Bastan stepped up to the door and checked it, twisting the lock. Unsurprisingly, it was locked. In the Caster section, many people would put a bar in front of the door, making it more difficult for thieves like herself—and Bastan, for that matter—from entering, but would they do that out here?

Bastan tipped his head to Sam. "Could you be so kind?"

"You don't trust yourself to open it?"

"I might be a little out of practice."

Sam chuckled and crouched in front of the door, pulling out her lock-pick set. She still carried it with her out of habit, though she hadn't needed it for some time. Bastan stood behind her, blocking people from seeing her along the street. Maybe that was the reason he had asked her to do it. With her petite frame, she wouldn't block anything other than a view of his backside.

She worked on the lock, and it clicked open with a soft sound. She stood, tucking the set back into her pocket, and stepped off to the side, giving Bastan room to go in first.

"What would a metalsmith have that you would be interested in?"

"Why wouldn't I be interested in a metalsmith?"

"With everything that's happened, I don't see you as needing to break in to have whatever it is you want."

"No, I suppose I do not."

"So?"

Bastan stepped into the store and waited for Sam to join him, then closed the door behind her.

It was darkened, and it took Sam a moment to let her eyes adjust. While she waited, she focused on augmenting her eyesight. It served several purposes, not the least of which was that she was able to practice placing the augmentations. She needed that practice so that she could be faster at it. At least, that was what Marin suggested. She wasn't able to help Sam much more than that, telling her that she needed to feel the power within her, and when she did, she would be able to manipulate it more easily, whatever that meant. Sam had seen Marin with her own augmentations, and she had seen her with those placed by her Scribe, and Marin was impressive either way.

As the augmentation settled through her, her vision became clearer. Everything within the shop took on a slight brightness, as if the darkness lifted away. As the sign suggested, it was a metalsmith shop. Glass-covered cases lined each wall, and Sam glanced in the first of them, seeing dozens of different pieces of jewelry sitting inside. She tried to lift the case, but it was locked.

"Are you here to steal something?" she whispered.

"Why would I need to steal anything from here? Haven't you already pointed out that my access to the palace has made it so I don't have the same need?"

"Then why are we here?"

"We are here because there is something else we need to look for."

They made their way to the back of the shop. A narrow stairway led to the likely living quarters above. It was similar to many of the merchant shops. Most had their homes above, which made it easier for them to know if someone was breaking in.

Bastan motioned for her to head up the stairs.

Sam frowned. "You want to go up?" she whispered. "If the merchant is here, they're going to know that we broke in."

"If the merchant is here, then it won't matter," he said.

Sam was confused about what was taking place. Why

was Bastan allowing himself the chance to get caught? It was unlike him. Then again, much of this was unlike him. Bastan had changed since the attack on the palace. It wasn't just that he moved openly and wore his sword and expensive cloak as if to flaunt his wealth and position, it was something else, but Sam hadn't been able to put her finger on it. Was it a sense that he needed to protect her? She didn't think that was the case, but she wouldn't put it past Bastan to feel that way.

At the top of the stairs, there was another door. She checked the handle, and it was unlocked. Why would it need to be locked? If the shop below was locked, then there should be no need for this one to keep others out.

Sam twisted and pushed the door open.

Bastan laid a hand on her arm and shook his head. He stepped forward, unsheathing as he did.

Kyza. What was this about?

Sam assembled her canal staff. The room wasn't huge, but it would be large enough for her to swing her staff if it came to that. She noticed a couple of chairs around the table, and there was a counter leading back to what she assumed to be the kitchen. A small hall led to what would likely be a back bedroom.

Bastan crept forward and raised his hand, signaling her for silence.

She didn't need him to signal that, but it did provide a warning. Wherever they were going—whatever they were doing—he was nervous.

In the back bedroom, he paused.

There was a small bed with a wardrobe positioned along the opposite wall. Two people slept on the bed. A narrow table was next to the bed, and a lantern rested on top of that.

Bastan made his way to the lantern and turned up the light.

He stepped back, his sword at the ready.

Sam frowned. Who were these people? One was an older man with graying hair. He was chubby, and she could see folds of flesh beneath the cover. Next to him lay a woman who was possibly ten years younger, with dark brown hair and a sharp jaw and much shorter, almost as short as...

Kyza!

The woman stirred and jerked her head around, seeing Bastan and then Sam. She jumped up and reached under the bed at the same time, pulling a staff free.

"A Kaver?" she shot at Bastan.

The woman started toward Bastan, twisting the staff, but he kept her at bay with the sword, flicking it around much faster than he should be able to without augmentations. Then again, if what Helen said about Bastan was right and he *was* djohn, it would explain his abilities.

Sam slipped forward and jammed her canal staff into the woman's chest, knocking her down. She stood over the woman, looking down. She didn't recognize her, though there were many Kavers she hadn't recognized who had returned to the city. Lyasanna had summoned them back, having them bring easar paper with them, and intending for them to help her with her attack on the Theln lands.

"What's your name?" Sam demanded.

The woman glared at her. "Do you think you can

succeed with this? Do you think we won't get her out? Do you think—"

Bastan slammed the hilt of his sword into her temple, silencing her. "Grab her."

The man on the bed started to stir, and Sam looked over. When he saw her, his eyes widened slightly, and then widened even more when he saw Sam grab the woman and fling her over her shoulder.

Sam turned back to him. "Go back to sleep. This was just a dream."

"But Camellia…"

"Camellia needs to return to work now," Sam said. "And you need to go back to sleep." She carried the woman down the stairs after Bastan and locked the door to the shop behind them as they hurried down the street and into the darkness.

5

MAKING PAPER

The smells that wafted out of the pot were almost overwhelming. Alec tried to ignore them, holding his breath when he had to, but he knew he needed to be close enough to it to tell whether the concoction was going to be useful or not.

He was careful with how he added each element. He mixed it slowly, bringing the water up to a steady boil, and prepared to add the svethwuud last. It would have to be last, because if he made a mistake and needed to scrap the entire mixture, he didn't want to lose the chunk of svethwuud.

He needed to experiment with it. How much of the wood was necessary to make the mixture effective? It was possible the entire chunk was required. That was how much he had used the last time, and though it had been successful, the paper was not quite as high quality as what could be obtained in the Theln lands.

When he was content the mixture of the other ingredients was appropriate, Alec cut off a quarter of the sveth-wuud root. He didn't even bother cutting it up, knowing from his previous mixtures that the heat of the boiling water dissolved the wood entirely. That was a surprising feature of the root. He didn't know of any other wood that would react quite that way, so he had to think it was something specific to the swamp tree, and not necessarily its interaction with the other ingredients.

With the addition of the svethwuud, the water took on a greenish tint. It was subtle, barely more than a hint of green, but the mixture hadn't been that color before adding the svethwuud.

Was there anything to the root that caused it? He was convinced the eels were somehow tied to the efficacy of the paper, but he still didn't know how. Maybe he never would understand without having enough time to experiment. The venom wasn't the key. He and Jalen had discovered it neutralized the effect of the paper, so it wouldn't help with creating it.

As he stirred the mixture, he wished he had someone who knew paper-making who could help him understand this better. He was trying to understand both paper-making and the nuance of how to create easar paper. Without a better understanding of everything that went into making paper, Alec didn't think he would ever be able to adjust the svethwuud ratio effectively.

When the hunk of svethwuud root was fully dissolved, Alec continued to stir, leaving the mixture boiling. The next step would be to strain it and then to filter it out over the screen.

Alec got lost in the process and took the pot and

poured it over the filter screen. When this was done, he took a flat metal tray and pressed it on top of the screen, pressing out more of the water.

He turned the screen over, exposing the mix to dry on the tray.

This time, the paper had a smoother texture to it than the last time he had done it. Then again, this time was a bit more controlled than what he had attempted before. He had been in something of a hurry, and the moment he had succeeded, he had hurried off, looking to find Sam to share with her what he had done.

Alec carried the tray with him and set it on a table against a wall. This was his own private lab, a place where he could experiment, where he didn't have to worry about others coming in and surprising him. That was one advantage of his promotion to master physicker. His gaze drifted to the door leading into his living quarters, another benefit of his promotion, and space much more substantial than he felt he deserved, but he was thankful for the setup since it gave him ready access to his lab.

There was only one thing to do, and that was to wait.

While he waited, he looked at the water that he had strained off the mixture. There was still a greenish hue to it, and he wasn't sure how much of that was useful, but considering everything he had learned about the eels and the fact that the easar paper he'd made the last time had been useful, he had to think that the pulpy residual mixture could be helpful for something else.

But what would that be?

Alec decided to run a few tests. He first considered trying it on himself, but given the fact that he had been poisoned by the paper mixture once before, he was a little reluctant. Then again, the paper itself wasn't dangerous, and Alec was confident that he had mixed it the same as he had before, if only using a slightly diminished quantity of svethwuud.

He took a cup and scooped out some of the water.

He brought it up to his nose and sniffed. It smelled the same as the pulpy mix—bitter and hot and somewhat foul, all scents that reminded him of the swamp, though intensified.

Alec squeezed his eyes shut and took a sip.

He knew that he shouldn't, but none of the individual items in the mix were dangerous. Even the svethwuud wasn't dangerous. He had handled it multiple times, and though he had never consumed easar paper, he had a hard time thinking the paper itself would be dangerous to him in any way.

Surprisingly, the water mixture was not nearly as awful as it smelled. It was almost sweet, though he could taste the edge of bitterness, almost like tea that had steeped for too long. He took a bigger drink, and it was warm as it rolled through him.

Alec set the cup down. He shouldn't drink any more, not until he knew whether he would experience any detrimental effects. Maybe the easar "tea" would allow him to avoid—or at least reduce—his consumption of eel meat. He doubted he would be so lucky.

Alec leaned back, relaxing as he sipped more of the tea. A part of his mind warned him that he shouldn't be drinking this mixture, not without knowing what it would do to him, and certainly not while by himself, in the event something went wrong. But there was something sweet about it, and he wanted to see what it might do for him. If the eel meat was beneficial, maybe the easar tea would be helpful.

He heard a knock on the door to his quarters, and Alec stepped out of his private room where he was running the tests and into his sleeping quarters. He closed the door behind him, not wanting anyone to catch a glimpse of what he was working on. When he reached the door and pulled it open, Sam waited on the other side. She was carrying someone and Bastan was with her.

"Good, you're here."

"Sam?"

She pushed past him and threw the person that she was carrying down onto the ground, unmindful of the fact that she tossed a woman on the floor. The woman was small and had dark hair, much like Sam did. She had a muscular build, and her skin was deeply tanned.

"This is Camellia," Sam said. "Apparently, Camellia is a Kaver."

Alec's eyes widened. "A Kaver? You found her?"

Sam nodded to Bastan. "I didn't find her, Bastan did. He has contacts throughout the city."

"Where in the city did you find her?"

"She was in one of the merchant sections," Sam said when Bastan didn't answer. "Bastan tells me that he has most of the outer sections monitored, and he's keeping an eye on who comes and goes."

"What I told you was that I'm keeping an eye on the outer section so that we can ensure your missing Scribe does not depart the city."

If anyone could ensure that Helen didn't leave the city, Alec had faith it would be Bastan. Not only did he control his section, but he had connections with other sections.

"What do you want me to do with her?"

"I want you to get answers from her."

"Sam—"

She shook her head. "Not like that. I don't intend for you to torment her in any way... at least, not too much. If it comes down to torture, I can do that or Bastan can."

"I don't want anybody to torture anyone."

"Even knowing what she is? Even knowing what she did?"

"We don't know what she is or what she did," Alec said. "All we know is what you've told me. If she's a Kaver and she's working with Helen, maybe we can help her. You saw what she tried to do to Beckah. If she is controlled by the easar paper, then we owe it to her to try and help her."

Sam glared at the woman on the ground. "If she's not controlled, then she has chosen to continue to work with Master Helen."

"Or she doesn't know the truth," Alec said.

"Fine. Either way, I need you to get answers."

"Sam, how do you expect me to find answers? I'm not the right person for this."

"You might not feel like you're the right person, but I don't know of anyone else we can go to."

Bastan took a seat on Alec's bed and clasped his hands together, looking over at Alec. "I could obtain information from her, Stross, but I think the way I would do it would be much less desirable than the way you might be able to."

Alec heaved a cautious sigh. "Bring her through here," he said, motioning to the door. He guided them beyond his private sleeping area and into his research room. He watched Sam as she entered, and her gaze drifted around the lab, settling quickly on the tray with the easar paper.

"Did it work?"

"I think so. I used much less of the root this time, hoping I would have enough to make a few more sheets, but it still takes considerable time and effort to make the paper. If we have to go sheet by sheet, this will be a very time-consuming process."

"Only if you're the only one making it," Sam said.

"We can't trust anyone else to make it," Alec said.

"Can't we?" She looked over to Bastan. "I imagine you could find paper makers in the city who might be of benefit to us."

"I imagine I could."

"Alec has other tasks he needs to be responsible for," Sam said. "And if he's keeping his focus on making paper, he can't be working on these other tasks."

"What other tasks do you intend for your friend?" Bastan asked.

Sam glanced down at the woman. "Tasks like figuring out what Camellia knows. Until we know, and until we know whether she was involved with Helen, we can't take the next step." Sam looked up and met Alec's gaze.

He knew what she was thinking and recognized the concern she had. She wanted to go after Tray, and until they managed to confine Helen, going after Tray would have to wait.

"I can try to find out what she knows. If I come up with anything…"

Sam nodded. "I can stay with you. I can help you question her."

"You mean interrogate her."

"I don't mean interrogate. I mean ask her questions."

"Are you sure that's safe?" Bastan asked.

"There are things I can administer to her that will sedate her enough that she can answer questions, but she shouldn't be able to overpower me."

"Shouldn't be able to?" Bastan asked.

"Sam was only able to overpower Master Jessup because I placed an augmentation on her."

"What makes you think the same won't happen with this woman?"

He didn't know. "Fine. I will be more aggressive with my sedation." He looked at Bastan, and he shook his head. "Sam has other things that she needs to do."

Sam stared at him for a moment. "More than I realized."

"What does that mean?"

"It means that Marin showed me some markings, and she thinks the Scribes are attempting to break into the prison to free Lyasanna."

"How can they break into the prison?"

"The same way that augmentations were placed on the building where I was captured once. They're using the structure itself as some sort of documentation. They're placing symbols onto the stone somehow, and it's weakening it. I don't know how long it will last. I have Marin trying to create other walls around it so that anyone who might break in will get confined, but I don't know how effective that will be."

"Do you need to have someone else there?"

"Who?" Sam asked. "Who do we trust that could go and sit that close to Lyasanna and could understand whatever symbols they are placing?"

Alec sighed. "There's one person who might know or would be able to figure it out," he said.

Sam frowned at him. "Who?"

"My father."

6

THE CAPTURED KAVER

S am glanced from Bastan to Alec then down at the woman on the floor. "I don't like the idea of leaving someone like this in your room unguarded, Alec."

"Nothing will happen while we're gone."

"Unless she manages to escape."

"I can sedate her in a way that will prevent her from escaping," Alec said. He disappeared into his lab and returned with a vial and began shaking it. "This is ashesl. Enough of this, and she will remain sleeping until I return."

"I think we need to keep her more than just sleeping," Sam said. "If she manages to come around, not only you but everyone in the university will be in danger."

"I doubt she will attack the university," Alec said. "Doing so would pit her against too many people."

"You think she would just sneak out? Helen has no qualms about attacking anyone who gets in her way. I'm sure she's trained her Kavers to behave similarly should the need arise."

Alec let out a heavy sigh.

"I know you don't like it," Sam said. "I know it's difficult for you to believe a physicker would do that, but I think we have to agree that she has proven herself as something more than a simple physicker. She is less interested in healing and helping than she is in maintaining a certain type of power."

"I know. I just… I just don't like it."

Sam took his hands. "You don't have to like it. I don't like it, either. But I like the idea of allowing her free rein in the city even less. We need to be able to question this woman." She glanced at the woman on the floor, then over to Bastan. "She's the first lead we've had. We can use her."

Alec poured some of the liquid from the vial into the woman's mouth. He massaged her neck, forcing her to drink. "This should keep her out for a while. It should give me enough time to go to my father and get back, and then we can see what else we might need to do."

Bastan glanced at Sam but said nothing.

What was he thinking? There was something on Bastan's mind, and maybe it was only his concern about leaving this Kaver in Alec's room. But then, Sam agreed that they needed to get additional help, and who better to help than Alec's father?

"I can't stay with her," Bastan said. "There is too much at stake, and—"

Sam shook her head. "No one was asking you to stay with her."

"We can't leave her here unguarded."

"No. I don't want to leave her, either."

Bastan let out a heavy sighed. "Let me send some men."

"You don't need to send anyone. She will be out," Alec said.

"Until she's not," Bastan said. "What happens when you return and she's awake? What happens when you come back, and she is waiting for you, ready to attack? What will you do then?"

Alec glanced from Bastan to Sam, almost as if looking for help from her, but Sam wasn't about to offer it. She agreed with Bastan, at least in this.

"Your men can't be seen in the university."

"And why not?" Bastan asked.

"Because the physickers will have questions."

"More questions than you would have if you had a Kaver running free, attacking?" Bastan asked. "I think I can keep my men concealed."

"I'll stay here until Bastan sends his people," Sam said. "Does that work for you?"

Bastan nodded. "That would make me happier than having this woman left alone."

Bastan slipped out the door, leaving Alec and Sam.

"Is this what we are to become?" Alec asked.

"I'm not sure what you mean by that."

"Are we going to continue to have to fight? To deal with this type of deception? Is that what we have now?"

"Only until this is all done."

"What happens then?"

"Then?" It was the question she didn't dare ask, but it was a question she knew needed an answer. Until she understood how to corral Helen and the others, there could be no peace for the two of them. There could only be more fighting. There was a need for the Kaver and the Scribe, not for Sam and Alec. "Then we get to find out. But until then..."

Alec took a deep breath and grabbed a jacket, though not his university jacket. "Don't let her escape," he said.

Sam smiled. "I have no intention of allowing her to escape. Just hurry back."

Alec departed, leaving Sam alone with the woman. She looked around for something she could use to bind her and settled on sheets. She cut several strips free and began to tie the woman's arms and her legs. She'd apologize to Alec later for destroying his bed linens.

She paced the room; her mind was buzzing. Not only did she need to find Helen, but she hoped that Alec's father would figure out a way to somehow prevent Helen from breaking the princess out of the prison. Would that even be possible? With everything they were going through, could they deal with that on top of everything else?

She took a seat and waited.

It was difficult to only sit and wait, but she had no choice, not with what else they needed to do. This was her task, at least for now. In time, she would have other tasks, and she would have other responsibilities, and if everything went well, she would finally be able to go after Tray, but until then, she had to sit here and wait until Bastan and his men returned.

She lost track of time until Bastan knocked. She nodded to the two men, recognizing both of them. Both were trusted men of Bastan's and had survived the attack on his tavern.

Ricken was large and had a sizable belly that matched his enormous beard. He was strong, and she'd seen that he was good in a fight. Paulie was not quite as big and didn't have as large a beard, but he made up for his less-than-intimidating stature with extensive tattooing along his arms and his neck.

"Ricken. I hadn't expected to see you again so soon."

"Is it your fault we keep getting these assignments?" he asked. He scratched the beard on his jawline and looked around the room, wrinkling his nose.

As he did, Sam realized there was a strange odor in Alec's room, though it was one that she had grown accustomed to. It wasn't a stink. It was more the smell of the various medicines that Alec kept.

"Don't blame me. I would blame Bastan. You know he doesn't think all that much of you."

Bastan glared at her. "Don't think to influence my men with your negativity."

Sam leaned to Ricken. "Did you hear that? Now you're his men. If I were you—"

Bastan grabbed her arm and pushed her toward the door.

Sam glanced back grinning. "Be careful with that one. She's tied, and she's sedated, but if she gets free…"

Ricken glanced down. "This one? Doesn't look like we should be all that concerned about her."

"Are you concerned about me?" Sam asked carefully.

Ricken frowned. "I've seen you fight."

"Know that she can fight as well as me."

Pulling the door closed, she and Bastan headed out of the university. Sam looked over to the hospital ward as they passed the double doors, wondering about the activity inside. Since Alec had been promoted to master physicker, he had changed much about the university, making it much more accessible than it had been before, and allowing others from the outer sections in the city to come for healing without repercussions and fear that they didn't have enough funds. It didn't take long for word to spread that the university had changed their policies. When Alec had loosened the restrictions, people had begun coming quickly, almost as if they had been waiting for just such an opportunity.

And probably they had. She imagined how many people were desperate for the kind of healing that could be found at the university. There were hundreds and hundreds of people needing healing throughout the city, many of them reliant upon apothecaries, many of the apothecaries with much less skill than Alec's father, and many people suffering because of that. Having the university to go to, having any place like that to go to where they could get the help they needed was a positive change.

"Where are we going now?" Sam asked.

"Unfortunately, I had intended for you to return to whatever it is you've been up to, but something has come up."

"What's come up?"

"Another visitor."

"Another Kaver?"

Bastan glanced over. "It's possible."

"One of them needs to talk," Sam said. "If they don't…"

"If they don't, we will find a way to make them talk."

They made their way through the city, passing over bridges, with Bastan nodding at men he knew. Sam still marveled at the fact that he was as well-connected as he seemed to be. She shouldn't be. She knew Bastan was quite connected in the city.

They reached a merchant section, Huls—a section where there was a preponderance of clothing shops—and Bastan slowed. This was a section Sam had visited many times over the years, having discovered that the people of Huls rarely kept their doors locked. It made for easier thieving that way. There was a limit to how much she had been willing to steal, not wanting to draw too much attention to her work, but this had been a place where she had come without Bastan's assignments.

"You recognize this section?"

Sam frowned. "I don't know what you mean."

Bastan chuckled. "You don't think that I've kept an eye on you all these years? I know you liked to come here and try clothing on before discarding it, choosing something much simpler." He looked over at her, almost sizing her up. "I know you prefer the cloak Marin gave you, and I must admit it does have some interesting qualities, but from the amount of time you've spent here, it seems you have another interest."

"My other interest was finding something I could steal."

"Steal. Wear. And now, you could purchase whatever you want."

"I don't have unlimited funds."

"Don't you? You have access to everything the palace

has. And you have learned that you are descended from the Anders, which gives you a certain connection to that wealth you didn't have before."

"I haven't thought much of that connection."

"I know you haven't, and there will come a time when you will need to, Samara. I know you don't like to think of yourself as a highborn, but everything you've learned about yourself has told you that you are much more than you ever realized. It's time to start acting that way—and dressing that way."

She frowned. "Now you're telling me I need to change my clothing?"

"I'm telling you that you need to stop dressing like a lowborn."

"Is that why we're here?"

"Partially."

He reached a shop and headed inside. There was a soft tinkling of bells when the door opened, and it reminded Sam of Alec's father's shop. Sam hadn't known what kind of place Bastan was taking her, but the inside looked like a tailor's shop. When he had mentioned he was taking her someplace to look at clothing, she half expected it to be a dress shop. That didn't fit Sam at all. She wasn't the kind to wear dresses, and even if she had been, they weren't practical for what she needed to do. She could only imagine a dress flying open as she sailed over a canal.

Instead, there were pants and jackets and shirts, all different sizes and colors, and Sam paused. She had been here before. Had Bastan chosen it because he knew that?

"Bastan—"

She didn't have a chance to finish. A small, elderly woman appeared from the back of the store. She had a strange-looking hat, and needles were stuck into it. Some had thread hanging from them. Deep wrinkles lined the corners of her mouth, and she had a serious set to her eyes.

"What can I do for you... Bastan. What are you doing here?"

Bastan tipped his head. "Madame Fornay. I brought someone that I would like you to help dress."

The woman glanced from Bastan to Sam before stepping forward. She took a measuring tape from around her neck and began stretching it down Sam's arms and around her stomach and then moved up to around her chest. At that, Sam pushed her back.

"Not the type for a dress, then?" the woman asked.

"Oh, I imagine she would love a nice dress, but the better question would be whether she would wear it."

"She would not wear it," Sam said. "And if that's what you think—"

Bastan chuckled. "She needs something that could help her fit in regardless of what section she visits," Bastan said to Madame Fornay.

"Which sections are we implying? If it's your typical places, that leaves a wide range, Bastan."

"It's not my typical. She needs to be able to visit both outer sections and all the way into the inner sections."

"What inner sections? There are some places where we can get away with a little less formality, but there are others where a young woman such as yourself should be seen only wearing a dress."

"This young woman would never be seen wearing a dress," Sam said.

"A dress is not necessary," Bastan said, as if ignoring Sam. "But it needs to be practical. Anything you have needs to have pockets deep enough to hold an assortment of items. And ideally, you would have something that would support this." He grabbed Sam's cloak and pulled it back, revealing her canal staff hanging from her belt.

"Interesting. Is she an acrobat?"

"Of a sort."

"I will see what I can come up with. I doubt I have anything ready-made for you, but I suspect it would only take me a few hours to create what you are looking for and have it sent wherever you would like."

Bastan tipped his head, and Madame Fornay disappeared to the back of the shop. Sam looked over to Bastan, shooting him an angry glare.

"Is this about you getting back at me? Did I do something that angered you?"

"You didn't anger me, but I have become increasingly aware of the fact that you are descended from the Anders, and with you spending time at the palace, I think you need to be dressed appropriately. The people need to see their rulers dressed in ways that they expect."

"I'm not a ruler. I'm not even one of the Anders."

"You are much more than you allow yourself to be."

"Bastan, I don't even intend to stay at the palace. When all is said and done, I intend to go after Tray."

And that might happen much sooner than Bastan wanted. If Sam had anything to do with it, she intended to finish with Master Helen and get out of the city.

"I understand what your intentions are. I'm also preparing you for what comes after."

"Bastan—"

She didn't get the chance to finish. Madame Fornay appeared and carried a jacket and pants. "This is mostly for sizing. Why don't we try this on?"

She held out the jacket, waiting for Sam, and she reluctantly slipped her arms into the sleeves. The fabric was much more beautiful than anything she was accustomed to wearing, and it fit perfectly. Madame Fornay made her way around Sam, tugging on the sleeves, checking the buttons, before nodding to herself.

"Perhaps a little longer, but not much. I think this will do. I should be able to place a few hidden pockets here that would allow for some concealment. And now these."

She held out the pants, and Sam slipped them on, not bothering to remove the pants she wore. They were worn and almost tattered, but they were comfortable. The pants fit nearly as well as the jacket, though she suspected part of the reason they didn't fit quite as well was because she was wearing her own pants underneath. Much like before, Madame Fornay made her way around, pulling on the inseam, patting Sam's bottom and then tugging on the hem near the floor. When she was satisfied, she stood and motioned for Sam to remove them.

"This will not take a long time. I have several items that would be satisfactory." She pursed her lips. "Though if I may be honest…"

Bastan tipped his head. "Of course."

"A lady like herself would do well to have at least one

gown. Especially if she intends to spend any time within the central sections."

Bastan glanced over. "Whatever you think, Madame Fornay."

"Bastan—" Sam growled.

Bastan ignored her. He and Madame Fornay had a brief conversation about cost, and Bastan whispered something in her ear, leading Madame Fornay's eyes to widen slightly.

"Very good."

She disappeared to the back of the store, and Bastan grabbed Sam's sleeve, tugging her out of the store.

Once outside, Sam looked over to Bastan, glaring at him. "What was that about?"

"That was about me helping you be more inconspicuous. I can't have you getting identified the moment you walk into a section that you aren't dressed for." He grabbed her cloak and fanned it open. "Look at you. Your clothing gives you away more than anything else. I know you don't care about the difference in classes, and I know you don't care about highborn versus lowborn, but others do. The moment they see you, they know you are from Caster."

"My clothing doesn't identify me as from Caster."

"It identifies you as from an outer section, Samara. That is enough." He took her by the elbow and started down the street, glancing around. "Why do you think I've never given you any jobs outside of Caster or the outer sections?"

"You gave me jobs in other sections."

"Nothing that required you to dress in a particular

way. It never mattered, not before, and perhaps it doesn't matter now, but I'm determined to see that you are dressed for the jobs that you might take. If you're going to continue working this way, and if you're going to continue spending time outside of Caster and those sections, you need to be dressed appropriately."

"And the gown?"

Bastan shrugged, but he did a terrible job of suppressing the grin. "There might be times when you need something a little more formal."

"What more formal do I need? I think the other clothing you convinced her to make will be enough."

"Maybe it will. Now, it's time for us to finish this job."

"And what job is that?"

"That is the two of us seeing if we can come across any more of Helen's people." He nodded to the end of the street.

There was a massive manor home that would have been almost as fitting on one of the more central sections as it was here in this merchant section. It was a sprawling two-story home with a short fence around it. There was a separation between it and the other buildings on either side, something that wasn't found in Caster. Sam imagined that the back of the home overlooked the canal. Considering the display of wealth, that would be expected.

Many of the people with money thought that having homes overlooking the canal was a display of their status. Sam didn't understand that, especially considering she had been in the canals more than once and knew what lived in those waters. Did they know? Did they not care?

Maybe it was more that they could flaunt the fact that merchants could pull up directly in front of their homes, though she hadn't seen any merchants willing to do that, at least not outside of the very center of the city.

"Why this one?"

"This one is a place that has drawn attention. While you were in there getting sized up, I was keeping an eye on it. My men sent word that there has been quite a bit of movement around this home, and while I was watching, I noticed there were several people who went inside."

"What kind of people?"

"Not merchants."

"How can you be certain?"

"Because one of them was foolish enough to wear a gray jacket."

7

SEARCH FOR KAVERS

Bastan led them on a meandering path, guiding them over to the manor house, but doing it in a way that would be least likely to elicit attention. Sam marveled at his skill. She'd only done a few jobs with Bastan, and because he rarely took jobs himself, it still surprised her how utterly silently he moved.

Some of that had to be related to his heritage. While she was a Kaver, Bastan was a djohn. She wasn't entirely sure what that meant, but she'd seen others in the city who had similar abilities. Most of them were minor abilities, but she had some experience with the djohn and their ability to face the Thelns.

"Do you intend for us to attack now?"

"Not attack. This is simply a scouting mission."

"And what if we find something that forces our hand? What if we have to take action?" Sam asked.

Bastan glanced over, one hand pressed against the side of a building, the other holding a rope with a hook on the end. He was preparing to climb, heading toward the rooftop. It was the same position she would have taken. "There are rarely times when you *have* to take action. There are times when action is beneficial, but there are rarely times when it is required."

"Then fine. What happens if we need to make a decision about whether or not we will take action on this supposed hideout of Scribes?"

Bastan frowned. "Are you mocking?"

"Bastan, you know I would never mock."

"No. You generally do much worse." He started up the building, and Sam followed, climbing onto the roof of one of the merchant buildings. This one didn't have a sign, and Sam wasn't sure what exactly it sold, but it probably didn't matter.

"You don't want to tell me what your plan is?"

"I plan to observe."

"Sometimes, you're too cautious," Sam said.

"It's the way I have maintained my position for as long as I have."

"No. The way you've maintained your position is that you send others into danger. You don't do it yourself."

"And I keep telling you that you were never in any danger, Samara. I was never going to put you in a position where you would have to do something that would pose a threat to you."

She crawled forward, crouching at the edge of the building so she could look out over the manor house. There were lights on inside, and shadows moved in front of the window. There was something about the house that reminded her of the last time she had attempted to break into a highborn house, and the easar paper she had been tasked with stealing. That had been the beginning of everything for her. It had been the change that had set her on a path toward a different life. Without that, she would have remained a thief, and though she might still feel like a thief—and a lowborn one at that—she was much more.

Everyone around her was much more too.

Except for Elaine. She was gone. Her mother was well and truly gone.

Bastan rested a hand on her arm.

Sam glanced over. "I'm fine."

"I can see from the tightness around your eyes that you're not entirely fine. Is it your brother you're thinking of?"

Sam sighed. It wasn't Tray, but it could have been. He had been with her the last time she had done something like this and had been the one looking out for her. His captivity had been the reason she had gone searching for other answers, the reason so much had changed for her. Everything had happened because of Tray, and mostly for the better.

Sam had found a mother, discovered Bastan was something of a father, and learned of her powers. And lost Tray.

"It's not Tray. Not only Tray," she corrected. "It's Elaine. I feel as if we never got a chance to really know each other, and now…"

"It's the reason you have to take every moment you have with someone and be thankful for it," Bastan said.

"If you're trying to get me to tell you how thankful I am that you're here with me, I'm not going to do it."

"That's not what I was after, but it wouldn't be terrible, now would it?"

Bastan grinned and then turned his attention back to the street, looking over at the building. Sam stared at it with him, looking for any signs of movement on the inside but didn't see anything.

"I haven't seen anyone heading in or out since we've been here," Sam said.

"I have not, either. That troubles me."

"Why?"

"Because I saw several people entering while we were in the shop, and I expected to see them leaving, but if they haven't, it suggests that perhaps there is some sort of meeting taking place."

And if there was a meeting, Sam needed to get inside.

She started forward, and Bastan grabbed her arm.

"What are you doing, Samara?"

"I'm doing what needs to be done. If they're having a meeting, I need to get in there and see what's going on and see if it has anything to do with Master Helen."

"If they're having a meeting, you cannot reveal yourself like that."

"I'm stealthy," she said.

Bastan arched a brow. "You might have been stealthy once, but ever since you've learned of your abilities, you have been anything but stealthy. I would argue that you're noisy."

"Nope. I'm not noisy. I'm stealthy." She jumped down, landing on the street below.

She started forward when Bastan joined her, moving much more quietly than she had managed.

"Fine. Maybe compared to you I'm noisy, but I'm still stealthy."

"I've tried teaching you stealth, but you have never wanted to be a good student of it."

"That's not true."

"Isn't it? Every time I have attempted to show you how to move quietly, you have refused my guidance."

"Maybe I would have taken your guidance if you wouldn't have kept me from taking the good jobs."

"I have given you nothing but good jobs."

"The jobs you gave me were the good ones? I'd hate to have seen the bad ones."

Bastan shook his head. They reached the short fence, and he leaped over, landing without making a sound on the other side. Sam assembled her canal staff and used it to flip over the wall, landing on a soft grassy lawn on the other side. A garden spread out before her, with flowers of many different colors filling it. A garden like this would be incredibly expensive to maintain.

"Whose house is this again?"

"I didn't say."

"I noticed. That's why I'm asking."

Bastan shook his head and nodded toward the house, creeping forward quietly. They moved around to the side rather than the main entrance, He reached a window and pushed on it. It opened, and he rolled inside.

Kyza!

She hadn't intended to force Bastan to do that. She had planned to enter on her own, but now that he was inside, she had to join him. She didn't want to put Bastan in any sort of danger. She had already lost Elaine, and she didn't want to lose the person who had effectively been her father all these years.

Sam propped herself up on her canal staff, balancing long enough to take a peek inside the window. The room was dark, and the shadowed form of Bastan waited for her. She flipped herself inside and carefully pulled her staff into the room.

Bastan nodded to it, his voice pitched at a whisper. "I doubt you will be able to use that in here."

Sam disassembled the staff and held out the two halves. "What about this?"

"Can you use it like that?"

"I can use it assembled or unassembled. I'm impressive like that."

"I have never doubted how impressive you are."

He started forward and reached a door. As he did, Sam glanced around the room and noticed that it was some sort of a sitting room. Chairs were positioned around a table with a few sheets of paper lying on it.

Sam hurried over to the table and looked at the papers. Could it be easar paper?

No such luck. It wasn't easar paper, but what she saw was some sort of notation on each of the sheets. She grabbed them and stuffed them into her pocket, determined to look at them later—or have Alec look at them later.

Bastan pushed the door open and paused, half in the hallway and half in the doorway. When he was content there was no movement, he stepped out, motioning for Sam to follow. When she did, nothing moved. She would've expected some activity, especially considering what they had seen from the street.

"Where is everyone?" Sam asked.

"Perhaps we should be thankful there's no activity."

"We saw movement. I expected to find people here."

Bastan went along the hall, checking door after door, and none of them were occupied.

"You think we go up?" Sam asked.

The narrow staircase led to the upper level, but if the people were all upstairs, there should have been some sound.

"I wonder if perhaps we need to go down," Bastan said.

There was another staircase that led down, and that was unusual this close to the canal. Few places were willing to fight with the moisture in a basement this close to the canal.

"This isn't a good idea. I know I said I needed to get in here to see what was happening, but we might be in over our heads."

"I won't allow anything to happen to you, Samara."

"I'm not worried about something happening to me."

"Then I won't allow anything to happen to me, either," Bastan said.

He started down the stairs, and Sam gripped her staff ends. As she made her way down after him, she focused on augmentations, trying to draw upon the power she could, thinking of what might be beneficial. She didn't know what they might encounter here and tried to bring on as many augmentations as she could.

Strength. Speed. Impermeability. Enhanced eyesight. Enhanced hearing.

They washed over her, one after another, a taxing effort, but she wanted to be prepared.

There was a door at the bottom of the stairs, and Bastan pushed it open.

Sam tensed, ready for whatever might be on the other side. Maybe Helen would be there, and they could end their search and capture her, then take her back to the university and interrogate her.

But no such luck. It was merely a storage room.

"We missed something," Sam said as she turned to head back to the main level.

"I don't know how we could've missed anything," Bastan said.

"We didn't go upstairs."

"If we'd gone upstairs, what do you think we would've seen?"

"I don't know, but the people must've gone somewhere."

When she reached the top of the stairs, she heard movement.

She looked over to Bastan, and he nodded. "I heard it, as well."

"What do you think it was?"

It came again. This time, near the front of the house.

It was a steady thumping.

Footsteps?

Not just footsteps. Several people's footsteps.

"We should get—"

Sam didn't get the chance to finish. The door at the end of the hall opened, and a man appeared. He carried a half-staff in his hand, and as soon as he saw her, he rushed down the hall, barreling toward them.

A Kaver.

Sam threw herself forward, positioning herself in front of Bastan, but it didn't matter. Another door opened, and another Kaver appeared.

"Where did they all come from?" she asked as she started her attack. She wasn't afraid to fight Kavers, especially if they were siding with Helen.

"How many Kavers do you think you can manage?" Bastan asked as Sam brought her staff around, preparing to attack. He was calm, but there was an edge of tension in his voice.

Bastan was nervous.

Sam wasn't accustomed to Bastan being nervous. He was always confident and calm, and for him to show any sign of nerves troubled her.

"I don't know. I guess you're going to find out. How many Kavers do you think you can manage?"

He grunted, bringing his sword around as he prepared to fight. "It seems we will soon learn. Perhaps we should have stayed outside and observed as I suggested."

"It's not really the time to say I told you so."

"I wanted to tell you before we died."

Sam smacked the staff against her attacker's staff. "What makes you think we're going to die?"

"Only the fact that there are many of them and only two of us."

"Fine. If you need to tell me you told me so before we die, then you said it." Sam spun her ends of the staff around, bringing one high and the other low. With her augmentations in place, she moved quickly, and the man she was facing wasn't able to compensate. She managed to strike him, catching him on one side of his head as well as one leg at the same time. He crumpled, falling in a heap, and blood pooled around the open wound on his head.

Sam backed into Bastan, getting close so that she could help. He whipped his sword around in a blaze, spinning quickly, and as she often was when fighting alongside Bastan, she was impressed by the level of skill he possessed. She didn't know if that was a djohn thing or if that was a Bastan thing, but either way, he managed to push back the Kaver who was attacking him.

There were two others in the hall with them.

Sam jumped over Bastan, kicking his attacker as she did, and the other two surrounded her. She whipped the ends of her staff, moving them in a quick circle. She was able to block one blow then another, but somehow, one of the attackers slipped through and struck her on the back of her leg. She staggered forward but didn't fall. She was thankful she had made her skin impervious. The blow didn't split the skin, and nothing broke; all she had to endure was the pain.

It did make her angry.

Sam swung one staff piece and threw it at the Kaver who was attacking her. It connected with the woman's stomach and threw her back.

It left only one attacker and Sam with just one half of her canal staff. "I might let you live if you lay down your staff," she said.

The other Kaver clenched his jaw. He was a little older than Sam, and he had close-cropped hair and sun-darkened skin. "You can't win. Your attack on the city and your intent to destroy everything that we are will not win."

"My attack? I'm only preventing Helen from making her attack. I've seen what she's doing and what she's willing to do."

"You don't understand. You have never been outside of the city. You don't know what's out there."

"My brother is out there," Sam said.

The man lunged, and she twisted out of the way, bringing her staff up at the same time.

Hers caused his staff to connect with his skull, and he fell backward.

She kicked, adding strength to the momentum that carried him backward, and he crashed through a doorway, landing on the floor on the other side.

Sam spun around, looking to see whether Bastan was in trouble, but he was sheathing his sword.

"How many of these do you want us to restrain?" he asked.

"I think we need to restrain all of them."

"And do you think we can?"

"Bastan—"

"It's a valid question, Samara. We either restrain them and see if we can keep them confined, or we have to realize that holding them creates a liability. Is that what you want?"

"I don't want to kill them."

"I didn't say that we would kill them."

"That's what you were implying."

Bastan looked over at the fallen Kavers. "I was implying that we simply eliminate them as a threat."

"Confine them. If Alec can sedate them, we might be able to get some answers out of them."

"And when they wake up? We can't stay here, Samara. And the two of us can't take four out. I don't know what sort of augmentations you have placed on yourself, but I doubt you have the ability to drag four people with you."

"I wouldn't have to bring four out," she said. "You could take two, and I could take two."

"They were right."

"They were right about what?"

"They were right about the idea that this is war. And if it is war, Samara, we must be prepared to do everything necessary for us to be victorious."

"Help me tie them up. We can drag them down into the cellar and come back for them."

"What if someone else returns before then?"

"One of us will stay and keep an eye on them."

"I will stay," he said.

"I need to be the one to stay here."

"With what you have been doing in the city, you are more valuable than I am."

"I'm not more valuable than you. You're the one who is helping to ensure that the outer sections are unified."

Bastan gritted his teeth and then nodded. "Fine. You remain. And if there is any danger, you depart. Do not stay here and risk yourself unnecessarily."

"I never do."

"I know that is not true."

They made quick work of tying up the Kavers, and

dragged them down into the cellar, securing the door behind them. Sam hoped there wasn't another way out down there, but there didn't seem to be. It seemed to be nothing more than brick and dirt.

"Go get Marin," she suggested to Bastan.

"I will find all the help I can," he said softly.

"We don't need an army."

"Are you sure?" He looked around the room before turning his attention back to Sam. "We don't know what we need. I saw a few people come in here, but none of them were the four that attacked us."

"None of them?"

Bastan shook his head.

Sam looked at the stairs and then looked up beyond. "Maybe before you go, we need to see what's upstairs."

8

THE BLOODLETTING

They reached the top of the stairs, and Bastan led. With her augmentations fading, she didn't object. She needed to reestablish them but doing so would take strength. If she tried it too soon, she tired more quickly, and her augmentations were not as effective. Nor did they last as long as when she gave her body a chance to recover.

At the top of the stairs, there was a single door. Bastan pushed it open and peered inside.

"What is it?" she asked when he didn't move out of the way.

"Samara—"

"No, Bastan. What is it?"

She pushed past and wished she hadn't.

Inside, she saw a woman in a corner, her still body suspended from the ceiling. Her head hung limp, her feet dangling above the floor, and her arms were outstretched to the sides, supported by additional rope. Her wrists had been slashed, and blood drained out, dripping into buckets below.

That wasn't even the worst part of it.

"That's Camellia," Sam said.

She looked over to Bastan, and he nodded.

"What's she doing here? We left her at the university, guarded by your men."

"It seems as if they managed to spring her free."

"And what is this? What are they doing with her?"

"She's a Kaver, right?"

She *was* a Kaver, and her blood was being drained out of her.

Was this how Helen was using the Kavers? If so, why would other Kavers fight on her behalf? If she was assaulting them in such a way, what would make them willing to fight for her?

"I'm going to see if there's anything around here that could help us," Bastan said.

Sam stood there numbly, unable to react. She needed to say something, but all she could do was stare at Camellia as she remained suspended from the ceiling. After a few moments, Sam dragged a chair over to her, standing on it so she could cut the woman's arms free. No one deserved this sort of torment. Not even a Kaver who had betrayed other Kavers.

She lowered the woman to the ground and gasped when she realized Camellia still had a pulse. "Bastan?"

He was facing a bookshelf and glanced over his shoulder. "What is it?"

"She's still alive."

"What? How can she still be alive?"

Sam shook her head. "Alec taught me how to assess for heartbeat and breathing and… All I can say is that she still lives."

Bastan turned back to her. "You need to get her to the university. If she knows anything, and if we can help her, she might be willing to share."

"She can't share with us if she's dead."

"That's even more reason for you to hurry."

"Bastan—"

He shook his head. "You can move more quickly than I can. Don't dispute that, as we both know it to be true. Get moving, see if you can help her, and then get Marin and return."

Sam bit back an angry comment. It seemed Bastan was going to get his way. As much as it annoyed her, he was right. She could move faster than he could, and with an augmentation, she could carry Camellia more easily than Bastan. And once she reached the university, she would have an easier time of getting the woman the necessary care.

"Don't think this changes anything."

Bastan chuckled. "What would it change?"

"Don't think it changes the fact that I know you're trying to stay here."

"Samara, I can assure you I couldn't care less whether I am here or not."

"No, you're trying to protect me in some way."

"Why stop what I have always done?"

"Would you stop saying that?"

Bastan grinned. "Does it bother you that someone else cares about you? It shouldn't."

"It bothers me that you keep trying to throw it at me that you're looking after me."

"I'm not throwing anything at you. I'm trying to remind you that you aren't nearly as alone in the city as you like to tell yourself you are. Ever since your brother headed off with Ralun, you have gone on as if you are isolated here, but that's not the case. You and I both *know* that's not the case."

"Is this your way of trying to make me stay?"

Bastan stared at her. "Go. Get this woman whatever help you can. And then bring that help back here. I will go back down to the cellar and guard our Kavers."

Sam didn't like the idea of leaving Bastan here to keep an eye on the Kavers, even restrained as they were. It took a moment to understand *why*. If something happened to him, she would be angry.

"Don't do anything stupid."

"Usually, I'm the one who says that."

Sam ran down the stairs and considered going out the front door before deciding to use the window. She carefully lowered Camellia out the window to the ground, and then jumped out, scooping her back up and running. As she carried her through the streets, she focused on her augmentations, needing to add strength and speed. This time, she needed to do it before she lost all of the augmentations that she already had, needing to ensure that she was able to reach the university in time.

Power surged through her in a cold wash.

Sam raced over bridges, ignoring the guards who tried to stop her, going much faster than they could keep up. She thought about using her canal staff and jumping the canals, but that would be too jarring for Camellia, and she thought she could manage more speed this way.

When she reached the university, Sam slowed. The line of people waiting for healing was much longer than it had ever been before, now trailing over the bridge and into one of the neighboring sections. The good news was that more healers were waiting than there had been before. But even with more healers, it would be impossible for them to keep up.

With so many people waiting, she wouldn't be able to cross the bridge, not easily, and not without trying to muscle through the crowd.

Sam had no choice but to jump the canal. She shifted Camellia in her arms and screwed the two ends of her staff together with her free hand. Running to the edge of the canal, she jumped, pressing off on her staff in the middle of the jump, using that to propel her over the water.

She landed on the other side as softly as she could and raced through the main doors of the university, not bothering to look back to see if anyone had seen what she had done. Inside, a few physickers moved along the halls, but Sam didn't go to them. She wanted to find Alec, but it was possible he wasn't back yet. He might still be with his father, which meant she would have to find someone else at the university who could help her.

Who could she find? Could she find Beckah? Sam had never really cared for the woman, but she trusted that she would do the right thing and would try to help Camellia.

She reached the hospital ward and pushed the door open and paused. It was so much busier than it had ever been before. There were hundreds of people in here now, and dozens of physickers making their way along the beds. Had Alec realized exactly how busy he would make the university by opening the doors in the way that he had? It made the physickers work that much harder, though knowing Alec, he probably didn't care. He probably enjoyed the extra work, and wouldn't have complained at all, except for the fact that he was not able to offer his own help because he was so busy with everything else he was working on.

Surprisingly, she saw someone she recognized and raced toward Jalen.

"Jalen. I need your help."

Jalen looked over. "Samara? Where is… Who is that?"

"I don't know where Alec is. This is a Kaver Bastan, and I caught. We had brought her to Alec, but she must've escaped, and now she's injured, and I don't know…"

Jalen took the woman from her and hurried to look for an open cot. There weren't any, so he was forced to set her against the wall near the back of the ward. Sam crouched down next to him. "It's unfortunate that we have not been able to keep up with the demand for our services," Jalen said. "As much as Alec wants us to help as many people as we can, there are limits to how many people we can support."

"Is there anything you can do for her?"

"Do you know what's wrong with her?"

"Look at her wrists," Sam said.

Jalen had started an examination, listening to her heart and her lungs the same way Alec would, but stopped to look at her wrists at Sam's suggestion. His eyes widened slightly, and he gasped. "Who did this to her?"

"I can only guess that it was Helen. As she did with your father, I believe she's stealing the blood of Kavers for whatever it is she has planned."

Jalen paused and looked up. His eyes scanned the ward until he settled on somebody in the middle of the room. "Beckah!"

Beckah hurried over, and when she saw Sam, she frowned slightly. Sam ignored the slight and pointed to the woman. Beckah crouched down next to Jalen, and the two of them began to perform a rapid assessment. Beckah checked Camellia's wrist and then her neck, leaning her head down to the woman's chest. "She still has a heartbeat," she said.

"I could see that. There is still blood spurting from these wounds. It's amazing she managed to make it this far."

"What do you think we can do?"

"I don't think there's anything that can be done for this much blood loss."

"We need to save her," Sam said. "We need to be able to question her to see what she knows and if there's anything we can learn about what Helen plans."

"Samara, I don't know that there's anything we can do. She's lost so much blood, and there's only so much support that we can give her."

"Do you have easar paper?"

"Sam…"

"You know how to treat her, right?" Sam stared at him, waiting for Jalen to argue, but he didn't.

"I know how to treat her, but there isn't enough time. Even if we managed to get easar paper, we wouldn't be able to buy her enough time to get her through this. I'm sorry, Samara, but she's gone."

Sam wasn't willing to accept that.

"There has to be something that can be done. We have to find some easar paper."

"Even if you did," Jalen started, "you would have to find both Kaver and Scribe. It won't work otherwise."

Kyza! Helen would win again.

"See what you can do for her. Just... Just try something. I have to get back to Bastan."

"I'll do what I can. I'm sorry, Samara. There are limits to how much healing we can offer."

Sam knew there were and had experienced the limitations before, especially when there had been nothing they could do for Elaine. She hated the limitations and hated feeling helpless and hated that Helen could take away the one person who might be able to offer some answers. Was that the reason that Helen had come for Camellia? Had she been in Alec's room?

As much as she wanted to go and check on Alec, helping Bastan took precedent, at least right now. She trusted Alec was well, but she couldn't shake her concern that this woman *had* been in his room. "Beckah, could you check on Alec? This woman was taken from Alec's room, and if anything happened to him..."

"I will."

Sam sighed and turned away, heading out of the building. She needed to get Marin and take her to where she'd left Bastan. She raced away from the university and jumped over the canal, now unencumbered by Camellia, landing on the palace section. When she ran inside, she stopped and asked the first set of guards, "Where is Marin?"

"I'm not certain."

"Is she still here?"

"I haven't seen her leave."

That didn't mean anything, and Sam knew it. Marin could have snuck out the same way that Sam was able to sneak out and could've crossed the canal without being seen.

"If you see her, send word to her that I need her help."

She ran back and jumped canal after canal, racing through the sections, heading back to Caster for help. She'd promised Bastan she'd return with Marin. When she reached Caster, she started keeping track of how long it had been since she'd left Bastan, realizing that had been far longer than what she thought was safe. If anything happened to Bastan, she would be angry. Hurt. Devastated. All of those thoughts raced through her mind.

When she reached Bastan's tavern, she hurried inside. She waved Kevin down. "I need your help. Bastan—"

"Say nothing else."

Kevin hurried away and spoke to a few of the men in the tavern. They immediately got up and went with Sam. It happened so quickly that she was almost taken aback by the speed with which they reacted.

"Is this all?" she asked as they lined up outside the tavern.

"We'll get more people as we go. Where are we going?"

"I'll show you."

Kevin turned to somebody and whispered something, and the man ran off. He wasn't anyone Sam recognized, but she trusted Kevin, which meant Bastan would have trusted this man.

They hurried through the streets, Sam no longer able to take the canals, wanting to stay with Kevin and the others, not wanting to get so far ahead of them that she would end up separated and running the risk of reaching Bastan—and possibly danger—before she had help with her.

There was no need to ask the others to go any faster. They hurried without any encouragement and reached the section far more quickly than Sam would have expected. She found the manor house and raised her hand as they approached.

There were probably fifty people with her now. What must it look like having Sam and so many others marching through the street? Bastan had already told her how little she looked like she fit in the section, and she suspected she wasn't the only one who stood out. Others with her probably stood out just as much, which would make it look like there was a mob descending on the manor house and attacking.

"Is he in there?" Kevin whispered.

"He's in there, and there's a cellar, and…"

"We'll get to him, Sam."

Sam took a moment and focused on an augmentation. She called upon strength and speed, deciding that they would be the most beneficial. In her fear and agitation, the augmentations came quickly, washing through her more rapidly than usual.

Sam kicked the door, and it splintered.

She raced inside, a dozen of Bastan's men following behind her. When she reached the door to the cellar, she knew something was wrong. It was cracked open. Bastan wouldn't have left it like that.

Sam ran down the stairs, already preparing her attack, but she needn't have bothered. The room was empty.

Sam hurried back up the stairs and met Kevin. "Search this level."

He made a motion with his hand, a similar gesture to Bastan's. She hurried upstairs, fearing that perhaps he had ventured up there again. That didn't fit with Bastan. He would have stayed down with the Kavers until Sam returned. The fact that he was not there suggested to her that something had happened.

Could Helen have returned?

Could the Kavers have awakened and somehow broken free?

Maybe Sam had been underestimating their abilities. Or maybe she was overestimating hers. Perhaps it was both.

Upstairs, there was something there that hadn't been when she'd left earlier.

Two of the Kavers they had attacked were suspended from the ceiling the same way Camellia had been. Blood poured down their arms, staining them, but there were no buckets, not as there had been for Camellia.

"What is this?" Kevin asked.

"This is the violence we're facing," Sam said. "This is—"

"Horrible."

"It is horrible." Sam made her way over to the first of the Kavers and climbed up on a chair to check for a pulse, but there was none. She made her way to the other and checked him, but like the first, he had no pulse.

They were gone.

And with them, any answers they could have offered as to what happened to Bastan.

"We have to find her," Sam said. "We have to do it quickly, or she will get out of the city."

"She can't get out of the city, not with everything that we have set up," Kevin said.

"Even with Bastan?" Sam asked. If Helen had grabbed Bastan, it was possible she could—and would—use him to escape the city.

Kevin paled. "We need to find her."

9

A SEDATIVE

Arrend had always been a place where Alec felt comfortable, and returning here now was no different. After everything that he'd gone through, having a sense of familiarity and normalcy was almost soothing. From the buildings lining the streets, each one with shop owners he knew from his childhood, to the sense of peace he felt when coming here, he appreciated it even more now that he had been raised to master physicker.

He reached the apothecary and found the door unlocked. Alec had offered him a place at the university, but his father had refused, at least so far. If Alec could continue to encourage the university to continue offering healing to anyone, regardless of their ability to pay or their station, maybe his father would find it in him to return.

For now, his father had not wanted to. Then again, there was something beneficial about having his father here at the apothecary rather than at the university. It gave Alec a place to go when he needed to get away.

The bell rang softly as he entered the shop, and Alec looked around. He waited for his father to appear, but he didn't.

Alec made his way to the back of the shop, passing row upon row of the medicines his father collected. There was a time when Alec had been convinced his father was simply altruistic, but all of that had changed when he discovered that his father had a more nefarious role. As a poisoner, he used his knowledge to work against certain people. That still troubled Alec, and they had not come to a complete resolution about it, at least not yet.

"I thought you would be preoccupied these days," his father said, stepping out from the rear of the shop. Ink stained his hands, and his face was drawn, as if he'd been awake for a long time.

Considering his father, Alec wouldn't have put it past him. There were times when his father would work in the shop all night, either healing or mixing up various compounds. "I need your help with something."

"My help?"

Alec nodded. "There's something I can't do."

"You? Alec, I've taught you the only limitations you have are those you place upon yourself."

"The only limitation I'm facing is time. I need to be doing other things at the moment, and I don't know that I have the necessary time—or temperament—for this."

"And what is it?"

"I can show you," he suggested.

His father frowned. "I need to finish what I'm working on before I can go."

"What are you working on? Maybe I can help?"

His father studied him for a moment. There seemed to be a debate warring across his face, and Alec wondered why he would hesitate. His father had always included him in everything that he did while working at the apothecary—other than working as a poisoner.

That had to be the reason for his hesitation.

"It doesn't matter what it is, I will help, Father."

His father nodded once. "I could use an extra set of hands, and considering your experience, you would be beneficial with this."

Alec followed his father to the back of the shop. A massive metal pot sat over the fire. A line of bottles rested on the table next to the pot, and a sheet of paper sat next to them, with detailed notes.

"What is this?" he asked.

"This is a sleeping draught."

Alec glanced at the page. There were probably twenty different items involved in mixing this, a much more complicated mixture than most that his father made. Most of the time, his father preferred simpler mixtures, and they consisted of two or three compounds, sometimes a few more at most, but never this many.

"What kind of sleeping draught is this?"

"Do you really want to know the answer to that?"

Alec pulled his attention away from the page and looked up at his father. "I do want to know. Who is this for?"

"I have many people who come to me for services."

"You have many people, but few would need anything this complicated. Why are you making something like this?"

"To be prepared."

"What kind of preparation do you need? What kind of preparation requires that you have a concoction like this..." Alec studied the list again before frowning and looking back up at his father. "This is for Helen and the other Scribes, isn't it?"

His father nodded. "Bastan thought that we had better be prepared. He suspected she might be able to counter most things but doubted she would be prepared for a complicated mix. I tended to agree. I figured if I could compound it in such a way that it masks all the possible ingredients, then it would be difficult for even Helen to determine what I used."

Alec had to agree that would likely be true. It surprised him that Bastan would be so thoughtful about what was used, but then should it? Bastan was incredibly intelligent. He had to be, especially for him to have gained such power throughout the city. Of course, Bastan would be making plans. But then, why wouldn't Bastan have shared with him and Sam what he was doing? Unless he had shared with Sam. Maybe Sam wasn't sharing with him.

"How did you come up with this particular recipe?" Alec asked.

"It has been a series of trial and error," his father began. "I started with the premise that I wanted to ensure anything I mixed could be masked. I feared that Helen, especially as intelligent as she is, would know if there was something to be concerned about. Most likely, she would know the moment she was exposed to something, which is reason enough for me to find a way to hide it."

"And have you?"

"Have I managed to conceal the presence of everything I've mixing in here?" His father shook his head. "There remains a bitterness to it, and I suspect someone like Helen would recognize immediately what that bitterness meant."

"What do you intend to do to counter the bitterness?"

"I have been trying various ingredients and ratios to see if I can counter it, but I haven't been able to find the right combination of compounds quite yet."

Alec studied the list. He didn't expect that he would be able to find anything that his father hadn't come up with. Everything on the list interacted with everything else, making it difficult for him to figure how his father had managed to mask the taste the way it was.

"How are you testing?"

"Slowly," his father said.

"Slowly?"

"I can only take a drop at a time. Anything more than that and I notice the effects. Even with the drop, I still notice the effects."

"And I assume that when you are testing, you are primarily looking for bitterness."

"Bitterness. Efficacy. Color. All of the above. I need to find whatever I can to conceal it."

Alec studied the list. Many of the ingredients would be used to counter the effect and taste of another. "Only bitterness?" he asked.

"That's primarily the issue. At this point, I can't come

up with anything that can mute it any more than I have."

"Why do you need an extra set of hands?"

"I thought I could continue to mix. You can add in the ingredients while I do, and maybe together we can find a way to conceal the flavor."

Alec dipped his finger into the mixture. He didn't need to be any weaker than he already was. Eel meat would help, but only to a point, and he hated that he was so reliant on it. Still, he was curious about whether he could detect the bitterness or whether this was something only his father was aware of. His father had a much more sensitive palate than Alec did, and it wouldn't be altogether surprising for his father to notice something Alec didn't think was quite as significant.

He needed only a taste. Just a drop. Anything more than that, and he worried that it would be too much for him.

Alec dabbed the liquid onto his tongue, letting it linger there.

There was definitely a bitterness. He was able to identify five of the various compounds within the mixture simply by the taste, and if he could, then he suspected someone like Master Helen, someone who was incredibly intelligent and skilled, might be able to detect even more.

The sense of the sleeping draught washed over him.

It happened all at once, hitting him quickly, and he staggered.

His father was there and guided him to a chair.

"I'd warned you that it was effective."

"You said you have been trying a drop at a time."

"Yes, but with everything I add, it grows increasingly

potent." His father took a seat next to Alec and studied him. "The good news is the effects won't last too long."

"Even with the poisoning I suffered?"

His father frowned. "It's possible that your effect may last longer. What were you thinking if you knew your weakness from the poisoning remained?

"I was thinking that I wanted to see if I could detect the bitterness that you were referencing."

"You didn't believe me?"

"No, I believed you, I just didn't know whether I would be skilled enough to detect it."

His father shook his head. "You continue to doubt yourself, Alec, when everything you have done has demonstrated there is no reason for that doubt."

"It's not a doubt, it's more a questioning. I'm confident in what I know and what I can do; I just wasn't certain I could detect the same bitterness you had noticed."

"And were you?"

"I noticed the flavors of varl leaf, orphum paste, coscar oil, bendrl, and loras root."

"You noticed all of that with a single drop?"

"I know there were probably more, but those were the only ones I could identify."

His father chuckled. "In a single drop. I can pick up perhaps the notes of varl leaf, but that's only because of how awful it tastes and the contribution that it has to the bitterness. That's what I've been trying to counter, but I don't think I've been as successful at it as I would like."

"Which is why you added the swere berry?"

"I thought that it might help counteract that bitterness. It mitigates it but doesn't eliminate it. Any more of the berry, and it becomes too sweet. What I need is something that will take the edge off but doesn't have quite as much sweetness to it."

The weakness and fatigue were beginning to recede. Alec suspected he would need more eel meat to completely eliminate the feeling, but for now, he was well enough that he could sit upright on his own once again. "What if I have something that might be helpful?"

"What do you have?"

"It's a combination of things, and I don't know whether it will be completely effective, but if it is…"

His father glanced over to the pot. "I think Bastan is right. We do need something for when we come in contact with Helen or those who work for her. If anyone will be able to counter the effects of these mixtures, it's going to be Helen."

"I don't know that it's wise for you to get involved like this," Alec said.

"I might be the best person to do so. I'm not a Scribe—not like you. I don't have the same connections as Helen. But I do have something she does not. I have experience with this." His father looked up and met his gaze. "I might be the only one who can do this, Alec. It's something I think is necessary, and I'm happy to do it if it will support you and the others."

"And when this is done?" Alec asked.

"What are you getting at?"

"What I'm getting at is whether you will continue to work as a poisoner when all of this is over."

"I don't know."

It was an honest answer, and Alec knew that he should

take it and be satisfied that his father had been honest with him rather than trying to lie to him, but he didn't like the idea of his father working as a poisoner and using his knowledge—knowledge that he'd acquired at the university —to harm others.

"You know that I have changed the requirements at the university."

"What requirements are those?"

"No longer is it necessary to have extreme wealth to obtain healing from the master physickers."

"You have done that?"

"I did it because it was the right thing to do. I have been fighting against the university's remuneration system ever since I got there. Now, as a master physicker, I've been able to effect real change. If my position within the university allows me to do that, I am happy to do so. Besides, from what I understand, the reason for the price and the requirement for coming to the university was so they had the necessary money to purchase easar paper."

"And now that you can make easar paper..."

"Now that I can make easar paper, it's no longer necessary for the university to charge what it had been for the services that others need."

"I... I am proud of you, Alec."

"That's not an answer."

"What was your question?" his father said.

"Will you come with me?"

"Where is it that I need to go before you help me?"

Alec smiled at his father. "To the palace."

"And why am I going to the palace?"

"Because I have need of the poisoner."

10

THE POISONER AND THE PALACE

A lec brought his father into the palace and was guided to the cells. He hadn't been here before and felt a chill as he went down the stairs and into the lower reaches of the palace, trying not to think of who had been held captive here. But these cells were a far cry from the city's prison. The prison where Tray and Sam had once been held was near the edge of the city, and it was nearly impenetrable. That was a place for common criminals. The cells beneath the palace were for uncommon criminals.

There was a part of him that wished Sam was with him when he entered, but it was probably for the best that she wasn't. When he saw Lyasanna, he resisted the urge to shiver. She made him uncomfortable, mostly because of her complete lack of remorse for everything she had done.

His father, on the other hand, had no such hesitation.

He stopped at the cell, and he studied her. The

princess sat inside, the room fairly unremarkable. She had a wooden cot, a bedpan, and a tray with half-eaten food on it.

"This is she," his father said.

"This is the princess."

His father snorted. "When she's confined, you don't need to give her the honorific. I think Lyasanna would be appropriate."

She stood and casually made her way to the bars, gripping them and looking out. "Ah, Samara's Scribe. Has she sent you here to see how you might best confine me?"

"She hasn't sent me at all. I think Marin has done an adequate job of holding you here."

"Marin won't be able to hold me for long. Even she has begun to realize that," she said, nodding to the end of the hallway.

Alec turned his gaze there. A half-built wall cut off the end of the hall, and behind it, he saw the section of wall where Sam said the other Scribes were placing markings, trying to erode the protections within the cells. He wasn't sure how that was possible, though it was likely a secret that Helen had kept from him. Maybe it had been kept from Eckerd as well, especially as he didn't seem to have any idea about how it was possible to place such augmentations from a distance.

"Marin didn't ask me to come, either," Alec said. "I've come on my own. And I brought someone who is even smarter than Helen."

Lyasanna grinned. "You had better hope that's the case. I believe Helen is far more gifted than you give her credit."

"I've given Helen plenty of credit. But I still maintain she's not nearly as impressive as my father."

Lyasanna's smile faded. She turned to his father. "The apothecary," she spat.

"You've heard of me?" his father asked.

"Who abandons the university to go and serve as an apothecary for lowborns?"

"I served as an apothecary for all who needed my services," his father said. He leaned forward, getting close to Lyasanna. "And I sold my services for other purposes. Perhaps you have heard of the poisoner?"

Her eyes widened slightly.

His father smiled. "Yes. From your expression, I can tell that you have. Know this. Helen may have experience as a Scribe, but I have other experience, and I intend to use it to capture her so that my son does not have to fear what she might attempt."

Lyasanna stared at him for a long moment before a smile returned to her face. "Interesting. I think you and Helen would've gotten along well."

"We never did," he said.

His father started toward the end of the hall and Alec followed, casting an occasional glance back at Lyasanna. He couldn't help it. She intrigued him, but equally intriguing was the fact that she had been willing to abandon so much of who she was and what she was for her to do what? How was siding with Helen and the Scribes helping Lyasanna?

Unless she wasn't working on her own.

He hadn't given that as much thought. Helen had figured out a way to control the Kavers, but they didn't know if there might be something else, some other way that she was controlling them.

"Alec?"

He turned his attention back to his father and noticed the way he was studying the far wall. He had climbed over the half-built section of wall and was now running his hand along the stone of the far wall. Alec joined him, scrambling over the half-wall and toward the back.

"I've wondered why it wouldn't be easier just to move her," Alec said.

"It might be easier, but if there's any way to draw Helen—and those who work with her—then we need to do it."

"So, you agree with Sam?"

His father glanced over at him. "This was Sam's idea?"

"Who did you think it was?"

"This is the kind of thing Marin would have considered, at least from what I can tell of her."

"I'm pretty sure Sam was the one who came up with this."

His father grunted. "She's an impressive woman. I would advise you to be careful with her too."

"Why careful?"

"Any woman who is creative enough to identify a way to capture someone like this will be creative in other ways. Don't cross her."

Alec shook his head. "I have no intention of crossing Sam. She's my…" He almost said Kaver, but she was more than that. She was more than his friend. Neither of them had been willing or able to express their emotions fully, but she felt the same way he did. Both wanted that time together, but until everything settled down, it didn't seem they would have it.

"She's yours. I understand." His father turned away from Alec and began to focus on the wall. "And what you would like is for me to help determine what these symbols are, is that right?"

"We need to understand the symbols, and we need to know how to counter them."

"I'm not sure I'll be able to help with that. These symbols don't mean anything to me."

"They don't have to mean anything. You just have to look and understand the pattern and see if there's any way that you can figure out how to counteract them."

His father took out a piece of paper from his pocket and withdrew a pen from the other, and then began to copy them. "I'll see if there's anything that I can work out. If new markings crop up, I need to know about them."

"You're not going to stay here?"

"If I stay here and try to work through this, we run the risk of me unintentionally destabilizing things." He looked over at Alec. "No. I don't think I can stay here. Let me work on this, and you… you work on that task that I gave you."

Alec tapped the jar of liquid his pocket. He would begin to test on his father's behalf, looking to see if he could eliminate the bitterness from his father's mixture, and see if the easar tea was effective.

When his father finished copying down the symbols, he turned back to Lyasanna. "It would go easier for you if you shared what you knew," he said.

Lyasanna smiled. "Easier for me? I think what you are

asking is for it to be easier for *you*. I have no intention of making it any easier for you. I doubt Helen does, either."

"Helen doesn't know what she has gotten herself into," his father said. "If she did, she wouldn't have attempted this with my son involved."

"Do you think that your threats mean anything to me?"

"Perhaps not, but they should. And, in time, they will. This is my warning to you, and my warning for her."

"I think you are making your warning to the wrong person."

"I'm not convinced that you aren't still in contact with her in some way," his father said. "So you tell her what I said. You tell her that Aelus will prevent her from harming anyone, especially my son."

His father left the room, and Alec hurried after him. When they stepped out of the row of cells, the door closed, guards standing on either side, Alec frowned at his father. "What was that about? What do you mean that she is still in contact with Helen?"

"I suspect someone here has been providing information to Helen. It's what I would arrange for if I were trying to get in. I will touch base with your friend and Marin and see what precautions they have taken."

"I suspect they have everything observed. Especially with Bastan involved."

His father stopped. "Bastan is involved with this?"

Alec nodded. "Ever since breaking Jalen out of prison, Bastan has been more openly involved in the politics of the city."

"That is surprising."

"You didn't know?"

"I wasn't certain. Most of the time, Bastan has preferred to move in the shadows, but what you're saying is that he is more open with his intentions."

"He is more than open. Because of him, the outer sections prevent Helen and the others from escaping."

"And does Lyasanna know this?"

Alec frowned, trying to think through what might've been said in front of Lyasanna. Could she know that? Could she know that Bastan and those with him were the key?

"I don't know. Bastan was seen at the university, so it's possible she understands exactly what Sam means to him."

"Yes. Another reason to be careful with that one."

"Bastan?"

His father shook his head. "Not so much Bastan, but the woman he considers a daughter."

They headed out of the palace, and Alec had hoped that he might run into Sam, but he didn't. He'd not seen her since she'd brought the Kaver Camellia to his rooms at the university. She and Bastan were probably out searching for Marin, which meant she was likely in danger once again. Would there ever come a time when she wasn't in danger? Would there ever come a time when he wasn't worried about her?

"Send word if you are convinced that your additive will make a difference," his father said.

"And you send word if you come up with anything about the symbols."

His father glanced down at the page that he held folded in his hand. "I will. I am... troubled... by this."

"By the fact that you don't understand the symbols?"

"By the fact that Helen knows something that is completely beyond me."

They parted, and Alec made his way over to the university, heading back across the bridge, no longer bothering even to flash any sort of sigil. He wasn't stopped, and with as often as he went between the university and the palace, the guards even knew him by sight. Alec made his way to the university and hurried up to his room. He was curious to determine whether adding the easar tea would make a difference. Would he be able to find a solution to his father's problem?

The door to his room was ajar.

Alec frowned. That shouldn't be the case.

He pushed it open cautiously and entered. His room was a disaster. Items had been tossed, and his table was a mess, leaving papers and books scattered all over.

Two men lie motionless on the floor. They were Bastan's men, and they were assigned to keep an eye on the Kaver... who was now missing.

Someone had not only broken into his room, but they had done so in the masters' quarters. That shouldn't have happened. His room should have been secure here, and there should have been no reason—and no possible way—for someone to have broken in and done this.

Was it possible the Kaver had managed to escape?

If that were the case, there would've been no reason for his room to have been tossed as it was.

Alec checked on the men. One of them had a pulse,

and he flipped him over, finding a big gash on his fore-head and a knot on the other side of his head. He would recover, but he would need some attention.

He turned his attention to the other man and found him pulseless.

He swallowed. Should he have stayed with the Kaver? He was convinced he had been able to sedate her, but maybe his concoction wasn't as strong as it needed to be.

There shouldn't have been any way for the Kaver to have escaped. Not only had he placed a sedation that should have been strong enough, but without augmenta-tions, she wouldn't have been able to break free. Even with augmentations, the men guarding her would have stood a fighting chance. She didn't have a weapon, and though he'd seen Marin fighting without weapons, these men wouldn't have been so easily overwhelmed.

That meant she had help.

Could it have been Helen?

He wouldn't put it past her to have known about another way to access the university.

If it was Helen—or someone who worked with Helen —then he was even more concerned. He didn't need Helen gaining access to the university and to his quarters, because if she did, it would mean it wasn't safe for him or others here. The university would no longer be a place where he could offer protection.

Even the palace might already have been compromised.

What about his back room?

Alec stepped past the fallen men and continued back into his area where he researched. Could somebody have made it all the way back here? If they made it into his outer room, it was likely they would search the entirety of his quarters.

He pushed open the door and looked around.

Surprisingly, it looked untouched.

Even the easar paper drying on the tray seemed to be untouched.

That troubled him. If the Kaver had awoken and attacked the guards, it seemed likely she would have at least checked to see what was back here, unless her only thought was on escape.

Maybe there was another explanation.

What of his chunk of svethwuud?

If the Kaver had discovered that, then Helen would have the answer to easar paper, and then she might be able to mix her own, which meant their one advantage over her would be gone.

He found the piece of svethwuud where he'd left it. It looked untouched and still had the slimy sheen that it had from when it had been extracted from the swamp.

As he looked around the room, he wondered whether anything here could be trusted. Anything could have been contaminated, which meant he would have to start over, even on the easar paper. He could test it, but did he dare risk relying on it?

Then he realized he couldn't even rely on the easar tea.

That was perhaps the worst part of all of it. It was bad enough that his room had been broken into, and the Kaver was gone, and bad enough that Bastan's men were injured and dead, but now all of his hours and hours of work, from making the easar paper to repurposing the easar tea were wasted.

It felt like a sick prank.

And yet, this wasn't a prank at all. The man lying in his front room was evidence to that.

Alec had to do something to help the one man who still had a chance. He could focus on the contents of his room later and could concentrate on trying to settle in and find safety later and could even send word to Sam then.

His first thought had to be on those he could help.

But before he left, he grabbed the chunk of svethwuud and stuffed it in his pocket. He should've kept it with him, but he had thought his room was safe.

When would all of this end? When would their world return to what it once was? Would they ever feel the sense of trust and security they once took for granted?

He shook his head to clear out those thoughts. One task at a time. He had to focus that way. He needed to find someone he trusted who could help him and get word to Sam.

11

SEARCH FOR BASTAN

Her search for Bastan had yielded nothing, so Sam decided to take a different tact and went looking for Alec, finding him in his quarters at the university. Her heart had not slowed since leaving Kevin at the building with the dead Kavers. She wanted nothing more than to race off and go searching for Bastan, but she needed answers. She needed to see if there was anything Camellia could reveal about Helen, or hopefully about where Helen may have taken Bastan. She wasn't about to lose him, not after losing Elaine and Tray.

She burst into his room without knocking and stopped short when she saw it in shambles. "What happened?" she asked.

He motioned to the men lying on the ground. "There was an attack."

"*You* were attacked?"

"I wasn't here, but *they* were attacked. I don't know if it was your Kaver woman, or if someone else came to find her. One of them will make it, but the other…"

Sam crouched down and realized Ricken still breathed. She was thankful for that, but she could see that Paulie was already gone.

"I don't think she escaped. They must have come for her. But how did they even get into the university? How did they know she was here?"

"I wondered the same. Now even the university is not safe. For any of us."

"We found a place Helen might have been," Sam said.

"*Might* have been?"

"I'm not sure if she was there or not," Sam said. "It's where we found Camellia with her wrists cut, but—"

Alec frowned. "Wrists cut?"

"Didn't Beckah find you?" He shook his head. "Where did she go, then? I asked her to find you to help save Camellia. I think Helen drained Camellia's blood to steal her Kaver ability. She was still alive when we found her, but I don't know if I got her back here in time. When I couldn't find you, I went to the ward and found Jalen, but…"

"Come with me," Alec said.

They hurried down the stairs into the hospital ward. Sam was exhausted after everything she had been through and from using all of her augmentations, but she had to keep pushing herself. For Bastan, she needed to keep moving forward, until she found where Helen would have taken him.

"There's Jalen," Sam said.

He was working on an older man on the far side of the room.

When he saw her, he shook his head. "Samara, I tried, but there wasn't anything that could be done. She was too far gone by the time you brought her here. I'm so sorry, but…"

Sam swallowed. If Camellia was gone, so too was any chance they would learn what Helen planned.

"Kyza! We needed to find out what she knew. Without her, there might not be any way for us to determine why Helen is killing her own Kavers and taking their blood in this way."

"That's not quite true," Alec said.

He started off and headed toward a cot in the middle of the room. When he reached a woman in her mid-thirties, he pulled back the blanket, revealing her arms. Sam gasped.

She had cuts on her wrists much like what Camellia had. "Who is this?" she asked.

Alec shook his head. "I don't know. I wasn't even sure what had happened to her when you showed me the other woman's wrists, it reminded me of her." He looked up at her with a grave expression. "And the king."

"Is she… alive?"

"She was close to death when I first came across her, and I did everything I could to support her, but we needed to know more. I sent the junior physicker to her section to find out more about her."

"And where is he now?"

Alec looked around. "I don't see him here."

"If he was out searching for information about her,

and Helen discovered, it's possible she would harm him, even kill him."

Alec gritted his teeth. "How many more people is she going to sacrifice to achieve her plan?"

"If Helen was doing the same thing with this woman, it's likely she was a Kaver."

"She's not dead, Sam."

"Fine. She *is* a Kaver." Sam looked down at the woman. She didn't recognize her, and it bothered her that there were so many Kavers she had not met. How could there have been so many? How could it have been hidden from her during her training?

Could it be that Elaine didn't know exactly how many Kavers remained?

If Lyasanna were interested in attacking in the city, it would fit that she would want to conceal the presence of Kavers.

"I don't know if she's a Kaver or not. I won't know until we are able to wake her up, but I don't know that it's safe to do that."

"We need answers," Sam said. "Bastan is gone, Alec."

"Bastan?"

"We found Camellia in a house Bastan's men had been watching. They had seen physickers going in and out. When we went in to investigate, we were attacked by Kavers. We found Camellia hanging from the ceiling, but alive, so I brought her here. Bastan stayed behind to guard the four Kavers who'd attacked us. When I returned to the house, he was gone, as were two of the Kavers, and now…"

She swallowed back a lump in her throat and wiped

away tears that had formed in the corners of her eyes. She wouldn't allow herself to cry. Bastan *wasn't* gone.

"You said there were four and then you came back, and two were gone. What happened to the other two?"

"The same as happened to Camellia and this woman."

Alec breathed out. "What is Helen using all of this blood for?" He pulled the sheet back over the injured woman. "I don't understand it. What does she think she can accomplish?"

"Isn't there anyone you can ask? I thought Master Eckerd was a Scribe."

"Master Eckerd is a Scribe, but he's not as knowledgeable as Helen. I think she was keeping certain aspects of her ability secret. And that's not all." Alec lowered his voice and leaned close to Sam. "I think she has been to the Theln lands and returned."

If that was true, then Helen might know more about what it meant to be a Scribe than anyone. Could Helen know how to use the blood in a way that would give her even more power?

Then again, a Kaver's blood drew upon the power of the Kaver. If the Kaver was dead, would the blood taken from the body still have any power?

She didn't think so. Which meant that an attack on the Kavers, draining them of their blood, wouldn't make any sense. It would only serve to weaken her position by removing her resources. She needed Kavers alive.

"We need to figure out the purpose behind bleeding out the Kavers."

"I don't know where to look. I've gone to the masters'

section in the library, but there isn't anything there that helps."

"And we've looked in Helen's rooms."

Alec nodded. "Virtually empty. Even though she's been at the university for as long as she has, there wasn't anything of importance."

Sam tried to think if there was anything in the palace, but they hadn't come across anything that would help her discover any secrets about Helen.

"What else do we know about her?"

Alec frowned. "Not much, but there is someone who might. I hadn't thought to ask him, because he was the one who…"

"The one who what?"

"He was the one I thought had betrayed me."

"This is your friend? Stefan?"

"He used to be my friend," Alec said.

"He was helping Prince Jalen," Sam said.

"I didn't know it at the time, and he didn't know what Jalen was. Which means he simply betrayed a friend."

"Or he was following the commands of his prince."

Alec let out a frustrated sigh. "That's possible too. Let's go find Stefan."

"What about her?"

"Until she wakes up, there's no way she will be able to provide you with any answers. And there's nothing more we can do for her without more information. I don't know how long it'll be, if ever. She lost a lot of blood, and it could be hours or days, but she's been given every chance she can to wake up." He thought of the young physicker he'd sent off into the city to learn what he could about her. "When she comes around, I will make sure they send word to me."

As Alec led her from the hospital ward, she glanced back at the woman. Maybe there was something familiar about her, but what?

They headed up a set of stairs that Sam had only been up a few times. It led to the students' section of the university, and Alec hurried along the hall until he reached a door halfway down. He knocked heavily. The door opened, and a tall young man with a narrow face looked out.

"Master Stross," he said.

"It's not master anything, Stefan. It's Alec. Can we talk?"

Stefan glanced from Alec to Sam, and he licked his lips, swallowing. "What is this about? Did I do something that will get me expelled from the university? You would need to talk to Prince—I mean King Jalen if you intend to do that."

Sam smiled to herself. If nothing else, Stefan seemed to have a bit of a spine. He was willing to stand up to Alec even though Alec was a master physicker, albeit one who had once been his close friend.

"You're not going to get kicked out of the university. I have questions about your grandmother."

Stefan's face paled. "I don't know anything about Grandmother. Others have come and asked me the same thing."

"Which others?" Alec asked.

"King Jalen has asked. Master Eckerd has asked. Master Carl."

Sam could see a mixture of emotions flicker across Alec's face. "They might have asked their own questions, but I have several of my own I need answered," Alec said. "Can we speak? You said your grandmother had a home in a section near here."

"She did—I mean, she does. Why?"

"We think Helen might have something that could be helpful to us."

"What do you think she might be keeping?"

"Information that would be beneficial to a certain subsection of the university. Will you help?" Alec asked.

Stefan glanced from Alec to Sam and then nodded. "When do you want to go?"

"Now," Sam said. She stepped forward and grabbed Stefan by the sleeve and pulled him out of his room. He didn't even resist. She had thought he had a bit of a spine, but maybe not.

They headed out of the university and across the bridge, ignoring the row of people waiting for healing. Alec didn't ignore it nearly as easily as Sam did, and his gaze drifted along the bridge, all the way out to where the line ended. She could see him calculating, trying to work through a problem, but considering what she had seen in the hospital ward, not only did they not have enough beds, but they might not have enough physickers to help this many people.

Stefan guided them toward a highborn section near the university. It was only one section over, and close enough that Helen wouldn't have had to stay at the university if she didn't want to. It made sense that she wouldn't have many belongings at the university, having a home so nearby.

"It's this one," Stefan said, motioning to a modest home. It was two stories and had a wide lawn, and a high fence—easily ten feet tall—encircled the entirety of the property. No light was visible in any of the windows.

Sam was hopeful no one was in there, but if they were, she was going to be prepared. She assembled her canal staff and looked over to Alec. "Do you have any paper?"

"I have the paper that I made, but…"

"But what?"

"But I'm not sure how effective it will be, especially after the attack. I don't know if they influenced or possibly contaminated anything I made."

Sam frowned. "Your back room was targeted?"

"It wasn't targeted, which is why I'm worried about it. Why would they have destroyed the front room, but left the back of the room untouched?"

"Maybe they didn't know about it."

"It's not much of a secret. There's a door there, which I don't lock. Would they not have at least gone in to see what was in there? And if they did, would they not have taken the opportunity to sabotage my work?"

"Maybe the focus was on getting Camellia out of the room."

"It's possible, but Sam, I'm just not sure we can trust the easar paper. I am nervous about attempting to use it on you. I don't want anything to happen to you."

She took a deep breath and then exhaled loudly. "Then we'll have to see if we can get by with only my own augmentations." She hoped it wouldn't come to that. As tired as she was, she wasn't sure she would have enough strength.

Alec studied her for a moment then reached into his pocket and pulled out a jar. He held it out to her.

Sam frowned at it. "What is this?"

"Just take one. I don't know how well it'll affect you, but it should at least restore you."

She reached into the jar and realized that it was eel meat. She had never consumed eel meat before, but it was a restorative, and if it could do anything to help, she should try it.

She braced herself and popped a chunk of the eel meat into her mouth and chewed it. It was bitter and awful and reminded her all too much of the swamp. She forced herself to swallow.

A wave of warmth washed through her. With it came a surge of energy. It was almost like an augmentation, but not entirely.

"How is that?" Alec asked.

"It's… It's better."

"I wish I knew what it felt like."

"You been eating it for the last couple of weeks. How do you not know what it's like?"

"Because I'm trying to counter the poisoning, I don't get to enjoy the benefit of it otherwise."

Sam sighed. "You're right. Let me just tell you that it feels like warmth, and then within a few moments, it's a feeling of alertness."

"That's what Jalen says too."

"How much of the meat has Jalen consumed?"

"Enough that he was worried about becoming dependent on it. He was going to stop, but I convinced him to keep using it."

"Using it? What does that mean?"

"It means that it can help him think more clearly. Until we get through this, we might need him to be able to think clearly enough to outmaneuver Helen."

Stefan had been watching them, saying nothing. He glanced at the jar, a question on his lips that went unasked.

"I'm ready," Sam said.

She tried the main gate in the fence and found it locked. She could jump the fence, but Alec and Stefan couldn't, so she pulled her lock-pick set out of her pocket and made quick work of unlocking the gate. As she did, she looked along the street to see if anyone was watching them, but there did not appear to be. Even if someone did, she wasn't sure she would have stopped. What would they do to her anyway?

"How is it she knows how to do that?" Stefan asked.

Sam straightened and stuffed the lock-pick set back into her pocket. She pushed open the door and glanced over her shoulder. "Because she's a thief."

The house reminded her of the manor house where she and Bastan had found Camellia—and where she'd lost Bastan, though this house was smaller in scale. There was a garden, though this one might have been larger. Some of the flowers had gone stale, and weeds had cropped up, marring the beauty that otherwise would have grown here.

Sam hurried to the front door. She tested the lock and

used her lock pick to open it. It popped open, and a musty odor emanated from inside the home.

Alec rested a hand on her shoulder. "We need to be careful."

"Why? Because the room stinks?"

"Because it smells like something has died in here."

Sam frowned and leaned forward, trying to smell into the room, but she didn't notice the stench of death. All she noticed was the staleness. "Are you sure?"

Alec nodded. "It's faint, but I'm certain."

"How can you smell it?"

He shook his head. "I don't know. I just do." Sam readied her staff and wished they had a lantern to carry inside. She stepped across the threshold and looked around as her eyes adjusted. Some light from outside streamed in, not enough for her to easily see, but enough to make out gradations in shadow. As her eyes adjusted, she was able to see that it was a well-appointed home. There were more decorations than had been in Master Helen's rooms at the university. A thick carpet covered the floor. Paintings hung on the walls, and there was a lantern on her desk.

Sam managed to get the lantern lit, quickly pushing back the room's shadows. A layer of dust covered everything. This might be Master Helen's home, and it might have been where she spent most of her time, but she hadn't been here for a while.

"I don't think we will find the answers we need here," Sam said.

"We came to look around," Alec said.

Sam surveyed the room but didn't see anything that

might help. The layer of dust that made it clear that Helen hadn't been here in some time troubled her. If this was where she had kept some secret stores, why wouldn't someone have been through here recently?

She hadn't been.

And if she hadn't been here, then Sam feared her hope of discovering what she might have done with Bastan was lost.

Alec joined her in the middle of the room and took her hand. It was as though he sensed her hopelessness. "We will find him," he said gently, squeezing her hand.

"What if we don't?"

"We will."

"We don't even know what she wants. We don't even know what she's after, or why she is doing all of this. All we know is that she's taken Bastan. She's hurt people, and…"

"We will find out what she wants," Alec said.

Sam didn't feel quite as confident in that. Without having any way for them to understand what Helen was after, she didn't believe they would be able to find her—or Bastan, for that matter.

He was lost to her.

12

A SURPRISING FIND

Alec made his way through Helen's house, searching for any clue that might help. Sam was struggling, and he needed to figure out if there was anything that could be done to help Bastan, especially with Sam unable to think clearly. It might not have been as bad had she not lost Elaine so recently, but losing her mother and now losing Bastan, Sam was not in a good place. It was his responsibility as her friend—as her Kaver—to help her find a measure of calm.

He didn't like the idea of looking around Helen's home alone, but Stefan was not going to be helpful, not with his grandmother involved. And Sam... Sam's mind was elsewhere.

He should have thought about this place before. He knew that Helen had some place beyond the university where she spent much of her time. She had to, mainly since she was often absent from the university for long periods of time. He hadn't expected it to be quite so close to the university, though.

He was determined to figure out what it was that she was after. Partly, it was a pride thing for him. He wasn't going to let Helen outsmart him. Wasn't he the youngest to ever be promoted to full physicker? Helen might have demanded testing in much the same way Alec had but hadn't she only been promoted to junior physicker?

He couldn't let himself think he wasn't smart enough to stop Master Helen. That mindset would only end up with him setting himself up for failure.

He surveyed the home. There had to be something here.

It was doubtful Helen would have returned—at least on her own—especially once she had been discovered. But could she have sent someone else? Could she have come in some other way?

And if she had, how would she have gotten here? There were no footprints on the ground outside, no disruption of the dust layering the floor, so either her last time here had been long ago, or she hadn't come through this way.

Alec frowned to himself. Of course, she wouldn't have come this way. If she had, someone would have seen her. Bastan had eyes everywhere.

He made his way to the back of the house. Stairs led up, and he searched for a stairwell going down, thinking of what Sam had described in the manor house she and Bastan had been in, but there was no evidence of a cellar here.

That meant up.

Alec looked back and saw Sam and Stefan making their way around the entry room. He would leave them. It might be for the best if he did. He started up the stairs, and as he did, he noticed that the layer of dust changed, disappearing, about halfway up.

"Sam?"

She came over and stood at the bottom of the stairs. "What is it?"

"Come up here."

Sam hurried up the stairs and joined him, and he pointed, motioning to where the layer of dust changed. "Do you see that?"

"I'm not sure what you're trying to show me."

"Look at the transition here. Do you see how the dust goes from a thick layer to nothing?"

Sam crouched down and stared at it. "I do now. How is it that you saw it so easily?"

Alec shook his head. "I think it was because I was watching for it." He continued up the stairs, and at the top, he found a wide room. There were no decorations here, nothing other than a few shelves. A single chair was angled so that it faced toward the window. Alec crouched down to lower himself so that he could see what view Helen would have from the chair and wasn't surprised to discover that the window offered a view of the palace.

"Why would this place be scrubbed of evidence of her presence?" Sam asked.

"Maybe it wasn't evidence of her presence." He looked over at her. "With everyone looking for her, Helen wouldn't have been able to get back to her home, not easily. She's a Scribe, and her abilities aren't that of physical finesse. But a Kaver? A Kaver would have been able to get upstairs without leaving a trace of evidence behind."

"You think that Helen sent one of the Kavers to her old home to find… What?"

Alec looked around. That was the question, wasn't it?

Helen was after something, and if he could figure out what it was, maybe they could figure out how to stop her.

What he needed was information that might help them understand what she knew as a Scribe that other Scribes apparently did not. Could it be somewhere here, in her house?

He turned his attention to the shelves. Unsurprisingly, most of the books on the shelves were incredibly old. Most were likely from the masters' section of the library, with information about injuries and ailments that should have been kept in the library. Alec began to frown as he looked along the row of books, thinking to himself that this wasn't the way knowledge was meant to be kept. It wasn't meant to be hidden and stored in one person's home. Knowledge of things that could help others was meant to be shared.

"What's this?"

Alec turned to see Sam with a book half out of the shelf. He glanced at the cover but didn't recognize the writing on it. There was some strange symbol…

"I've seen that symbol before," he said.

Sam stared at it for a moment before her eyes began to widen. "The cells."

Alec nodded. "Grab that one. See if there are any others like it."

Sam began to look with different interest and focus.

And now that she had discovered something that at least had some connection to the mystery, Alec was increasingly confident they would find something of use here.

He continued searching the shelves, and there were three other books with symbols on them. He took all of them. He went title by title, moving along the shelf, deciding that it was worth it to move slowly, especially if they were able to discover what Helen might have been hiding here. Some of the titles were obscure. That didn't surprise him. In the brief time that he'd spent in the masters' section of the library, he had seen various obscure titles. A few here were strange, and he pocketed those on the off chance that they might help him understand what Helen might have known about Scribes.

"I'll have to send somebody here to collect the rest of these," Alec said. "I'm sure they belong in the university library."

"You don't think they are important?"

Alec shrugged. "Important to the university, but maybe not for our immediate needs. Those," he said, pointing to Sam's pocket where she held the books with the symbols on them, "are likely to be something more, though I don't exactly know what, yet."

"I can help," Sam said.

Alec nodded. He would like that. He would also see what his father might know. There had to be something else that his father would have uncovered about the symbols by studying the books.

"Alec?"

Stefan's voice drifted from below, and Alec went to the

top of the stairs and looked down. "What is it? Are you okay?"

"I'm fine, but I think you need to see this."

Alec glanced over at Sam and then shrugged. He took another look around the room, feeling as if they might be missing something. "Can you check to see if there's anything hidden here?"

"Hidden?"

"You were the thief. See if Helen might have been keeping something from us."

"You keep commenting on the fact that I was a thief. If it bothers you that much—"

Alec grinned at her. "I only comment on it because I find it funny."

"Funny?" Sam slipped over to him and jabbed him in the chest with one end of her canal staff. "I'll show you funny."

"Just see what you can come up with," he said.

She glared at him before tearing her gaze away and turning her attention to the room. Alec hurried down the stairs, once again noting the transition of where the dust layer had been wiped away. It was obviously intentional, but who would have come through here and thought to erase away any traces of their presence? And why start halfway up the stairs? What had they hoped to accomplish?

"What is it, Stefan?"

He found Stefan standing in front of a wall. A painting was set on the ground, and as Alec approached, he realized that it looked to be of a younger woman with flowing brown hair. She had a slightly crooked nose, but her eyes were warm and almost welcoming.

"I found this here."

"What is it?"

Stefan handed a book to him.

It was a thick book, thicker than most that he had seen up in Helen's upstairs room. The cover was a dappled leather, and much like the ones they had collected upstairs, there were strange symbols on it.

"What made you think to look behind the painting?"

"I didn't look behind it," Stefan said. "I was going to take it with me."

"The painting or the book?"

"The painting. It's of my mother."

Alec turned his attention back to the painting. "What happened to her?"

Stefan shook his head, sighing. "I don't know what happened. All I know is that she was sick, and Grandmother was unable to help her, regardless of how much she tried."

An illness a Scribe was unable to help with? Many such illnesses came to mind, but there was something about this instance that troubled Alec. Could Stefan's mother have been tainted by the Book of Maladies?

"Why don't you see if there's anything behind any of these other paintings," Alec said.

Stefan looked down at the portrait that rested on the wall and shook himself before he began pulling portraits from the walls and searching them. As he went, Alec started to flip through the pages of the book. At first, he thought this would be nothing more than a series of symbols, nothing that he would understand, but two pages in, he found only blank pages. There were markings in the upper right corner, but nothing else.

His hands began to tremble, and his breath caught.

The sound on the stairs pulled his attention away, and he turned back to Sam.

"What is it?" Sam said, staring at him. "I didn't find anything else up there, so I don't know if there's anything hidden in those shelves that we need, or that might be beneficial, but so far, it's just these books."

"Stefan found something."

"What'd he find?"

Alec swallowed and handed the book over to Sam. She flipped through the first few pages much the same way that he had, her gaze narrowing as she noticed the symbols, and then her eyes widening, color draining from her face as she came to the blank pages with the symbol in the corner.

"Is this?"

Alec nodded. "It has to be, doesn't it? This has to be the Book of Maladies."

13

THE BOOK OF MALADIES

"The Book is not a single book. It never has been," Aelus said.

Sam couldn't take her attention off of the book. The last time she'd seen pages like that had been when she had broken into the highborn house. At the time, she'd blamed Ralun, but now she wasn't quite as certain he was responsible for the Book.

What if Helen was the one responsible for it?

"What do you mean that it's not a single book?" Alec asked.

He stared at the pages no differently than Sam did, and every so often he would reach over and finger the paper. It *was* easar paper. Sam had determined that, but there was something about it that seemed a little different from the easar paper they used.

"It's a series of volumes." Aelus shrugged. "I'm afraid I can't tell you much more than that."

Alec looked over to Sam and then back at his father. "If

it's not a single book, then how do you know which volume has been used on a person?"

"Alec—you're asking me questions for which I'm not entirely certain of the answers. I don't have the same knowledge of the Book as some might. I'm not even a Scribe, so all I know is based on rumors, and those rumors are likely born from other rumors."

"You seem to know enough to understand that Sam had been targeted by the Book."

"Only because it made sense. But this? I can't read the page, and though there might be some way of revealing the writing here, even if you knew how, it's of little use."

"How do the Thelns use the Book?"

"Again," Aelus said, looking at Sam. "I don't entirely know. Much of what we know is conjecture. The only people who truly know and understand the Book are the Thelns."

Sam frowned. There had to be some reason Helen had a copy of the Book. And the secret to it seemed tied to the symbols, though without being able to interpret them, there wasn't anything they could do. All of it appeared interrelated, but complicated, nonetheless.

"Have you figured out anything with those symbols?" Alec asked.

His father sighed. "That's the strange thing. I think I've identified a pattern, but I haven't been able to determine what it means. It's a sort of writing, but it's not any sort of writing I've seen before."

"What of the things that mother had?"

His father shook his head. "Anything we had was lost

in the fire. And your mother… Well, she didn't keep many things from her homeland."

"Other than the book on how to make paper."

His father nodded. "And even that, I was surprised you were able to uncover its secrets. Without a Theln translator, there wasn't any way for us to interpret what was there."

Sam glanced at the books of symbols that she and Alec had taken from Helen's. There were four of them, and each was filled with symbols much like they had discovered on the wall inside the palace prison. The symbols were similar to those on the first few pages in the Book, but not so much that they were able to translate them.

"The book of Mother's was different from those," Alec said. "Hers was written in a different language, but it was written. These are…"

His father nodded. "These are."

Sam couldn't help herself and continued to flip through the Book. Even as she did, she felt something from it. Perhaps it was nothing more than the fact that it was old—and *felt* old. There was power in the pages. There was power in the words. But she wasn't entirely certain what the intent of it was.

"I don't understand this," Sam said.

"What is it you don't understand?" Aelus asked, looking from Sam to the Book.

"This book. What's the point of it?"

"The point is assassinations."

Sam frowned. "It doesn't seem to make any sense. It's extensive if it's this long. What was the point of having so many ailments here?"

"As I said—"

Sam looked up. "I know what you're saying, and I know what we've believed about the Book, but what if that's not it?" She looked over at Alec. "I think of the things you do and the way you document each illness and injury. How is that any different from what would be documented here?"

"Well, presumably, it's the fact that the Book seems to allow someone to be influenced in such a way that they are poisoned, or at least, effectively so."

That idea troubled her, though Sam couldn't put words to why that was.

"What are you trying to figure out?" Alec asked.

"I'm trying to figure out what we are going up against. And why Helen would have this copy in her home. Why would it have been hidden, especially when it could have been so useful?"

"Useful? Sam, you're talking about a copy of the Book of Maladies."

"Not a copy," Aelus said. "Like I've been saying—"

Alec turned to his father and threw up his hands. "Fine. Not a copy, but still, it is a book with the same writing as the Book of Maladies. Whatever else it is, it's dangerous."

Aelus sat back, staring at the Book. He said nothing, and Sam pushed the Book away from her, standing. "I'm going to have to trust that the two of you can figure this out."

Alec looked at her. "What are you going to do?"

"I still need to figure out what happened to Bastan. If you get a chance, maybe the woman at the university can help. See what she might know. I need—*we* need—to know what Helen is after so we can get him back."

Alec stood from the table and wrapped his arms around her. "We will find him. Bastan isn't helpless."

"Against a group of Kavers? He might be more helpless than we realize. I've always thought of Bastan as this incredibly strong and talented person, but there are limits to what he's capable of doing."

"The same can be said for you."

Sam clenched her jaw. "See if you can find anything out. If you have to go to the university and ask others there, then do it."

"Eckerd might be able to help," Alec started, scratching his chin. "Although, Eckerd has been strange since all of this started."

"He's probably strange because he isn't quite certain which side he needs to be on," Aelus said. "Or how all of this might involve him."

"It's possible, but…" Sam turned away from them, letting Alec and his father have their discussion about the various master physickers. What did it matter to her? What did anything matter until she figured out what had happened to Bastan?

He couldn't have merely been dragged out of the city. He was too well connected for that.

That meant she needed to go back to Caster. She had to be the one to coordinate things in Bastan's section. If there were anyone who would have the necessary connections, it would have to be her, wouldn't it?

She reached Caster near midday. A bank of thick clouds hid the sun, obscuring it and leaving the day dreary. It matched her mood. She reached the tavern, and inside, she found a dozen men all scattered around. Voices stopped when she came in, and when Kevin—sitting near the back of the tavern—nodded once, the voices resumed.

Sam made her way over to Kevin and threw herself into a chair across from him. "What's the plan?"

"I've been trying to see what we can come up with. I haven't been able to find any word of Bastan yet." When Sam opened her mouth, Kevin waved his hand, silencing her. "That doesn't mean I won't; it only means I haven't, not yet. I'm certain he's not out of the city. If he were, we would've heard that. It's too hard to move anything in and out of the city without notice, and we have all the potential avenues under watch."

"All of them?"

"There are only a few ways people can be moved."

"We don't even know that the intent is to move him out of the city," Sam said.

"No, but from the activity we've observed, that's the most likely plan. There is enough activity that tells us something significant is happening, even if we don't yet know what." Kevin leaned back and crossed his arms. He let out a heavy sigh. "Bastan has enemies, Sam."

Sam smiled slightly. "Of course he does."

"They are enemies who would be of great benefit to those who seek to regain control of the city." He leaned forward and lowered his voice. "Have you ever wondered why Bastan has stayed in the outer sections of the city?"

She shrugged. "Because he has his network here. Because he's connected and set up. It's because—"

"It's because he protects the city."

Sam would have laughed, but there was an earnestness to Kevin's face that warned her against it. "What do you mean that he protects the city?"

"Just that. Bastan is responsible for providing a certain level of protection to the city."

"You mean that he was asked?"

Kevin shook his head. "It's nothing quite so formal as that. I think Bastan took on the role for himself, wanting a certain level of stability. There are other beings of power in the world, Samara. You've seen some of them."

"I've seen the Thelns. So have you."

"The Thelns. They are but one part of it. Bastan himself..." Kevin paused and shook his head. "No. I shouldn't be the one to even share that."

"I know about Bastan."

"Then you know he is something more than he appears. There are others like him, and there are others outside of the city that would like to gain entry. *That* is why I'm concerned he will be taken out of the city."

Sam could see the value in using Bastan in that way. If he was able to prevent access to the city by those who shouldn't be here, it might be beneficial to others for him to be removed. What would happen then? What kind of attack would they be facing if Bastan were gone?

A better question might be, would they be strong enough to withstand it?

"Do you think you can hold the city if something changes?"

"Hold? Sam, we're doing all we can to maintain the outer section. If something happens in one of the inner sections, there might not be anything we can do."

There was more to the city than Sam knew, but there was one person she could ask. She slapped the table and stood. "Keep looking for him," she said.

Kevin arched a brow at her. "Of course I will. Bastan means as much to me as he does to you."

She knew that he did and gave Kevin a warm, but worried smile before heading out of the tavern and making her way toward the center of the city, planning her conversation with Lyasanna and Marin. The two of them would need to provide information, though Marin might not know anything more. Lyasanna, on the other hand, likely did. There were things that she was hiding, and it was that information that Sam was determined to obtain. If Lyasanna knew what was taking place in the city, she was about to give it up.

As Sam crossed the bridge leading to a merchant section—Isand, a place with mostly warehouses and canal barges all tied up along the edge—she had a growing suspicion someone followed her.

Every so often, Sam glanced back, looking to see whether she could spot anyone. It would be easy enough for her to turn and shake them free, but she saw no evidence of anyone behind her.

As she made her way forward, she still couldn't get rid of that sensation.

Someone *was* there.

Sam assembled her canal staff and started focusing on an augmentation. With everything that she had been through, everything that she had experienced, she was tired—far more tired than she had been in quite some time. Finding the energy and the focus to place an augmentation was difficult. She thought about Alec's eel meat and recalled the energy it had given her, albeit temporary. She'd have to get some for herself if her need for multiple augmentations continued.

Sam abandoned the attempt at the augmentation and decided to vault herself onto one of the rooftops nearby. Doing that didn't require an augmentation, and she had enough strength in her to launch herself onto the roof, kicking up with the staff so that she could swing herself into a position where she could observe the street below.

Given that it was still daylight, movement like this was almost guaranteed to draw attention. Sam hated that she might, but she didn't have much choice.

When she landed on the roof, she pulled her canal staff up and rested it on her knees. She looked around, surveying the street below. There was no movement.

That wasn't entirely true. There was something, but it was what she would have expected. There was the activity of people who belonged here, that of merchants and a few highborns. There were even a few lowborns. Though they were better dressed than most, Sam could still tell. The clothes couldn't disguise the way they carried themselves. Lowborns know their own kind.

Maybe Bastan had a point about her clothing. It announced where she came from in a way she didn't necessarily want.

Thinking of Bastan sent a surge of irritation through her, but also determination. She would find him. She *would* help him.

Once again, she had a sense of movement behind her.

Sam shifted, glancing over her shoulder, and was almost too late.

Two men approached.

Both carried canal staffs.

Sam vaulted into the air, pushing off with her staff, and attempted to reach for an augmentation.

It didn't come. She was just too tired.

She spun her staff, bringing it around, trying to fight, but she wasn't fast enough.

One of the staffs caught her on the leg, sweeping her feet out from under her.

Sam rolled, bringing her staff around, and was rewarded with a gentle *thunk* as her staff connected with one of the men on his leg. It wasn't as solid a blow as she preferred, but it was enough to elicit a soft cry of pain. Even without augmentations, Sam was able to generate enough strength to cause injury.

"Get back," she said, swinging the staff around.

"I think that you are mistaken in our intentions," one of the Kavers said.

She realized too late that he was behind her.

He swung his staff around and connected, catching her on the back of the head.

Sam fell forward, losing the grip on her canal staff, and her vision went black.

14

BOUND

Pain throbbed in Sam's head. It had been a while since she had been beaten quite like that. Long enough that she had almost forgotten how much it hurt. She tried to blink open her eyes, but they were sticky, either gummed closed or coated in blood. When she attempted to move her arms, she couldn't.

They were tied over her head, and she was bound, trapped and unable to move.

Over her head?

The thought jerked her awake more than anything else did. Her heart hammered in her chest. The same thing had been done to other Kavers.

Were they going to bleed her out the same way they had the other Kavers? Was this what Helen wanted them for?

She managed to pry her eyes open and looked around. She was in a small, sparsely appointed room. She was indeed suspended from the ceiling, her arms spread wide, like Camellia's, her legs not able to reach the ground. She kicked, but to no avail.

She was trapped.

Her heart hammered again.

Had they already cut into her arms to bleed her out?

If they had, she might already be dead. No one knew that she was here. No one knew that she had come to this section. No one would know what happened to her.

She'd made a mistake moving through the city so openly and freely. After the attack, she had thought herself essentially safe, and no longer worried about hiding her presence, or hiding the fact that she was a Kaver, but she should have known better. She should have known that with Helen and the others roaming the city she wasn't safe. She should have known that there would be no safety until Helen was stopped.

"Help!"

Even as she screamed, it sounded weak in her ears. She tried to yell louder and to put more force into her words, but there was none.

She looked up at her arms, fearing that she would see blood dripping down her skin and that she was dying, but all she saw were her arms spread, suspended above her head.

Not bleeding out, not yet.

She tried to kick again, thinking that if she could flip her legs up, she might be able to hook her legs somehow and release her hands.

That didn't work.

Could she pull on an augmentation?

When she had tried up on the rooftop, she had been

unable, failing because of fatigue and everything she had been through. Considering that, it was likely to be more of the same, but she had to try. If she didn't, Alec would never know what happened to her.

Sam focused.

She thought of what she wanted: strength, skin that would resist injury, and speed so that she could escape.

Her head throbbing made it difficult for her to focus on those augmentations. Even as she tried, she knew she would not succeed. She had no more strength or ability to focus, not anymore.

Kyza. She hated that she was trapped.

She hated that she would die like this.

The door opened, and someone entered.

Sam was facing the door and expected to see Helen.

"Lyasanna?"

The princess approached, a slight grin parting her mouth. "I told you that you would not be able to hold me."

"How did you get out?"

"There is much you and your Scribe have failed to understand about your abilities, but there is much more you have failed to understand about others who live in the city."

Sam frowned. "Where is Bastan?"

"You demand to know where your friend is as you hang here like this? I don't think you're in any position to be demanding anything, Samara."

"I will get out, and I will—"

Lyasanna darted forward, and faster than Sam could react, she slashed at one of Sam's wrists.

The pain was unbearable.

It burned through her. Warmth ran down her arm, and a trickle of blood that dripped from her wrist landed in a bucket below.

Lyasanna darted back, holding a bloody knife.

"What is it that you will do? I think you will provide the answer to many of our problems."

"How?" Sam could already feel her strength training from her. There was no way she would be able to place an augmentation, not now, and not as the last of her strength was fading.

"One common misconception is that Kavers are needed for augmentations." Lyasanna leaned close, and she grinned. "When it's truly all about the Scribe. The Kaver's blood adds strength to the Scribe, but the Kavers themselves aren't necessary, not for what must happen."

"Why are you doing this? Why are you attacking others like this?"

"It's time for a reckoning. We were thrown out, but now, we will return and be more powerful than ever before."

"Thrown out?" Sam wasn't sure whether it was her weakened state that made it difficult for her to understand or whether it was something that Lyasanna was saying that made her struggle to comprehend. "What do you mean you were thrown out? The palace?" That had only just happened, so that couldn't be the reason Lyasanna and Helen attacked this way.

"It's the secret the Anders have long hidden." Lyasanna came close again, and Sam was afraid that she was going to slice her other wrist with the knife and drain her more rapidly, but she didn't. "I didn't want

Elaine to know. I was afraid she would reveal this secret."

"What secret?"

"It's the secret only the Scribe Council has known. The Scribes were sent away. Exiled. The Anders were merely their defense, the Kavers who protected them. But the Scribes have always ruled in the city."

"Exiled from where?" Sam asked. Even if she were to die, she needed to know. She *needed* the answer.

"Exiled from our homeland."

She darted forward and slashed the sharp blade through Sam's other wrist, and hot agony burned once again.

"And now, we will return. With Kaver blood, we will be able to overpower everything they have done to prevent our return."

Sam licked her lips. Even her tongue was weak. Her mouth didn't seem to want to move the way it should, and there was a strange lightheadedness that worked through her, almost as if she were swimming.

"You could have had peace with the Thelns," Sam said. "Marin told me it was within your reach. You could have returned."

"We could have returned and been subjugated," Lyasanna said. "The conditions of the return were such that we would never hold the position of strength we deserve. And now? Now with Helen's help, we have gained enough knowledge and insight that we will be able to overpower anything they can think of to prevent our return."

Sam tried lifting her head, but it was too heavy.

"You should be thankful. You will be a part of it. Integral, even. Your blood will help us defeat your precious Trayson."

"He should have been *your* precious Trayson."

The princess chuckled. "He was never precious. He was a means to an end. He was meant to be a bargaining chip, but when that failed…"

Sam couldn't move. Lyasanna was a horror. A monster. She had intended to use her child as a bargaining chip? But then had she not, would Sam have known him? Would she have known Bastan? Would she have…

Her thoughts started to jumble together.

"You were formidable, Samara. Much more formidable than I think Helen anticipated. Marin did well concealing you from us and training you in her own particular way."

"Marin?"

"Unfortunately, even Marin won't be able to help you now."

Sam tried moving, but her arms were too heavy. Her legs were too heavy. Her head was too heavy to even lift.

Was Lyasanna still speaking?

She didn't hear her.

All she heard was a steady sort of swishing, a heaviness in her head that thudded within her.

Her mind went blank.

The only thought she had was that she was dying, and with it came a certain sense of disappointment. She would die, and she wouldn't know anything more about what happened to Tray. She wouldn't know anything more about what Helen planned for the city.

And she wouldn't know any more time with Alec.

"Alec…"

"Shush, Samara."

Was that Lyasanna?

She thought she was being moved, but she couldn't tell. If she was, were they bringing her down because she was already gone? But if she was gone, why would her mind still be running like this?

Maybe it wasn't.

Maybe this was the After, and perhaps she was with Kyza, though she doubted she deserved that blessing. With everything she had done during her life, could she really be granted a blessing to spend eternity with Kyza?

She tried to open her eyes, but they didn't open for her. Once again, all sensation began to fade around her. There was blackness, and then there was nothing.

15

UNDERSTANDING THE BOOK

A lec stared at the pages of the Book of Maladies. There was some way to activate the writing, there had to be. Otherwise the Book was useless. Yet without understanding the symbol and the intent behind it, there was no way for him to know the purpose behind the Book.

His father flipped through the pages in one of the smaller books of symbols, trying to come up with an answer. He had the page on which he'd copied the symbols from the wall of the palace prison in front of him, and every so often, he would glance up, a crease wrinkling his brow as he studied it.

"None of this will make sense without some way of interpreting it," Alec said.

"I still believe it's all about the pattern, and not the actual translation," his father said. "I think if we can discover the meaning to the pattern, we might be able to get a sense of what Helen intended, if nothing else."

"Even if we figure out what she learned from the books, we don't know how she was able to do it. She shouldn't have been able to place these patterns from a distance."

His father frowned and set his hands on the table and finally looked up. "From a distance." He breathed out in a heavy sigh. "You're right. How is it she would be able to place them from a distance?"

"That's what I'm saying. It doesn't make sense. That's not how augmentations work."

"What if it *wasn't* from a distance?"

"What do you mean?"

His father glanced from the book to the page and then up to Alec. "What if it wasn't from a distance? What if the symbols are on the wall, but the *other* side of the wall. Could they have somehow pressed them through the wall?"

Alec's breath caught. He hadn't considered that possibility, though now that his father said it, there was a certain sort of sense to it. It *was* possible that the markings could have been made on the other side of the wall, but if that were the case, it meant someone had access to the palace—at least to the part of the palace where they were confining the princess.

"I need to go and see what I can come up with."

"You go. I'm going to keep looking at this, and I will see if there's anything here I can discover."

Alec glanced at the Book. There was a part of him that thought he should take it with him, but doing so wouldn't be of any help. He had no intention of attempting to use it, and worse, he had no way of understanding what was written within it. Until they figured out the key to the symbols, they might not be able to determine what each page in the Book referred to. It might be that there was no way for them to understand without having someone from the Theln lands who could explain it to them.

He made his way out of the apothecary and hurried toward the palace. When he reached the university section, he glanced over, thinking about stopping in, but decided against it. Doing that would only delay him, and right now, he wanted to uncover whatever he could to see whether Lyasanna had some way of actually escaping the prison. She shouldn't be able to, but then, she knew the palace much better than he or anyone else in it.

Alec hurried across the bridge and was quickly waved through. He hadn't expected to be stopped, but even as he went across, he glanced back to see if he recognized either of the guards but didn't. Were they Bastan's men? He had managed to secure much of the city himself, which both impressed and troubled Alec. The fact that Bastan had so much control was surprising, as was the fact that he was able to use it so effectively.

He reached the palace and raced toward the back. Once there, he nodded to the guards, and they waved him through. Had he been here enough that they recognized him?

Once inside, Alec stopped.

The cell was empty.

Lyasanna was gone.

"Kyza!"

Alec never swore, but this seemed to be a time for it if any was.

How had Lyasanna managed to escape?

Alec yanked the door open and yelled to the guards. "The prisoner escaped. Send word to Marin."

One of the guards looked inside, and his eyes widened before he hurried off, disappearing down the hallway and into the palace. The other followed Alec back into the row of cells.

Alec pulled on the door to the cell and found that it was unlocked.

He turned his attention to the wall. Marin had masons building another wall, creating a barricade that would prevent Lyasanna from escaping, but obviously that hadn't been as effective as it needed to be. Somehow, Helen had managed to gain access and had broken her out.

He still didn't know why. There was a benefit to having one of the Anders, but it had to be more than that. How was Lyasanna important to what Helen planned? She was a Scribe, but Helen had other Scribes.

There were so many questions. And now they wouldn't have answers.

"What happened?"

Alec spun. Marin stood behind him. She carried her canal staff as she strode forward, an augmentation obviously in place with the fluid way that she moved.

"She's gone."

"I can see she's gone. How?"

Alec shook his head. "My father and I were wondering if maybe there was another way she could have been placing augmentations on the wall. Is there space behind this?"

Marin studied the cell before turning to the wall, not stepping over the new wall they were building. "There shouldn't be anything behind that wall."

"We need to excavate it to find out."

Marin went to one of the guards and whispered something to him. He raced off.

"What did you say to him?"

"I want to summon an excavator."

She guided Alec through the cells and into the room that had been formed by the new wall. There wasn't any sign of where Lyasanna could have gone here either. She had simply vanished.

"I presume she didn't go out through the main part of the palace?"

"If she had, I would've heard," Marin said. "I should have kept closer tabs on her. Or maybe I should have moved her, but Sam was confident that we would be able to hold her here."

"She didn't want to hold her. She wanted to draw out Helen."

Marin tapped her staff on the ground, the sound ringing out. Her fingers wrapped around the wood, squeezing much harder than necessary. "*We* wanted that. It was something we discussed and decided on. In that, Sam was right. To find Helen, we had to draw her out."

Alec traced his hand over the symbols that were on the wall. There were more now than there had been before. Each of them was thick, and he had seen some of them in the books that they had taken from Helen's home, but he didn't know what they did other than create some way of getting in.

"You think they weakened the wall in some way?"

"No," Marin said, tapping her canal staff on the stone. "If they weakened the wall, we would have detected that. It would've been easy enough to repair. What they did…" She shook her head. "I'm not entirely certain. I have plenty of experience with augmentations, Alec, but these are nothing like any I've ever experienced."

"Because they were placed by a Scribe of great skill."

Marin frowned.

Alec heard the sound of another voice behind him, and he turned. Jalen appeared, his face flushed and sweat beading on his brow. He had run the entire way from the university.

"You summoned me…" Jalen looked around, seeming to finally take in the emptiness. "Where is she?"

"That is what we are trying to determine."

"And that's why you called me here?"

"I called you here because I have need of an augmentation."

Jalen frowned. "I don't have much easar paper remaining. None of us do, not with Helen having stolen it from the city."

"There is enough for this."

"What would you like?"

"I would like strength, large hands, and bones that will not shatter."

Jalen nodded. He held out his hand and picked it with a knife, and Marin did the same with hers. They pressed their hands together quickly, something that Alec suspected they had practiced, and Jalen took a seat on the ground and pulled a slip of paper out from one of his pockets. It was little more than a scrap of easar paper. Not much to write on, but for what Marin wanted, it would be enough. Jalen made a few quick notes, and when he was done, he looked up at Marin. "That should be it."

Marin took a step toward the wall. She closed her eyes, and as Alec watched, her hands began to enlarge. She punched, powering through the stone.

"I thought she sent for an excavator," Alec said to Jalen.

"Apparently, she's the excavator."

Alec watched as Marin destroyed the wall, ripping stone free from it. It was an impressive display of augmentations and the kind he had never even tested with Sam. What limits did their augmentations have? Those were questions he still didn't know the answers to. Maybe there weren't any limitations, but then again, the limitation seemed to come from the power of the Kaver and Scribe.

As she tore away the stone, Alec saw space behind the wall, an opening that should not have been there.

"Kyza!" Jalen said. He stepped up behind Marin and peered into the darkness. "How is that possible?"

"Either they had planned this, or this has always been here," Marin said.

"We need to follow it," Jalen said.

"Not alone. And not in the darkness," Marin said.

"We don't know how long she's been gone."

"If Helen came for her, she has more Kavers than we do. We might need numbers and the ability to place augmentations." Marin glanced from Alec to Jalen. "Find Samara. I will gather Bastan's men, and we will pursue this, but we need to do so in a careful way."

Alec glanced over to the opening in the wall. How much time would they waste waiting? With Lyasanna gone, it might already be too late. The damage might already be done.

"I'm going go in there to see what I can find," Alec said. Sam would be angry, but she would understand. She would have to.

"You don't want to wait for Samara?"

"If it's only Lyasanna, she's a Scribe—"

"A Scribe who has been effective at having augmentations placed on her before," Marin said. "It's the reason we need to be careful with her."

Alec let out a frustrated sigh. Marin was right, but he didn't like it. He didn't like the idea that they would have to wait, especially not with whatever Lyasanna and Helen might be planning.

"We must ensure no one else uses this passage to enter the palace. How do you intend to keep this protected?" Alec asked.

"I intend to stand guard myself."

"And what happens if you're attacked?"

"If I'm attacked, then it might already be too late." Marin waved a hand to Alec. "Go find Samara."

He glanced over at Jalen before making his way out. Other than knowing that she had gone to Caster, he wasn't even sure where to begin looking for Sam, so he decided to see if any of Bastan's people might be able to help.

Alec ran.

What choice did he have? He went as quickly as he could, racing through the streets, heading toward Caster.

He was tired after going barely halfway. He paused long enough to pull out his jar of eel meat and took a bite, needing to replenish his strength. The bitterness seemed less today than it had been, though he suspected that was nothing more than his imagination. There was nothing about the meat that would have changed in the last few hours since he'd taken a bite.

He looked around. He was in a merchant section. It was one he thought he'd been in before, rows of warehouses looking familiar. There was also a manor home that reminded him of the one Sam had described.

As he looked at it, he realized people were entering the front door. Two of them carried long staffs. Canal staffs.

His breath caught. Could they be Kavers? Could this be the same manor house where they'd found Camellia?

He needed to find Sam, but he also needed to understand what it was that Helen was up to. If he could discover something here, it would be of value to them.

Alec crept forward, trying to be as quiet as he had seen Sam doing. He didn't have the same experience with sneaking through the streets as she did, but she had tried to teach him stealth, and though he had never quite mastered it, he was better than he once had been.

A low fence surrounded the property. Alec jumped over it and crept forward, reaching a window. He pulled himself up, hanging carefully from the edge as he tried to peer inside. It reminded him of when they had gone to Helen's house and had looked inside. But this house wasn't empty. He counted four people, and the two with the canal staffs troubled him the most. Could the others be Scribes?

Would Helen be inside?

He lowered himself to the ground. Now that he knew this was here, he would come back, but not until he had Sam with him. He wasn't going to come by himself and wasn't willing to try to attack, not without someone who could fight more effectively than he could. He was nothing more than a physicker—a Scribe. He had no abilities to fight.

Alec turned back toward Caster and ran. As he went, the sound of boots thudding across the stones chased him.

He darted into an alley, not wanting to be overrun by someone here.

As he stayed in the darkness, he saw the people making their way along the street. Bastan's men. Alec stepped out, recognizing Kevin.

"Stross. Come with me."

"What?"

"You're needed."

"I'm needed? What happened?"

He said two words that caused Alec's heart to lurch. "It's Sam."

16

SAVING A FRIEND

His father's apothecary shop was dark, and there was a coppery scent that Alec recognized—blood. A lot of blood—far more than what anyone could survive.

When Kevin led them to the back, Alec staggered forward.

"Sam?"

She was lying on a cot, her arms at her sides, and her face pale.

"She was found like this, Alec."

Alec spun and saw Bastan. "Bastan? What happened? How are you free?"

"Help her."

Aelus was already working on Sam, and Alec quickly began to tamp down the emotion, focusing on engaging his mind, knowing that for Sam to survive, he would need to use everything ounce of his knowledge, every skill he'd ever learned from his father.

"What do we know?" Alec asked.

His father glanced up. "She was found bound to the ceiling with rope. There were these slits in her wrists. I have sutured them, but there has been a significant amount of blood loss."

Alec quickly checked for a pulse. It was there but thready. Her breathing was regular but weak. The sutures his father had placed were stable, and the lacerations over her wrists were significant.

"How much blood loss?"

"It is difficult to know," his father said. "With as pale as she is—"

Alec turned to Bastan. "You were the one to find her?"

Bastan nodded.

"How much blood loss did she have?"

"I don't know. There were two buckets beneath her. I brought them with me, but…"

Bastan motioned to two buckets on the floor underneath the cot. He glanced at them, and his heart skipped a beat. With that much blood loss, there might not be anything that could be done for her.

"It's contaminated, Alec. I would have suggested using it, but…" Bastan pulled one of the buckets out, and there were traces of dirt and something else in it.

She couldn't have her own blood replaced. Even if it were successful, the likelihood of infection would be too high. That left only one option.

It was risky, but for Sam, Alec was willing to do it.

"She needs a donor," Alec said.

His father looked up, shaking his head. "Alec, that's not possible."

"It is. I've seen records of it at the university. She needs someone who can donate blood to her."

He made his way to a closet and grabbed a few supplies. There was a syringe, and he took it, grasping a needle made of a fine reed. He would need that to find a vein to administer the blood. Even if he were successful, there would be a risk of infection.

"Easar paper," he said to Bastan. "I need any you can find."

"Where?"

Alec squeezed his eyes shut. The only easar paper they had was what he had made recently. Did he dare trust it?

Did he dare not?

"My room at the university. In the back. You'll find it on a tray there."

"I will get it myself." Bastan ran out, and Alec turned his attention back to Sam.

"Alec—" His father tried to caution him.

Alec prepared the syringe. He didn't know how much blood would be needed to help Sam, but he was willing to do whatever was necessary to help her.

He took a seat and pumped his arm a few times, and then felt for a vein beneath the skin. As his father watched in horror, Alec jammed the needle into his arm, found a vein, and drew out blood.

He wasn't certain how much would be necessary, but now that Sam's bleeding had been stopped, she needed the lost blood replaced. He wasn't sure whether this would work, or if their blood would even be compatible, but the fact that they were Kaver and Scribe made it more likely it would be.

As he pulled the needle from his arm, his father reached for his wrist. "This isn't going to save her."

Alec didn't look up. "There's nothing else that will. I'm going to try this."

"Alec..."

He glanced up. "I'm the master physicker."

His father fixed him with a strange expression and then nodded, removing his had from Alec's wrist.

Alec reached for Sam's arm and checked for a strong vein, but with as weak as her pulse was, it was difficult for him to find one. He moved up to her neck. The vein there was larger, and if he pierced it the wrong way, it was possible that it would lead to more bleeding, but if he didn't do anything, she wouldn't survive this, anyway, so it was worth the risk.

Alec placed his fingers on either side of the vein, stabilizing it beneath the skin. He brought the needle out, and slowly pierced her skin and began to administer the blood.

He went slowly. With as sick and injured as she was, he wasn't confident how much she could tolerate. It might be she couldn't tolerate much at all, but he had to try.

When he was done, he looked over at Sam, noticing that her pulse was only slightly better. Her color was unchanged.

He needed more blood.

He pumped his fist when his father grabbed his wrist again. "Use mine."

Alec looked up at his father. "We don't know whether you would be compatible."

"You are, so we can presume I am."

Alec wasn't sure it worked that way, but maybe it didn't matter. At this point, Sam needed anything, and he was determined to see that she had the necessary support to come back from this.

He plunged the needle into his father's arm and withdrew a syringe full of blood. He returned to Sam and administered it to her.

By the time he was finished, it seemed as if her pulse was somewhat better. It was still fast, and it was still thready, but he had hope.

The door to the apothecary jingled open. Alec looked over as Bastan raced inside. He held out the sheet of easar paper.

Alec took it and stared at it. It would weaken Sam for him to use it, but then, he could use a ratio that was mostly his blood, and less of hers. If he did that, it was possible she wouldn't need to use quite as much of her own strength for recovery.

A drop or two. Nothing more than that. And he wouldn't even need to draw it from her. He could take it from the bucket. It didn't matter that it was contaminated.

He grabbed a bowl and added two drops of Sam's blood. Then he pressed on the skin on his arm where he'd pushed the needle in and squeezed out a dozen drops that he added to the bowl. Between the two of them, he had enough for ink. Would it be enough to help her?

Alec reached for the sheet of easar paper and stared at it.

He dipped his pen into the ink and began to write.

The words flowed across the page. They were a desperate plea, not the same impartial description he typically used. This was desperation. This was a desire for help—any kind of help—and he prayed it would work.

When he was finished, he sat back.

He knew the augmentation had taken hold as a cold washed over him. It was a powerful surge that burned through him, stronger than that of any augmentation he'd ever placed. Distantly, his mind worked through the reasons why that might be, coming to a decision that it must be from the ratio of blood used.

There was nothing for him to do but wait.

At least Sam still breathed. Every so often, he would check her pulse, and his father nodded, looking at him with a worried expression. "I can keep an eye on her. You have done everything that you can. I will let you know if anything changes."

"I'm not going to leave."

His father shook his head. "I wouldn't ask you to. But you need to rest. What you've done will take strength out of you, and with what Helen has done to you, you don't have much strength to spare."

It reminded him of the eel meat. He took the jar out of his pocket and took a piece, chewing it slowly. Would it help Sam? He had to believe that it would. He took another few pieces out of the jar and found a knife and used it to chop it up into tiny pieces. He took the chopped meat and gently pried open Sam's mouth, and stuffed it toward her throat.

He massaged her throat, trying to help her swallow it.

Then he got up.

Bastan took his place, looking down at Sam.

"What happened?" Alec asked. It was the first moment

he'd had since arriving with Kevin to even think about asking.

"I was captured. I escaped."

"It's not as simple as that."

"It *is* as simple as that. They thought to trap me, but they underestimated me."

"Who were they?"

Bastan glanced over at him. Tears welled in his eyes. "The damned fools who thought to do this to Sam."

"We need to know what they intended," Alec said.

"Whatever it is, they think her blood is the key."

"And Lyasanna escaped," Alec said.

His father gasped. "How?"

"It was like you thought. There was an opening on the other side of the wall they were placing their augmentations on. They used that and somehow gained access to the cell."

"Could Lyasanna be responsible for what happened to Sam?" Aelus asked.

"She is the one responsible, but she wasn't there when we found Sam. There was a Kaver I didn't recognize. He's dead now." Bastan turned his attention back to Sam. There was a quiet intensity to him, almost a rage that boiled beneath the surface. Alec had not seen Bastan angry before, not like this. He was frightened by it, but he thought that Helen should be even more frightened. Bastan was not the kind of man anyone wanted as an enemy.

Could Helen have finally made a mistake?

If so, maybe they would be able to figure out what she was after.

"I don't want to lose her, not like this," Bastan said.

"I don't want to lose her, either." Alec stood near Sam's head, and he trembled. "I don't want to lose her at all. We haven't even had a chance to have any sort of normalcy. We haven't had a chance to have a life where we weren't trying to figure out what it meant to be Kaver and Scribe and trying to fight off the Thelns and…"

Bastan breathed out. "She's strong. The strongest I know. She'll pull through this."

Alec looked down at Sam. He couldn't tell if her color was any better, and out of habit, he checked her pulse and found it still thready. It wasn't getting any better, despite the blood they had administered and the augmentation he had placed. Maybe it was too late. Maybe she wouldn't survive this. Maybe Sam was already lost.

And that means Helen will have won.

"One of us needs to go tell Marin," Alec said.

"I can go," Kevin said behind him. Alec hadn't realized that the other man had remained with them the entire time. He had been quiet, standing off to the side, watching as they worked. "At the palace?"

Alec nodded. "She will be in the cell."

Kevin departed, and Alec couldn't help but pace, every so often coming over to check on Sam, his mind racing and prayers forming that he never had formed before. Sam swore to Kyza, but Alec thought he should pray to her god. If any looked over her, it would be the one who viewed lowborns like her in a favorable light.

He took a seat on her other side and gently lifted her hand. It felt helpless. There was nothing that he could do for her. Waiting.

"How long do we need to wait?" Bastan asked.

"I don't know," Alec said. "I thought that with the augmentation…"

Bastan nodded. "We just have to be patient. She'll come back to us when she's ready," he said, sounding like he was convincing himself, not Alec.

Alec hoped that was true, but what if she didn't? What if she wasn't strong enough to pull through this? What would he do then?

17

AWAKE

Sam awoke slowly. Everything was a blur. Her mind was a jumble of thoughts, and she couldn't focus when she tried to think. Her mouth was dry, and her eyes felt like they were gummed closed. It took a moment for her to remember what had happened, and when she did, she jerked. A medicinal stench filled her nostrils.

"Easy, Samara."

Samara? She recognized the voice, but she shouldn't have.

"Bastan?"

He patted her hand. "I'm here, Samara."

"How?"

"It doesn't matter." Bastan made a strange, strangled sound that in anyone else Sam would think was a sob. Not from Bastan. He wasn't the type to cry.

"Where am I?"

"You're in the apothecary shop."

That explained the odor. Now that Bastan mentioned it, the smell was familiar. She'd been here often enough to know what it was. "And Alec?"

"Sleeping next to you."

"Sleeping?" She managed to pry her eyes open and rolled her head to the side. Alec rested with his head on the cot, and his hands were gripping hers. She wouldn't let him go. Never again. "What happened?"

"He saved you. He took blood from himself and gave it to you."

"How?"

Bastan shook his head. "I've never seen anything like it. He is quite an impressive young man. When he was done, he used blood ink and the easar paper, though I think he used most of his own, and less of yours."

Bastan took a deep breath and sat up. He rubbed a knuckle into his eye, and Sam frowned. Was he crying?

"What's wrong, Bastan?"

"We thought you were dead, that's what's wrong, Samara."

Sam looked over to Bastan. "Dead?"

Even as she said it, she knew what he meant. She remembered the way that she felt, the way that everything had gone black, and she had thought she was going to die. Lyasanna had intended to bleed her out, to use her blood for... What? What purpose did Lyasanna have for her blood? What would she gain from it?

The better question was what would Helen gain from it?

"If they have my blood, they can do—"

Bastan pulled a bucket out from underneath the table.

"They don't have your blood. I grabbed the two buckets when I brought you out."

Sam frowned at the buckets. "Why would Alec not have used that? He could have given my own blood back to me."

"We were concerned about whether it was safe to do it. There's something in the blood that likely contaminated it."

"What would be in the blood?"

Bastan frowned. "It wasn't safe, Sam, and Alec is particular about how he does things. Considering that you still live, I think we should allow that, don't you?"

Sam tried to chuckle, but it came out as a cough. "We need to find Lyasanna. Now we know she is part of whatever Helen is planning."

"There is no doubt they are working together. I learned that much from my captors before I escaped."

"Why would they talk around you?"

"Because they had no choice," Bastan said.

"What?"

"I gave them no choice but to tell me what they were planning."

Sam would have shivered, but with what Helen had attempted on her—at least, what Lyasanna had done to her—Sam had a hard time mustering the necessary empathy. "What did they share?"

"They believe the Kaver blood is key to some sort of plan to overtake the city."

"Not the city. They intend to overthrow the Thelns," she said, remembering what Lyasanna had shared.

"Why the other Kavers are going along with it is beyond me."

"What if they're not all going along with it?" Sam asked.

She was beginning to feel a little bit better, not strong —not quite—but better than she had been when she first woke up. If this were all about an augmentation, even with the easar paper, it would take a while for her to feel back to normal, if she even could. After losing as much blood as she imagined she had, her recovery would be slow.

"About the Kaver we found. Camellia. What if they aren't all going along with it?"

"The other two I escaped from didn't have any difficulty with sharing what they were a part of," Bastan said.

Sam's head throbbed. She had a hard time thinking through things in any way that would allow her to come to a solution. "I feel like I need some eel meat."

Bastan grunted. "It just so happens that Alec has a supply."

He shook Alec, and he awoke with a start.

Alec glanced from Bastan down to Sam, and seeing her awake, his eyes widened. "Sam. You're back."

"Thank you. I feel like I've been beaten in a way I haven't in a long time, and my head throbs and I feel rundown and…"

Alec could only nod. "But you're alive."

"I'm alive." She glanced at Alec's jacket. "I understand you have eel meat with you?"

Alec nodded. "I have to keep it on me. It's the only thing that keeps me going sometimes."

Sam sighed. "Can I have some?"

Alec reached into his pocket and pulled out the jar he always carried, and when he popped the top, the familiar bitter stink emanated from the jar. He pulled out a chunk and handed it to Sam. She took it gingerly. Her wrists throbbed from where Lyasanna had cut her. She would have to have that healed at some point too. An augmentation would make short work of her recovering from that injury.

Sam chewed on the piece of meat. As she did, a sense of warmth washed over her. Strength gradually returned, and she let out a heavy sigh and propped herself up on her elbows. She looked around the apothecary. Other than Bastan and Alec, there was no one here.

"Where is your father?"

"He went to see what else he could learn about these markings. I told him where we came across the books in Helen's house, and he thought he would go and take a look."

Sam took a deep breath. That was a good idea. "I don't know how Lyasanna escaped."

"I do." Alec told her about the opening in the cell, the way the markings had been pressed through from the other side, augmentations placed on the stone that either weakened it or turned it into some sort of doorway.

"We're dealing with someone who is incredibly intelligent, has knowledge we don't have, and is using Kavers for some horrible purpose we can't figure out."

The door to the apothecary opened with a tinkling of bells. Sam looked over and saw Marin race in, carrying her canal staff. She stopped abruptly in front of Sam.

"Samara. You're alive."

Sam nodded. "A refrain I've heard several times."

"I was warned you might not pull through."

"I'm still not clear how I got here, but Alec managed to bring me back from the edge of death."

Marin sighed. "Lyasanna did this?"

"She did. She was augmented, and she taunted me, gloating that we could not hold her. Then she slit my wrists and watched as I bled out."

"When she recalled all the Kavers to the city, we knew she was planning something."

"But it's not that she is using them in any way that would make sense. I thought she would use the Kavers to attack, but that's not it at all. She just wants their blood. As she wanted mine."

"I don't understand why she would want Kaver blood without a living Kaver."

"She claims it doesn't matter."

Her strength faded. Could the benefit of the eel meat fade so quickly? Sam sagged back down onto the cot. How much longer would she be able to stay awake? With what happened, she needed to get up and get moving; she needed to begin her search for Helen and the others, but with the way she felt, she wasn't sure that she could.

"We need to discover where the tunnel from the cells leads," Marin said.

"The tunnel Lyasanna escaped through?" Sam asked.

Marin nodded.

"And what it doesn't matter? What if she has enough Kaver blood and doesn't come back? She plans to go after the Thelns. We need to stop that." She looked at Marin, wondering how much Marin knew of the connection between the Thelns and the Anders. From what Lyasanna said, only those on the Scribe Council knew.

Sam now knew there was only one way for them to really find the answers.

"We have to leave the city," Sam said.

"Sam, you're not in any shape to even think about that now," Alec said.

"Maybe not now, but I *will* get stronger, and when I do, we need to go and see what it is that Helen plans with the Thelns." She looked at Alec and then to Marin. "You've been there before, so we will need your help. And Alec, I think you need to come, regardless of the warnings we've heard about Scribes not returning. We need to understand just what the Scribes in the Thelns lands know. There's something there, some reason they do not return when they leave."

And maybe it was all about being invited to remain. If what Lyasanna had said was true, then the Scribes had been exiled from the city. But perhaps they didn't have to be exiles. Maybe they hadn't been allowed to return, and if that were the case, then it would explain why Scribes never came back.

"Who will guard the city if we all travel to the Thelns land?" Marin asked.

Sam turned to Bastan. "You will, won't you? You've always been willing to look out for the city. Kevin told me exactly what it was that you do."

"Kevin would not have shared anything like that with you."

"Fine, he didn't tell me *exactly* what you do, but he did

say you have a larger role than what most know. It's a role you chose for yourself."

"I only intend to ensure certain other undesirables don't make it into the city."

"If you can do that, then you can help keep the rest of the city safe. You can keep an eye out for Helen and the others while we travel to the Theln lands for answers."

Bastan breathed out. "I don't care for this, Samara."

"I don't care for it either, Bastan, but what choice do we have? We need to have answers. Everything seems to be pulling us toward the Theln lands. Not only because I want to find Tray, but because all of this seems to have started after Lyasanna returned from her brief fling with Ralun."

"I don't like that you will be leaving and I am not accompanying you."

"I will be as safe as I can be," Sam said. "And I won't be going alone. Marin will be coming, and Alec, and—"

"And Jalen will need to come," Marin said. "If we are going to face any sort of opposition, I would prefer to have someone along who can place augmentations on me."

"That means no Anders will remain in the city," Bastan said. "That puts the city in danger if there is an attack."

"You can stay in the palace, and you can ensure that the city is protected," Sam said.

Bastan snorted. "Samara, you have an awfully high belief in my abilities."

"When have you ever given me a reason not to?"

Bastan stared at her, and then he nodded. "If you do this, everything changes."

"Everything has already changed, Bastan."

Bastan watched her for a long moment before sighing. "Indeed it has, Samara. Indeed it has."

18

OUT OF THE CITY

The barge was a narrow one, just wide enough for the four of them to travel on. Marin used the barge pole, pushing them deep into the swamp at a quick pace. Trees jutted out of the water on either side of them. Could they be svethwuud, the same trees used to make the easar paper? Maybe they were something else.

The swamp had a strange humid stink to it along with the familiar scent of rot. "Do you notice that?" Sam asked.

"Notice what?" Marin asked, her gaze sweeping over the darkened swamp. They chose to leave at night, thinking it would draw less attention, but now that they were out here, Sam wished that maybe they had chosen to come in the daylight. It would have been easier to navigate. She had considered placing an augmentation to improve her night vision, and even Marin's, but knew it was best to conserve their strength.

"There's a smell," Sam said.

"There's always a smell in the swamp," Alec said.

"This is one I haven't noticed before."

Alec wrinkled his nose as he took a deep breath. He was dressed in a cloak that matched Sam's, and the shadows drifted off of it. Marin and Jalen each wore one as well. Bastan had found them, and she didn't want to know where he had come across them. Madame Fornay had provided clothing, and Sam was now dressed in much nicer garb than she had been before.

"I don't smell anything," Alec said.

"Maybe it's just me," she said. Since awakening from her near-death experience, she smelled everything a little differently. Then again, she had been consuming more of the eel meat, believing she needed to in order to have the necessary strength to continue with their plans. *Her* plans.

"I smell it as well, though I have smelled the swamp like this before," Jalen said.

"Maybe it's always been like this," Sam said. "I just haven't noticed it."

They were making good time, but Sam still wished they could move faster, wanting to reach the edge of the swamp and then... Then they needed to pass through the forest, and on the other side of the forest was a dense plain.

"What is it?" Alec asked.

Sam shrugged. "I'm just thinking about what we have to face before we can get through this."

"I might have been exaggerating a bit about how difficult the terrain would be," Marin said.

Sam glanced over. "What do you mean exaggerating?"

"I didn't want you to leave the city before I managed to

get free. I thought if I presented a challenging enough passage, you would bring me with you."

Sam grunted. "So, there's no dangerous forest beyond the swamp?"

"Oh, there is a dangerous forest, but it's not quite as dangerous as it would appear, and there are ways to safely navigate it, especially when you have a Scribe with you."

Sam shook her head. "So much deception."

"I am sorry. Truly," Marin said. She looked at Sam, and she met her gaze, holding it for a moment. "I wish I could have done things differently. I wish Tray didn't need such protection, and that his mother wasn't interested in seeing him dead, and I wish…"

Sam shook her head. "I wish you hadn't stolen my memories."

"You blame me, but it was never my intention to take that much from you. I just didn't know what I was doing. When I came across the Book, I used it on Tray, but I didn't know it would carry over to you."

Sam stared out at the swamp. Hearing for the first time that Marin's stealing of her memories had been nothing but a mistake left her numb. There'd been a time when she wanted nothing more than to understand everything that Marin had stolen from her. She'd wanted her memories back, memories of a time before she had lost her mother and father, of a time when she wasn't an orphan and destined to run the street, but so much had changed for her that she no longer felt the same way. She no longer felt she needed to have her questions about her past answered. And even if she were to recover those memories, would they provide any of the answers she sought? It was possible the only answer that was relevant was that the life she lived was the one she was meant to live.

And would any memory she regained change anything?

"While we're here, we should harvest a few eels," Jalen said.

"We shouldn't delay," Marin said.

"Alec might need us to have eel meat. And I…" He shook his head. "I might need us to have eel meat."

Marin looked at him, and there was almost something of irritation on her face. "We don't know what it will do to you long term," she said.

"We know it enhances focus. With where we're going, all of us might need enhanced focus. And Alec might need the simple benefit the eel meat has been providing."

Alec pulled the jar out of his pocket, and he tipped it over. "I have some left, but depending on how long we're gone…"

Marin pulled the pole out of the water. "Fine. We can stop long enough to replenish Alec's, but none for you," she said to Jalen. "I don't like that you've allowed yourself to become reliant upon it."

Sam suppressed a smile. Seeing Marin like this and seeing how she was harassing Jalen about the eel meat amused her. And she didn't entirely disagree. If Alec didn't need the extra support of the eel, she might have felt the same way.

They drifted into a cluster of trees. Sam didn't bother to ask Marin how she knew eels could be found there.

When they reach them, Marin handed the barge pole over to Sam. "Keep us steady," she said.

"I can do this, Marin."

"That might be, but I don't know how fatigued you are. I think it's best if you continue to recuperate." Marin stood at the edge of the barge and jumped in. There was a soft splash, and she was gone for a few moments before she jumped free of the water and flopped two eels onto the deck. She looked over at Jalen. "You get to clean them."

Jalen cocked his head, and there was a hint of a smile on his face. "Gladly."

He withdrew a belt knife and started to cut open the eel. As he did, Alec crouched down next to him and joined him, making quick work of cutting out the eel flesh.

"What do you think we should do if we come across Helen?" Sam asked.

"Helen won't be here. She wouldn't do anything that would put her at risk," Marin said.

"If she intends to attack the Thelns, she would have to come this way, wouldn't she?"

Marin nodded. "There isn't another way to reach the Theln lands."

They continued forward, Marin now pushing with a vigorous pace that told Sam she used augmentations to do so. Marin didn't seem to have any limitations with how long she could hold an augmentation, which could mean she either had more strength than Sam did to begin with, or she had enough practice with using augmentations that she had developed better control with them.

Could Sam someday get to that point? Seeing Marin with augmentations had been a revelation. She was incredibly powerful, and with them, she had been able to not only overpower nearly half of the soldiers in the palace, but there had been something incredibly supernatural about the way that she moved and fought.

The night passed quickly and transitioned into day. Marin allowed Sam to pole the barge, and she resisted the urge to draw on augmentations, as she had resisted ever since her healing. There was a part of her that worried about how she would feel when she finally did attempt an augmentation on herself. Would she be able to do it? Could she ever be as strong as Marin, and not fatigue so easily when attempting multiple augmentations. It was that fatigue when being pursued by the Kavers that got her caught. She would eventually need to try to place an augmentation again. She had to know whether she could, so she would know what she could and couldn't rely on if attacked.

It was late in the day when the edge of the swamp came into view. Beyond the swamp, the forest rose up. It seemed as if the swamp trees—the svethwuud—blended into the trees of the forest and essentially joined them.

"Is that it?" Sam asked, pointing to the forest.

Marin had joined her at the bow of the barge. Jalen was manning the pole, giving both Sam and Marin a break.

"That is the forest. Once we cross through there, we will reach the plains, and from there, it's only a short stretch to the Theln lands."

"I thought the swamp would be harder to cross."

"Normally, it would take a lot longer, but I was

drawing on significant augmentations to speed us through here," Marin said.

"I thought you were."

"I didn't want to linger too long in the swamp. If Helen decided to send attackers after us, Kavers would have little difficulty reaching us if we moved too slowly."

"What about in the forest?"

"We're going to have to tie up the barge, and then we will have to see how quickly we can move across the forest. We won't be quite as fast as if you and I were alone; we are going to be limited by them," she said, nodding to Alec and Jalen. "Both of them are capable, but the forest is tricky."

Sam stared out at the forest. "You don't think they can make it?"

"I think they can make it, but not without our help. We need to be prepared to be more involved than you are accustomed to being to ensure they make it through safely."

"Are you saying we're going to have to carry them across?"

Sam glanced back at Alec. It wasn't that he was tremendously large, but considering what she had just been through and how weak and rundown she felt, she didn't know whether she would have the strength necessary to carry Alec for an extended period of time.

"It's doubtful, but..." Marin stared into the forest, and worry creased her brow. Sam had seen that worry on her face before, and it made her uncomfortable.

"What aren't you telling me, Marin?"

"I've told you everything you need to know about this," she said.

Sam laughed at her. "First you tell me the forest is dangerous, and then you tell me it's not. Now you're telling me it is. Which is it? Do I need to be concerned about what we're going to encounter or not?"

"It has been over ten years since I've crossed that forest," Marin said. "In that time, I've come to the swamp, and I have navigated around here, but I haven't made it as far as the forest. There hasn't been a need. Why would there be when going beyond the forest would put me in contact with the Thelns, and I know better than to risk myself like that."

"What makes the forest so dangerous?" Sam asked.

"I wasn't deceiving you when I said there is a certain level of danger to the forest. I wasn't deceiving you when I told you that there are creatures you need to be careful of. Those are realities in the forest, but it's not a given we will encounter them. If we navigate directly through, we should come out on the other side in less than a day, and hopefully encounter-free."

A day. Another day when Helen could have started her attack on the city. Another day for them to be in danger.

As they neared the forest, Sam could see how dark it was inside. Daylight had begun to creep into the sky, sending streaks of color through the clouds, and though the swamp was never a bright and cheery place, there had been the promise of sunlight.

Though she had typically operated at night, welcoming the darkness and not afraid of it, going into a place like that, a place where the trees would conceal everything, shrouding it in darkness, left her more than a little uncomfortable.

"What happens if we lose the barge?" Sam asked.

Marin glanced over at Alec and Jalen. "We had better not."

Sam followed the direction of her gaze. Assuming they made it where they were heading and then were able to return, they would need the barge to return to the city. Without it, Sam and Marin could cross the swamp using their canal staffs, but Alec and Jalen needed help. Sam had carried someone before, but right now, she didn't have much faith in her strength to carry Alec with her. Marin could likely carry Jalen without a problem.

Alec and Jalen noticed them looking over their way. Alec stood and joined Sam at the bow of the barge, looking out into the forest. "There aren't any stories about the forest here."

"The stories that we get are from Marin," Sam said. "And she claims that it's both dangerous and that it's not," she said, glaring at Marin.

"I think… I think we should be prepared for the possibility that we will need to place an augmentation."

Sam reached out her hand. Alec pricked the palm and collected her blood in a small metal vial that he stuffed into his pocket. He did the same for himself. When he was done, he nodded.

"That's it?" she asked.

"What do you mean?"

She cocked her head to the side. "Only you? I would like to have a supply of blood in case things take a turn."

"Sam—"

Sam shook her head. "I don't want to be so dependent on you that I can't place an augmentation if it comes to it, Alec."

"I only have these two vials."

"Then I'll take yours, you keep mine, and you can give me a scrap of easar paper." She didn't need anything more than a scrap. If it came down to her needing anything more than that, they probably were in more trouble than they'd get out of.

Alec let out a frustrated sigh and pulled one of the metal vials out and handed it to her. "I don't like this." He pulled a piece of easar paper from his pocket and tore it in half, handing it over to her.

Sam took the paper and stuffed it into her pocket, folding it up tightly so that it would stay anchored into the bottom of her pocket rather than falling out every time she stuck her hand in. She looked at the vial of blood, holding it up and shaking it. "How do I know this is yours and not mine?"

"Sam?"

She grinned and stuffed it into her pocket. "Fine. I'll trust you."

She turned to see Marin and Jalen watching them. Jalen had a certain tension around the corners of his eyes.

"I'm guessing you don't have extra vials like that?"

Jalen shook his head.

"According to Alec, we probably won't need them anyway."

"We shouldn't be separated from them," Marin said. "If we end up separated…"

Sam nodded. If they ended up separated, then it might not matter.

The barge reached the edge of the forest. It was a gradual change, the wet swamp transitioning to soggy ground. The trees at the border were more like clumps of the svethwuud, only occurring more frequently. The trees themselves were somewhat more significant than those out in the swamp, and as they began to grow closer and closer together, they grew taller with more massive trunks.

Marin pushed the barge into the forest as far as she could before motioning for them to climb out. The ground was soggy, and it was unpleasant beneath Sam's feet. She tried to ignore the fact that it squished the way that it did. She was used to having solid footing beneath her. It would take some time to adjust to this.

"We need to find some way to conceal the barge," Marin said.

Alec and Jalen both helped drag the barge into the forest. They found a clump of strange shrubs that they covered it with. Sam propped the barge pole up along the trunk of one of the trees, using a length of vine to secure it to it.

"Now that that's done…"

Marin turned away and headed into the forest. Shadows swallowed her as she disappeared.

19

REACHING THE FOREST

Alec looked over at Sam. She was quieter than she usually was, though nearly dying likely did that to her. Her color seemed to have returned to normal, and she appeared to be maintaining what little strength she had, though not gaining any. It might only be his imagination, but she seemed more hesitant than was usual for her.

Perhaps this journey was a mistake. Heading out into the swamp, by barge or by canal staff, was dangerous, even if she had been completely well. And she was not at all well. And now the forest lay ahead with its own dangers lurking.

The forest intrigued him. The trees here all appeared to be svethwuud, though they were different from those found in the swamp. Would they make easar paper, or did it require the presence of the eels growing around the roots? The ground remained spongy, almost as if water from the swamp seeped up through the bottom layer of the forest, threatening to soak through. He didn't relish the idea of needing to stay in the forest overnight, but if Marin was right—that it would only take a day—they could avoid an overnight stay. If all went well, they would be through the forest by the end of the day.

None of that made him feel any better.

He followed Jalen, admiring the way that he moved so comfortably. Part of that likely came from his training as a Kaver, his way of concealing that he was a Scribe. But part of it was simply him, Alec thought. Jalen was an impressive man.

"How long have you and Marin known each other?" he asked after they had been walking for a while. Sam and Marin walked a few paces ahead of them, far enough that it gave him and Jalen some space so they could talk.

Jalen glanced over. "Marin was the head of the Kavers. She still hadn't found a Scribe, and when I was beginning to understand what I was…"

Alec frowned. "But why would you have gone to Marin?"

"We knew each other as children," Jalen said. "We have known each other for a long time. I trusted her."

"Did you trust your sister?"

"I thought that I could," Jalen said.

"Did you know anything about her son?"

Jalen shook his head. "She has kept that from everyone, including my parents."

"Has Marin told you what Lyasanna intended?"

Jalen's jaw clenched, and his eyes tightened. "I have heard what Lyasanna intended for her child. I don't blame Marin for what she did, and I see there are times that

Samara does, just as I see the way she looks at Marin, almost as if she can't decide whether she likes her or not."

"I think Sam looks at everyone that way."

"It's different with Marin."

Alec climbed over a fallen log. Even that was somewhat squishy. "For Sam, she has gone through a wide range of emotions lately. For the longest time, she only knew Marin as someone she worked for. She would take jobs, but…"

Jalen glanced over. "But what?"

"I think Marin was probably training her, even if Sam didn't know it at the time. When she learned that Marin was something more than a talented thief and employer, she began to hope she could learn something about her mother. She never dreamed that her mother still lived."

"I don't necessarily agree with how Marin used Samara. I understand that she thought it was necessary to provide protection for Tray, but…"

Alec sighed. "I don't even think that bothers Sam, not anymore. It did for a while. For a long time, she was angry with Marin, but the more she has come to understand the city and the Kavers and Scribes, the more she has come to terms with the fact that it might've been better for her to have been kept from everything."

Sam glanced back at him, almost as if she knew he was talking about her. He flashed a smile. It was difficult for him talking about Sam in this way. If Sam had grown up knowing who she was and what she was, it was possible Alec would never have learned about his potential as a Scribe.

"Have you ever wondered how it was that the two of you met?"

Alec glanced over at Jalen. "It was chance. She was attacked by Ralun, and nearly dead when she staggered into the apothecary."

"I just think it's an interesting chance that she would happen to make it to the one person who might be able to help."

Alec frowned. "What are you saying?"

Jalen nodded at Marin. "I wonder if she had a hand in that." He glanced over at Alec and flashed a smile. "Or maybe it was only chance. If so, it was quite fortuitous that Samara managed to find you at a time of such need."

They continued onward in silence. Alec hadn't given that much thought. Now that he put his mind to it, he realized that it *was* fortunate that Sam had stumbled into his apothecary shop. She had been injured, the crossbow bolt poisoned and likely fatal, and what would have happened had he not been there? What would have happened had she not had that paper?

Could Marin have known about his father and suspected that Alec would have the ability to work with Sam?

No. For that to be the case, it would have meant that Marin knew he would find the easar paper Sam had stolen. It would have meant that Marin knew he would discover the secret to writing on it. It would have meant that Marin would... have been far cleverer than what he thought was possible.

It wasn't Marin, but it did raise the question of some greater influence. Perhaps there was something to the gods, even though Alec had never prayed to them, not like so many did. He didn't swear at them the way Sam did, either. In his mind, it was better to not anger the gods than to risk their attention.

Jalen occasionally glanced over at him as they walked, saying nothing more about what he had suggested. Alec was thankful for that, and the day passed slowly. Marin gave them a few breaks, during which they would drink from water flasks, and Alec would take bites of eel meat to keep himself as energized as possible. It was a good thing they had stopped for those two eels, otherwise, he might not have enough to survive the travel through the forest.

"How much farther do we have to walk?" Sam asked as they took a break late in the day.

Marin looked up at the forest canopy. It was dense and created thick shadows around them. Little light came through, nothing more than the sense of daylight. "I don't know. It's difficult to ascertain this deep into the forest."

"We haven't seen any sign of the creatures you claimed we would," Sam said.

"That is good."

Sam frowned at her but said nothing more. Alec could tell that she wanted to, and from the way she clenched her jaw, he suspected she was biting back some comment. It had to be difficult for Sam, but he was thankful she resisted. It served no purpose, not with what they were trying to accomplish.

As the forest grew darker, night likely falling around them, Alec thought he heard movement. He jerked his head around but saw nothing. With the growing shadows, even if something were there, he'd likely not see it.

"What is it?" Jalen asked.

Alec shook his head. "Probably nothing."

"But you noticed something?"

Alec shrugged. "It's probably only my imagination. With the way the shadows are…"

There it was again. It was a sense of movement and with it almost a scraping sound.

"Marin," Jalen said in a harsh whisper.

She glanced back, a question in her eyes.

"Alec thinks he—"

She raised her hand, silencing him. Marin assembled her canal staff. Alec wasn't certain how effective that would be in the forest. With the trees growing as close together as they did, it would be difficult for the staff to be of any use. Were she to try to swing it, she would likely smack into trees rather than have the freedom to spin it as he had seen her do before.

The sound came again, and this time, Alec was sure he heard it. It was over his head, he looked up, scanning the branches.

Sam had made her way over to him and grabbed his arm, forcing his attention down to her. "What is it?" she asked.

"I don't know. I hear something."

Sam froze and looked up into the trees, following the direction of his gaze. She frowned, and he wondered if she was attempting an augmentation. She no longer needed him quite the same way, and now that she could place them without his assistance, he didn't feel quite as important to her. Then again, it didn't require them to draw their blood to write on easar paper for her to place those augmentations, so there was an advantage to it.

"I don't see anything."

"With an augmentation?" he whispered.

She shook her head. "I haven't…"

"Why not?"

"Ever since the injury"—Alec noticed the way she said *injury*, rather than remarking on how she had nearly died—"I haven't been sure whether I should try them. I really need to. I think practicing with them could make me stronger, much like I think that is the way Marin developed her skills, but…"

Alec took her hand and squeezed it gently. "I understand."

"It's more than that," she said.

She looked around and kept her voice low. No one had seemed to want to speak very loudly in the forest, and Marin continued to scan the treetops, having not started them forward again. That bothered Alec. Was there something more here? The way Marin searched the trees, led him to believe it was a possibility. Could it be the creatures she had warned them about?

"Something feels different now," Sam said. "I don't know how to explain it any better. It's not what's happening around us that's different. *I* feel different."

"I think you're just tired from the loss of blood."

"Don't you think the easar paper augmentation would have made that better by now?" She glanced over at him and bit the inside of her bottom lip. "Every time we used the easar paper in that way before, the effect was fairly rapid. It has been days since you placed it. I should be completely recovered. Weakness shouldn't linger, not like this."

Alec sighed. "What if it's the effect of what Helen did to me?" He hadn't considered that before, and he should have. "I gave you some of my blood. What if that is making you feel the same malaise I've felt ever since I was poisoned?"

Sam frowned. "I don't know if that's it."

"Do you get any benefit when you eat eel meat?"

"What kind of question is that?"

"When I eat it, I don't feel the same thing as Jalen or others. All I feel is normal."

Sam held her hand out, and Alec pulled the top off the jar and handed her a hunk of meat. Sam chewed it slowly, her nose wrinkling as she did. When she swallowed, she closed her eyes.

"I feel warmth, no different than I have the other times I've taken it. I feel a strange surge of energy within me. I feel... good."

Alec smiled to himself. "That's reassuring."

"Why?"

"Because if my blood somehow carried the poison, you wouldn't feel that at all. I don't feel that at all. What I feel is nothing."

"Have you tried not taking it for a while."

Alec swallowed. He couldn't imagine what would happen if he were not to use the eel meat. How tired would he be then? How rundown would he be? "I haven't tried, and I don't know that I should. I don't know what would happen to me if I did that."

"Yeah. And maybe now is not the best time to try," Sam said, looking around.

Alec started to laugh, but the sound came again.

Sam tensed, and she pulled her hand free of his, looking up at the trees. She reached for her canal staff, pulled one end of it out, and gripped it almost like a club.

"I heard it that time," she whispered.

"What do you think it is?"

"We need to move," Marin said.

"Is this what you warned us about?"

"I don't know. I can't see it, and if it is, and if they're directly overhead…"

She started off, moving at a rapid pace. Sam somehow kept up with her, even in her fatigued state, but Alec had a little harder time. He wondered again about the eel meat's effectiveness. Even Jalen struggled, though maybe that was only for his benefit. They reached a log that blocked their way, and Sam scrambled over, flipping with a twist of her half canal staff, leaving Marin with Alec and Jalen.

"What is it, Marin?" Jalen asked.

"Not yet," she said.

"Not yet? If not now, then when are you going to share anything about this with us?"

Marin frowned. "Knowing about it will do nothing but frighten you."

"I think I'm getting frightened enough just from the fact that you aren't sharing something," Jalen said.

Alec started to smile. There came a soft gasp from the other side of the fallen tree.

Sam.

Marin jerked her head around, grabbed Jalen and Alec, and jumped, carrying them up over the tree.

Alec barely had a chance to marvel at her strength or the fact that she hadn't needed her canal staff to clear the fallen trunk. When they landed, the ground absorbed the jarring, and they sank softly into the ground.

Where was Sam?

They had heard her gasp, but she was nowhere to be seen.

"Kyza!" Marin said.

"What happened? Where is she?" Alec asked.

Marin scanned the treetops. "I need an eyesight augmentation, and quickly," she said to Jalen.

He didn't argue and quickly withdrew a knife from one pocket and a slip of easar paper from another. He jabbed the center of his hand, and Marin stretched out her hand. They slapped their palms together, mixing the blood, and Jalen scraped the blood off her palm with the edge of his knife and quickly used that to write something on the paper.

Alec stared up into the trees, trying to see what might be up there, and what might have grabbed Sam, but could see nothing.

"Maybe she only went to explore."

"She didn't go to explore," Marin said.

"Maybe she—"

Marin's eyes changed. There was a slight widening, and Alec didn't know whether that came from the augmentation or from something that she observed in the trees. Either way, her breath caught, telling Alec more than the changing to her eyes did.

"Kyza!"

"What is it?"

"I'm going to need you two to stay here," Marin said.

"Stay here?" Jalen said. "Marin, if something happened to Sam, I don't think it's wise for you to go running off into the trees after her, especially if—"

"If I don't go after her, she will be lost."

Jalen fell silent. Marin jumped, using her canal staff to slip into the trees, landing on a branch. She scrambled away, quickly disappearing from view. With her gone, Alec felt a surge of nervousness. They had no Kavers with them now.

"We should probably find someplace to conceal ourselves," Jalen said.

Alec looked around. The trees were large enough that they could rest near them, but the ground around the trees was soft and spongy, making it unpleasant for them to stand, much less sit.

"We could go and hide near that fallen tree," Alec suggested, pointing to the trunk that Marin had jumped them over. It was enormous, and the trunk should provide some decent protection from whatever it was that was out here in the forest.

Jalen stared at it for a moment. "That's probably a good idea."

When they reached the tree, Alec found the trunk unpleasantly mossy. He didn't want to stay too close to it, but at the same time, he didn't want to remain exposed any more than was necessary.

"How long do you think she'll be gone?" Alec asked.

"I don't know. Marin hasn't told me a whole lot about this forest, but I can tell it makes her nervous."

"She was trying to downplay it with Sam."

"I don't know why she would. Marin isn't comfortable here."

"I'm not comfortable here. There's just something about it. It's almost as if we're being watched."

Jalen chuckled. "I'm glad you said that. I thought I was the only one thinking it."

Alec looked around, staring up at the trees, but he didn't feel that same sense of movement and didn't hear anything, not the same as he had before. How long would Marin be gone? How long would they be left alone?

"How good are you with that sword?" Alec asked.

"Why?"

"If something happens, I want to know that you are skilled enough that you can defend us."

Jalen shrugged. "I'm good enough that I was able to pass as a Kaver for years."

"Yes, but a *lazy* Kaver."

Jalen smiled at him. "It was easier to play up the idea that I was lazy rather than to reveal that I was simply a terrible Kaver. Laziness creates a better excuse, I think."

Alec noticed the sound again.

It came as a softness, almost a scraping, and it was almost directly overhead.

He looked up, trying to stare into the darkness, but saw nothing.

"What you think it is?"

"I don't know," Jalen said. He unsheathed his sword,

and having him here, with his sword and with his armor, made Alec feel only slightly better.

Jalen might survive this, but would Alec?

There was a flash of shadow.

"Kyza!" Jalen darted forward, moving rapidly, but not the same as Marin or Sam would move with augmentations. He swung his sword and slammed it down. It hit the trunk of the tree with a loud *thunk*, and Jalen swore again.

"What was that?" Alec asked.

"I don't know—"

Jalen was shoved forward.

Alec caught him, and wetness covered his hand.

Not wetness. Blood.

Jalen lost his grip on his sword, and Alec picked it up, holding it out, trying to understand what happened.

There was another flash of movement, and he heard a strange howl that quickly faded.

Kyza!

Sam's swear seemed to fit here, especially with the strangeness he had experienced.

"What happened?" a voice called from the darkness.

"Marin?"

She appeared next to him, almost as if coalescing out of the shadows. She carried her canal staff, and a bruise had formed on her brow.

She crouched down next to Jalen, rolling him over.

"I don't know what happened. You disappeared, we crouched near the tree to see if we could stay shielded, and then we saw movement."

"It was good you moved closer to the trunk, but he's going to need help."

"What kind of help?"

"The kind only a Scribe and Kaver can provide."

Alec reached into his pocket for his easar paper, but as he did, he froze. "What happened to Sam?"

Marin shook her head.

"Marin? Where is Sam?"

Marin looked over, and he noticed the anguish in her eyes. "She's gone, Alec."

"Gone? What do you mean she's gone?"

Marin grabbed the slip of easar paper from him, quickly pricking her finger and mixing it in her palm with a drop of blood from Jalen before scrawling a few words on the paper.

"Marin?" Alec pressed.

When she finally looked up, she could only shake her head. "She's gone."

20

DECISIONS AND RETURNS

A lec watched Marin as she guided them further into the forest. It was dark, and with every passing moment, he feared for Sam. There had been no sound of anything other than her startled gasp, and whatever had happened to her had torn her away. Now what would happen to her? Would there be any way to get her back?

"Marin?"

Marin glanced back at him. She had a determined set to her jaw, and she gripped her canal staff tightly. "I'm doing as much as I can, Alec. I don't want anything to happen to Samara, either."

"I know you don't, I'm just saying…"

Marin shook her head. "I know what you're saying. And I'm telling you that I am doing everything possible to rescue her."

"What if there is no rescue?" Jalen asked. When Alec looked over at him, frowning, Jalen only shook his head.

"I understand what we're trying to do, but what if there is no rescue? What if we have already lost Samara?"

"I don't think we've lost her," Alec said.

"Because you don't want to believe it, but you're a physicker—a *master* physicker—you need to be realistic with what we know."

"I know that Sam has seen worse," Alec said. "She's come through it."

"Even if she has, do you really think she can get free?"

"Not without knowing what happened," Alec said. He looked over at Marin, and she paused near the trunk of a massive tree. Deeper into the forest now, the trees were still somewhat similar to the svethwuud, but not the same. Different enough that Alec wasn't sure whether they would even be useful for creating easar paper. Then again, getting to the roots may not matter, not when there were no eels that swam around them the same way they did in the swamp.

"We know what happened," Marin said.

"We know that she disappeared," Alec said. Sam had been gone for no more than half of an hour, maybe less, and already he felt that getting to her was hopeless. As much as he wanted to find and rescue her, he had already begun to think it wouldn't be possible. And if they failed, if *he* failed, what would happen to him then? What would he do?

"I've already shared with you that there are dangerous creatures in the forest. If one of them grabbed Samara—"

"They would eat her?" Alec asked.

Marin sighed. "Not eat her. That is not what they would do."

"Then what?"

"The chamyn serve the Thelns."

Alec blinked. "Those creatures? The ones that you described? How do they serve the Thelns?"

"They are the reason the forest has been so difficult to cross. Without the chamyn here, it wouldn't be nearly as difficult. I warned Samara about the sinkholes, but they are easy enough to avoid if you stay near the trees, which is why I have been guiding us in this direction. But the chamyn prowl the treetops, and they watch for signs of outsiders, of people who should not be here. Most of the time, it's easy enough to avoid them."

"It doesn't seem easy enough," Alec said. Why would Marin not have shared with them that these creatures worked for the Thelns?

Maybe it didn't matter. If they could avoid them—if they had *managed* to avoid them—then it wouldn't have mattered.

"They aren't usually found this far out in the forest. I hadn't expected to need to watch for them."

"And now that you know they are here?"

"Now that I know, we need to keep an eye on them. If they have come this far, it's possible we will be limited on where we can go in the forest."

"Limited? How so?"

"In that there are certain places in the forest where—"

Marin spun and twisted her canal staff, thrusting it into the air. There came a strange muted cry, and Marin sucked in a breath.

"Kyza," she said, backing into Jalen. "There are more."

"These creatures?"

"Look into the treetops. You can see them there. I count five—no, six."

Alec looked up, but he didn't see anything. Everything beyond the lowest branches was nothing more than blurs of shadows. He couldn't make out anything up there, not enough that revealed the chamyn.

"We need to move back," Marin said.

"Back? We can't go back. If we do, we won't be able to help Sam."

"If they grab us, there won't be anything we can do to help Sam."

Alec started backward and felt movement behind him. He spun around, and one of the creatures was there.

"Marin!"

She flipped and moved quickly—so quickly that Alec knew she had an augmentation—and landed near the creature. She smacked it with her staff, and it jumped back into the trees. It managed to do it with such speed and grace that Alec knew the creature was augmented too. There was no natural way for a beast to move like that.

"I think we need to move quickly," Marin said.

"Where?" Jalen asked. He had a sheet of easar paper out and was frantically writing on it while standing.

"We have to get back to the swamp," Marin said.

"If we go back the swamp—"

Marin turned toward Alec. "I'm well aware of what happens if we go back to the swamp, but if we don't, these creatures will drag us into the Theln lands. Trust me when I tell you that you don't want to experience that. We have lost too many that way."

"Lost who?"

"Scribes, mostly. Kavers have been captured, but Scribes are typically the ones who are captured. It's the reason few Scribes ever ventured this way. I thought... It doesn't matter what I thought. What matters is that we need to keep moving to reach the barge."

Alec resisted, but Marin grabbed him and pushed him forward.

"If you get caught, what can you do to help Samara?" she asked.

She jumped and spun with her staff flying out from her. Alec heard the solid thud of it striking something—or more than one something. When she landed, she grabbed him and Jalen and began running.

They streaked through the forest, and every so often, Marin would pause, whipping out with her staff, attempting to strike, but she never managed to catch one of the creatures again.

Alec hated that they were going the wrong way. Away from Sam. It felt like they were abandoning her. She wasn't lost to them, not yet. He wouldn't believe that. And yet, what choice did he have? What else could they do but return to the barge? The creatures wouldn't be able to reach them there.

Finally, the edge of the forest appeared. Marin single-handedly grabbed the barge and threw it into the water. Alec marveled at the sheer strength she managed, the way she was augmented and was able to do that, but he didn't dare stop. Marin grabbed him and tossed him onto the barge. Jalen came after, and Marin stood on the shoreline in the forest, remaining there long enough to strike at another one of the chamyn.

Once out of the forest, Alec had a chance to get a better look at the creatures. They were enormous. He had read about horses, never having seen one since they didn't exist in the city, and the creature reminded him of what he'd envisioned based on the descriptions he'd read. They were large enough to ride, and large enough to grab him and carry him off to the Thelns.

The creatures had elongated snouts and large ears that flopped forward. The eyes were the strangest. They glowed with a greenish sort of light. Three of the creatures surrounded Marin, crouched as if to jump.

Marin leaped, but one of the creatures grabbed her by the leg and threw her back to the ground. Marin spun, whipping her staff around, and she caught that creature on the side of the jaw. It withdrew, but two others jumped forward and grabbed Marin and began to drag her back into the forest.

Somehow, Marin managed to free herself. Something came flying out, and for a moment, Alec hoped she had somehow managed to jump, but he realized it was the barge pole.

"Go!" she screamed.

"Not without you," Jalen said, standing near the bow of the barge.

Marin was dragged again, and once more, she managed to kick and got free long enough to make it back to the edge of the forest, and Alec thought that perhaps she might get herself free, but then she was dragged again away. "Go," he heard, though her voice was weak.

Alec took the barge pole and stood at the end of the barge, staring into the forest. He kept waiting for Marin to return. She was augmented, and there was no way she should've been able to be dragged away like that, but she never returned.

"We have to go after her," Jalen said.

"How?" Alec asked, turning to him. "You saw what they did to her. You saw the way they were able to drag her. What do you think you and I can do?"

Jalen rounded on him and reached for the barge pole as if to jerk it from Alec's hand. "We can't leave her!"

"I said the same thing about Sam, and Marin forced us out of the forest. Do you think you and I can do anything to rescue them? Even with your armor and your sword, do you think either of us is equipped to go after them?"

Jalen glared at him before turning and facing the forest. "I need…"

Alec rested a hand on his shoulder, trying to reassure him. "I need the same, but I don't think either of us is skilled enough, or strong enough, to go after them."

"I thought I'd lost her once, and I didn't want to lose her again. Not this way."

Alec studied Jalen. "You care for her."

Jalen looked over at him. "Of course I do. We have known each other for nearly my entire life. When I believed that she had died, I…" Jalen shook his head. "Why would she not have come back to me?"

"The chamyn took her. I don't think that she could—"

"I'm not talking about now."

Alec swallowed. "I don't know. I think she was doing what she thought was necessary to protect Tray."

"If she was trying to protect him, she could have come and found me. I would have helped."

"Could you?" Alec asked.

Jalen shot him a hard look. "I could have."

"You weren't willing to reveal that you were a Scribe. How is it you think you would have been able to help her?"

Jalen stared at him, and then he took a seat on the deck of the barge. "Is that it? She didn't tell me because she thought I was too cowardly?"

"I don't think that's it, not at all. All I'm saying is that there is more to Marin—much more—than what we know."

"There *was* more to Marin," Jalen said in a whisper.

"She's not gone. Not yet."

"You saw those creatures," Jalen said. He pointed toward the forest that was growing increasingly distant. They seemed to be drifting even without using the barge pole.

"I saw those creatures, but I also heard what Marin said about them. If they serve the Thelns, then it's possible they will drag her to the Thelns." Alec had to hope that was what would happen. He had to hope that was all that would happen with Sam. If they were lucky, Sam would reach Tray, and he would help her. She's as much his sister as he is her brother. Surely, he would help, and she could return, and...

And what?

Alec had no idea what Tray's standing was with the Thelns. If they had Sam, there might not be anything Tray could do. Alec wasn't even certain how Tray felt about

Sam, not after everything he had been through. He had been in the Theln lands a long time now, long enough he might even consider it his home. He had his father now, and he knew nothing of his Lyasanna, not like a son should know his mother. He only knew that she had wanted him dead for merely existing.

But Sam might be alive.

That was what he had to hope for. Alec needed to believe Sam still lived. He needed to believe the chamyn hadn't killed her.

He took the barge pole and began to push. What choice did he have? What choice was there but to return to the city, maybe find help, and wait to see if Sam and Marin returned?

Jalen looked over at him, and Alec hated the hopelessness in his eyes. It matched the fears in his heart, but he was determined not to let them overwhelm him. He had seen Sam survive much worse, and he had to believe she could survive this too.

But in truth, he worried this might be something more than she could survive. He feared the Thelns would take revenge for what she had done to them. And he worried Tray wouldn't be strong enough to oppose them.

21

CAPTIVE

S am flew through the air.

It was a strange sensation. She had been standing on the soft, spongy forest floor, and the next moment, she was soaring.

Something had grabbed her and carried her.

She tried to determine what it was, but she couldn't. All she knew was that it had grabbed the back of her cloak, but it had done so in a way that didn't hurt her.

At least she still had her canal staff. She thought about swinging it, but as she was flung from branch to branch, jumping with whatever creature carried her, she wasn't sure she dared do that. If she did, she could end up falling from a great height and dropping down to the forest floor. Without Alec with her, she wasn't sure she would survive it.

Instead, she focused on trying an augmentation.

Her first since being injured and nearly dying at

Lyasanna's hand. She was hesitant, but if she was ever going to do it, now had to be the time.

What would Alec do? How would he document an augmentation for her? His style had changed somewhat since going to the university. He was just as diligent with his documentation, but there was something to it that had changed. He used less embellishment. Everything was simple.

Strength. Speed. Bones that wouldn't break. He likely would have a combination of medicines he would administer that would ensure the augmentation was effective, but Sam didn't think she could use that herself. Instead, she wanted only those augmentations and hoped they would take hold.

Had anything changed?

Alec had worried about the poisoning affecting her. The fact that he was still affected by it bothered her, but she didn't think that was the reason for her weakness. She didn't think his poisoning was the reason she felt different. Maybe it was just that she had lost so much blood and had nearly died.

As the augmentation took hold, washing up through her with a flash of cold, power surged through her.

It was almost unexpected. The strength she managed was more than she ever had before, at least when creating an augmentation alone. This was almost overwhelming.

Whatever creature had grabbed her landed on a branch, and Sam spun, jerking herself around. The force of it freed her.

She twisted while getting free and landed on the

branch, grabbing it and holding tight, afraid she might slip and fall.

An enormous cat stared back at her.

The creature crouched on the branch, holding on to it with long claws. As Sam studied the creature, she realized it wasn't merely a cat. The nose was longer, and the ears flopped forward, and the eyes were wide and gleamed with a soft, almost greenish light. Fur was dappled and blended in with the tree branch.

Sam hesitated, freezing in place. Was this what Marin had warned her about, the creature she feared?

And yet, the creature hadn't tried to hurt her. It had only grabbed her, carrying her into the upper branches, but hadn't harmed her.

Not yet.

She crouched on the branch and glanced down, trying to gauge how far up she was, but it was difficult to determine. The forest floor was little more than darkness, a blur beneath her, and far enough away that she wasn't sure she could reach it safely were it to become necessary.

The strange creature watched her, almost as if trying to predict what she might do.

She gripped her canal staff, but would it be enough if the creature tried to attack her? It was better than nothing but by how much? If she were attacked up in the trees, her precarious perch would make using the staff a challenge.

The creature rested its head on its paws and stared at her, almost as if trying to decide what to do with her.

"Well?" Sam said. She felt more than a little ridiculous attempting to speak to the creature, but the way it looked at her was almost as if it wanted her to say something. "Now that you have me here, what's your plan for me?"

The creature's ears swiveled, almost as if trying to listen for something, and then it stood. Before Sam could react, the beast lunged and grabbed her by the back of her cloak and started running.

This time, she did fight. She tried to thrash, but the way the creature had bundled her cloak kept her trapped within it. There was no way for her to escape, no way for her to get free, and the only thing she could do was go along for the ride.

The creature jumped from branch to branch, carrying her through the forest, high above the forest floor, and moving with much more speed than Sam would have managed. With each jump, Sam braced herself for a jarring landing, but it never came. She felt the speed as they soared through the air, jumping from place to place, and struggled to maintain a grip on her canal staff. Wherever they landed, she needed to be prepared for what might come next.

Would this creature bring her to a pack of others? She wasn't about to become lunch for some strange forest cat, but as much as she struggled, trying to twist her way free, she wasn't able to do it.

Kyza, but she felt stupid.

She tried bringing her arm around, but every time she tried, the creature jumped, carrying her farther and farther from where the others were.

Was Marin even coming after her?

If she did, there might not be anything that Marin

could do. There were limits to her ability, even though she was as skilled a Kaver as any Sam had ever encountered.

In that case, Sam wasn't sure she wanted Marin coming after her. She didn't want the others to risk themselves and end up getting captured—or worse—by these creatures.

The only part she cared about was that Alec wouldn't know what happened to her.

Light filtered through the trees.

At first, Sam thought it was imagined, but the longer it went, the more confident she was there was light in the distance.

Was the creature carrying her to the edge of the forest? Or had they returned to the swamp? Maybe this strange cat had decided it didn't want her in its forest and was trying to push her out.

With two more jumps, the creature soared down, landing softly in a field of tall grasses.

It was the end of the forest, and it wasn't the swamp.

Kyza. Was this creature going to drag her into the middle of the field and eat her? Why bring her here? Why not have his meal in the forest?

There was another possibility, but how likely was it that the creature would drag her all the way to the Theln lands?

It broke into a run as soon as they landed on the ground. On and on they ran, and Sam was little more than baggage, little more than something the creature kept clamped in its jaws as it continued to carry her across the plain. At one point, she bounced off the ground briefly, long enough that she struck her head, and Sam was sure she lost consciousness, however briefly. It didn't slow the creature at all, and it continued to run, moving with terrific speed.

There was something different about the air here. It was almost... clean.

Sam was so accustomed to smelling the swamp or the canals or the overall dankness of the city that having the air smelling of flowers and grasses and earth was unexpected.

She tried twisting so she could look around, but she couldn't see anything, not with as quickly as the creature was moving. All around her was a blur, nothing else.

The grasses tugged at her canal staff, and she struggled to hang on to it. There might not be any use for the staff, not the same way there was in the city, but Sam was not about to lose that weapon. If there was one of these creatures, there were undoubtedly more, and she had to be ready.

As the time stretched past, the landscape around her started to change. It became almost a rolling sort of hillside, and sunlight shone down. A heavy wind began to gust, tousling her hair even more than the movement from the creature did.

Were she not so worried about what was happening, she might have almost enjoyed this, but she wasn't able to enjoy it. She worried about Alec and Marin and Jalen. Were they looking for her? How would they find her? Or would they have to save themselves and retreat to the swamp and back to the city?

It might have just been her imagination, but it seemed as if the creature began to slow.

Maybe it was getting tired. Or, more likely, it had arrived wherever it was taking her. As it slowed, Sam started to focus on trying to pull on an augmentation. If she could manage that, if she could do anything that would get her free, she would use this opportunity to escape.

Finally, the creature came to a stop.

It dropped Sam in a heap and bounded away, leaving her in a clearing. She stood and checked to make sure her canal staff was intact and looked around.

The forest wasn't visible from where she was. Even the grassy plain was little more than a memory. She was on a hillside with a massive city in the distance.

Sam's breath caught. That had to be a Theln city.

How? Why?

The creature had brought her where she was planning on going, but now she was here without Alec and Marin and Jalen, and she wasn't certain it was safe for her to remain.

Returning would be difficult. It would force her to walk back the way she had come, if she could even figure that out. As she looked around, she realized she had no idea from which direction the strange creature had come.

Kyza!

Could she figure it out based on the position of the sun? Even that was difficult to do. When she'd been in the forest, the sun had been shielded from her, preventing her from determining which direction it rose. The creature could have gone in any direction, other than south which would've taken her back to the swamp.

And from where she was, could she even get free?

Where was the cat?

It troubled her that the creature had left her here. If it intended to come back for her, if it intended to turn her into some sort of meal, she wasn't about to stay here and wait. No, she would be ready to fight.

Only... now that she was here, she was curious.

Could she learn anything about the Thelns? She didn't want to endanger herself without knowing exactly what was down there, but she could observe and see what she could learn. If this was where she had intended to go, shouldn't she take advantage of it?

And it was better to keep moving than to remain here. It would be better to get free before—

Something thudded toward her.

Sam spun, looking for what she heard, but there was nothing.

She paused and listened. There was no doubting what she heard. It was a thundering, practically coming from beneath her.

There might be a way she could see.

She used her canal staff and propped herself up, climbing to the top of it to look around. It made her visible, especially in a landscape otherwise open, but if she didn't, she would have no way of figuring out what was coming in her direction. She wasn't about to be surprised again.

She'd made a mistake.

A dozen of the strange creatures bounded toward her. And they weren't alone. Thelns.

Kyza!

Sam flipped off of her staff and began running, trying

to get away, but she couldn't outrun the creatures or the Thelns. Even with augmentations, she had no chance.

They reached her near a wide, hard-packed road leading into the city in the distance. Sam spun, trying to use her staff to prevent them from getting too close, but one of the creatures simply grabbed it and jerked it from her.

Sam struggled, preparing to attempt an augmentation, but she wasn't quick enough.

Two of the Thelns grabbed her and held her.

She was trapped.

22

ASALAR

A sound startled Sam, and she jerked her head around. It was the sound of footsteps, and she had heard them often enough over the last few hours that she was convinced someone was coming for her, but they never did. She was left alone in this room, staring at the blank walls, nothing but the surprisingly ornate door keeping her confined.

Her eyes traced an outline around the door, and it hadn't taken her long to recognize the markings. They were the same sort of markings Helen had used to break the princess out of the prison cells beneath the palace. Sam imagined they created some kind of augmentation for this door and some way for it to resist any method she might have of opening it.

It didn't surprise her that the Thelns would have those markings. She had been convinced Helen had stolen the knowledge from the Thelns, and this was even more proof of that. What did surprise her was the color splashed on the walls. It was far more than she had expected in these lands, and it gave them a sort of vibrancy. One wall was a bright orange while another was yellow, and still, another was red. The only wall that wasn't quite as vibrant was the one with the door, and it was painted a pale blue, the color the sky had been when she was captured.

She was unharmed. That surprised her as much as anything. When the Thelns had captured her, dragging her with them into the city, they had merely confined her. They didn't beat her or knock her unconscious, and they hadn't made any attempt to harm her.

They had covered her face. Sam saw nothing as she entered the city, nothing that could help her know what a Theln city was like, and nothing that would reveal to her where they had brought her. She had noticed sounds, but it was nothing more than the sound of voices, murmuring sort of noise that reminded her of the streets of Verdholm.

The smells within the city were different. There was a pungency, like that of animals, and a stink of dung that hung in the air. Every so often, she was convinced that she heard animal sounds, though she wasn't sure.

And now, she stared at these walls. It was too dark in the room to make out much detail, but there was a bed and a basin of water. Nothing else. And she wasn't bound. That surprised her.

They had taken her cloak and with it everything that was in the pockets. That included the easar paper and the vial of Alec's blood. Without that, she had no way of augmenting herself other than ones she could place on her own. Those augmentations were useful, but not nearly as effective as the combined Kaver and Scribe blood written on easar paper.

If they found that, what would they use it for? Would they use it against Alec?

That idea troubled her.

And they had taken her canal staff.

She imagined it broken, tossed aside as they carried her into the city. The canal staff was a part of her and losing it left her feeling almost as naked as not having her cloak. Were she to have to choose, she would prefer to have the staff rather than her cloak. She would almost rather have the staff than any clothing. At least if she were to have her staff, she could fight. Without it...

Sam didn't know what she was without it.

The sound of footsteps faded.

Maybe it was nothing more than a patrol.

There was a regularity to those footsteps, and she wished she had a better way of keeping track of how often they came past. If she could figure that out, she might be able to figure out how to time an escape. She wouldn't give up on the idea that she *would* escape. She was determined to do so, and return to Alec, but now that she was here, now that she was a captive of the Thelns, she had to believe there was some way of finding Tray. She had to be able to reach him, didn't she?

When she was convinced the steps were gone, she made her way to the door and tested it. It was locked, and without any way of picking the lock, she doubted she would be able to escape, not easily.

What about with an augmentation?

She focused on strength. It was the only one she focused on. If it worked, and if she managed to get herself free, she could try for other augmentations, but strength first. With enough strength, she could tear the door off, much the same way as she had torn the door off when Jessup had captured her.

The feeling of the augmentation came, washing through her with a cold wave.

Much like the last strength augmentation she'd placed on herself, this one felt more powerful than what she had expected. Could it just be that she hadn't tried in quite some time? Or was there more to it? Maybe she really wasn't any more powerfully augmented than normal, it only felt that way. It could be dangerous for her to believe she had a greater augmentation than she did.

When the augmentation took hold, she grabbed the door and jerked.

Nothing happened.

She tried pushing, shoving on the door, but there was nothing. Whatever augmentations they'd placed on the door prevented her from doing anything other than wasting the augmentation.

What about the walls?

Sam tapped on the orange wall. It was a solid sound. She pushed against it and realized that it wasn't painted wood at all, but stone. As she made her way around the room, she discovered that each of the walls was stone. The paint had only masked that, making them appear to be wood.

She had no way out.

She had already been trapped, so that realization

didn't trouble her any more than knowing that her augmentation failed her so spectacularly.

If they knew how to suppress her augmentations so efficiently, would there ever be any way for her to escape?

The sound of footsteps came from outside the door again, and Sam stepped back, moving against the wall and not wanting to be too close to the door were it to open.

When they made their way past, she turned her focus to the symbols on the door again. Maybe there was something there that she could determine, some way she could counteract the augmentations the Thelns had placed.

But she couldn't figure out any way to do so. Even attempting to pick at the symbols, trying to weaken them in some way, failed her.

Footsteps returned, sooner than they should have.

Kyza! She hurried back, getting out of the way, and was just in time.

The door opened.

Sam expected Thelns to greet her, so she was surprised to see a thin man with graying hair, wearing a flowing jacket striped with colors. He frowned when he saw her.

"You. You are to come with me." He had an accented voice and a clipped way of speaking.

"I'm not going anywhere until I know what's going on."

The man glanced back at her. "It's my understanding that the chamyn captured you?"

"It didn't capture me—"

"You were carried here out of the forest?"

Sam frowned but decided to go along with it. "I was. I

was looking for my—"

The man turned away and started off down the hall-way. Sam stayed in the room, but a pair of muscular men stepped inside and stood off to either side of the door, giving her no choice but to go along with the other man. He didn't strike her as a Theln, certainly not like Ralun or the others who had attacked the city, or even like the Thelns who had captured her and brought her here.

At the end of the hallway, the man stopped and looked back at Sam. He waited with his hands clasped in front of him for her to join him. She looked over her shoulder and saw the two others waiting. They did not appear to be armed, but they were considerably larger than she was, and she doubted she would be able to escape them easily.

Sam hurried off down the hallway after the thin man. She glanced at the walls as she made her way through the hall, frowning to herself. They were vividly painted like her room, as was the tile that she walked on, all in orange and red and yellows. Paintings on the walls were done in the same bright colors. There was a brightness to every-thing around her.

It didn't fit what she had expected of the Thelns, though Sam no longer knew what she should have expected of them. She thought about the strange creature that had dragged her to that field nearby, and then seem-ingly returned with Thelns and more cats. Were they that well trained? There was so much she didn't know about this land.

She continued to follow the man and occasionally glanced back, looking over her shoulder, realizing there was no way for her to escape. Any attempt to do so would be thwarted by the two men who trailed her. Every so often, she encountered others in the hallway, what she assumed to be guards much like the other two and standing at attention, as if barricading the doors.

Were they keeping people out, or were they preventing those inside from escaping?

Maybe others were being held here against their will.

She hadn't considered the possibility that there would be other Kavers here. If she could find them and free them, they could work together, and they could break free of the Theln lands and return to the city. There might even be Scribes she could help, and if she could free them, maybe this could be about more than finding her brother. It could be a rescue mission.

The smallish man stopped in front of a set of double doors and waited until she reached him. The two men standing behind her, preventing her from running, took a position on either side of the door.

"When you go in, you will be polite," he said.

"Polite?" Sam frowned.

"Do not make the mistake of thinking that your abilities will allow you to attack. If you try, you will find that the chamyn will prevent you from going very far."

Confusion washed through her, and Sam could only nod dumbly.

What was this about?

The small man pushed the door open and waited for Sam to enter.

She glanced at him before heading inside, and half expected to find Ralun waiting for her on the other side. What she saw was nothing like what she expected.

242 | D.K. HOLMBERG

A petite woman sat in a chair near a fireplace, holding a mug of tea, a book open on her lap. She looked up from the book when Sam entered. Much like the man who had guided her here, she wore a long, flowing robe that was striped in as many colors as his. She closed the book and looked over at Sam. "Thank you, Belden."

The man bowed. "Of course, Your Grace. I must advise you—"

The woman waved her hand, and Sam recognized a dismissal. She had received many of them herself over the years. "There is no need for you to advise me on anything. I am well aware of what she is."

"And the chamyn?"

"I trust that you will see to their reward?"

"Of course, Your Grace. It's just—"

"It's just nothing, Belden."

The man glanced over at Sam and frowned. "I will make certain that you have the necessary protection."

The woman shrugged. "You may do as you see fit, as you often do, Belden."

The man took his leave, pulling the door closed behind him. When he was gone, the woman stood and approached Sam. There was a certain grace to the way she moved. It wasn't like an augmentation, at least not entirely, and she studied Sam with an appraising eye that reminded her of the way that Alec would study someone.

"What are you doing in Asalar?"

Sam frowned. "Is that where I am? I wasn't trying to reach Asalar, I was trying to reach—"

The woman stopped in front of Sam. She was taller than she had appeared when seated, though not much.

Her shiny dark hair was pulled back and tied with a lace ribbon. She smelled of mint, or perhaps another spice, something that Sam couldn't quite place. Alec would have been able to.

"I know what you were trying to reach. You have reached Asalar."

Sam knew nothing of the lands outside the city. All she knew was that they were dangerous. Everyone in the city knew that. It was why they were protected where they were, and considering some of the dangers present within the city, the outside world would have to be deadly dangerous.

But this place did not strike her as terrifyingly dangerous as rumors depicted the outside world.

"Where am I?"

"You are where you attempted to come. You are not the first."

"What happened to the others?"

The woman's eyes narrowed. "Many of them have departed."

"And where have they gone?"

"I was hoping you would provide that answer," the woman said.

Was she talking about the Kavers who had returned to the city? If that was it, then it meant the Thelns had known all along what the Kavers were up to. Maybe the Thelns had allowed Kavers to observe.

That idea troubled Sam, but mostly because it meant the Thelns had not bothered the Kavers. If they had known they were there and didn't do anything, perhaps she knew even less about Thelns than she realized.

"Who are you?"

The woman stared at her for a moment, and the smile faded from her face. It was replaced by a frown, and the woman cocked her head to the side, watching Sam with what she could only think was irritation or amusement.

"You come to my lands, and you question who I am?"

"I was only looking for someone. I didn't mean to come and threaten."

"You have not threatened at all. I don't know why you would even make such a suggestion."

She was so dismissive that Sam was almost taken aback.

"Then why have you captured me?"

"Because you were brought here by chamyn."

Sam shook her head. "So?"

"How is it that you know so little about Asalar?"

"Why don't you explain it to me."

"It is unfortunate that I must. The chamyn brought you here, which means they found you as no threat."

"It didn't feel that way when the creature was dragging me through the forest."

"I imagine not. For that, he is sorry."

"He? How do you know he's sorry?"

The woman turned and looked at the back of the room. Sam followed her gaze and realized that one of the creatures sat there, curled up on a carpet. Kyza. How had she overlooked that? The cursed thing was here all along.

Sam took a step back, feeling incredibly uneasy.

"Why would it bring me here?"

"Because you have returned. Why should you not be welcomed back, cousin?"

23

LOST COUSINS

S am could scarcely breathe. She looked at the strange woman who stood so serenely in front of her, her hands clasped together, the multicolored robe flowing around her. "Cousin?"

"You didn't know?"

"What are you talking about?"

The woman smiled. She waved for Sam to follow and started out of the room. The two men who had followed her through the building took up position on either side of them as they strode through the hallways. Sam had a strange feeling as she went through the halls and a sinking sensation.

What was this woman going to show her?

"Who are you?" Sam asked.

"I think the better question would be, who are you?"

"I know who I am."

"It is possible that you do not. If you knew who you

were, you wouldn't have come here. You wouldn't have questioned."

They continued along the hallway and reached what appeared to be a massive and ornate entryway that opened to the outside. The tiles were the same bright colors and stretched along walls arching overhead. Carved lanterns marked either side of the door, and Sam realized they were shaped like the symbols that had been used on the doorway.

The woman guided her outside of the building, and Sam stopped, unable to take another step.

They stood in a vibrant, grassy courtyard. An enormous garden stretched before them, filling the air with its fragrance. When she managed to drag her attention away from it, she noticed two pillars rising on either side of the garden. They were made of gleaming white stone, but each was inset with colorful tiles that matched what she had seen inside the entryway.

"Where am I?" she asked.

"Asalar."

"I was looking for Thelns. I was looking for my brother."

"And who is your brother?"

"Trayson. Ralun captured him and—"

The woman turned to Sam. "How is he your brother?"

Sam couldn't take her eyes off of the pillars or the garden. She looked from one to the other, feeling overwhelmed. The palace in Verdholm was amazing, as was the university, but neither was anything quite as striking as this. Everything around her was wondrous, beautiful, and...

Squeezing her eyes shut, she forced the vision from her mind. It was all designed to distract her. She felt that with a sudden certainty, and she knew that whatever else was happening here, the building and the garden were designed to distract her from what she needed to do.

"It's a long story. We were raised together, and we believe that we were brother and sister, and—"

"So, you are not his sister?"

Sam's eyes snapped open. "I'm his sister as much as anyone can be. I would do anything for Tray."

"Anything? You would fight on behalf of your 'brother'?"

"Don't say it like that," Sam said.

"How would you have me say it? Is that not what you have said?"

"I'm done answering questions. Tell me, who are you and where am I?"

The woman smiled. "I have already told you where you are. As to who I am, that is perhaps less important. You may call me the Master of Records."

"What kind of title is that?"

"What kind of title is Kaver?"

The woman knew who she was, knew what she was, and Sam wasn't certain what to make of it. How much should that concern her?

"Who are the Thelns?"

"I believe you already have experience with them. If you need me to help you better understand who they are and what they can do, I will gladly do it, but I would have thought your previous experience would be enough."

"That's not what I'm asking. Who are they to you?"

Sam glanced back to the door that they had come out of. The two guards were enormous and muscular, but they didn't have the same build as the Thelns. Why would this woman have guards like that, mainly if this Asalar was somehow situated in the Theln lands?

"It amazes me how little you know."

"What is there to know? I know the sections of my city. I know the city itself. I know how to navigate it."

"And yet you know so little of anything beyond its borders."

"I've traveled the swamp and the forest, and I've walked across the steam fields. I think I have done more than enough to know the land beyond my city."

"You speak of the places around your city, but nothing beyond that. Can you have such a narrow-minded view of your home that you don't recognize that there are places beyond it?"

Sam bit back a response. She knew there were other places outside the city. They had ships that came in and out of the harbor, often with trade from outside places, though it was difficult, and those ships were infrequent. There were plenty of others in the city who represented those outside of the city, enough that she knew the places beyond their borders, even if she had never ventured there herself.

"Everywhere outside the city is dangerous."

The woman laughed. "Are they? Or is it the city you call home that is dangerous?"

The woman turned back toward the building and started inside. Sam took one more look around the garden and at the spires of the building and shook herself before turning and following the woman inside.

When she entered, she expected to go back the way they had come. But the woman led her another direction, pausing at what seemed to be a throne room with a gilded chair and nothing else in it, almost as if she wanted to demonstrate her power and authority, but she turned away and headed down a narrow hall. Sam passed a few people in colorful clothes, some in bright orange gowns and some in yellow, while others wore striped clothing much like this Master of Records.

Sam remained silent as she followed, not sure what there was to say. They reached the end of the hallway and took some stairs, heading up. At the top, the woman continued along another hallway, the floor having the same colored tiles. The woman stopped at a set of doors, and Sam was surprised when they stepped through and were back outside in the bright sunlight. They crossed an arched bridge, which was as ornate as anything she'd seen so far, and Sam could hear the sound of rushing water below. Not a canal, but a river. It was nothing like home. On the other side, the woman took them into another building. It wasn't as ornate as the first building, but Sam had the same sense of awe as she made her way through here. Instead of the colorful floor tiles, these were just black and white. The architecture was simpler, and rather than arched doorways, these were flat, with simple stone headers, and the doors were metal rather than wood. She saw none of the symbols she had in the other building. Nothing that struck her in the same way as what she had seen there. Still, there was the same unmistakable sense of strength about it all.

"Where are we?"

The woman glanced over. "You wanted to find your brother."

"Is he here?"

The woman turned away and continued down the hallway, leaving Sam staring after her. What was this? What was all of this? None of it made any sense to her, and she couldn't shake the feeling that there was something she was missing.

The woman had made a comment about how Sam knew so little, as if Sam should have known more... about the world, and about this place. And though she liked to think she had a sense of the world, from her brief forays beyond the city into the swamp and steam fields, she realized she knew little. She'd not even known of the Thelns or their lands until they had come to her own city and endangered those she cared for.

They reached yet another door. This one was a deep brown, almost coppery color, and metal. Sam reached for it, feeling a warmth radiating from the metal. The woman grabbed her hand and pulled it back.

"That would be unadvisable."

"Why?"

"You must be welcomed before you can enter."

"What would happen if I were not to be welcomed?"

"Likely, you would die."

The woman slipped her hand into a glove and reached for the door, knocking twice. The sound rang out like a bell, and it tolled through the hall.

Sam could only stare.

After a few moments, the door opened, and a massive person stood in the doorway. Sam took an involuntary step back.

Ralun.

When he saw her, his face twisted into a sneer. "What is this, Irina?"

The woman glanced over at Sam, and Sam couldn't tell from her expression what she was thinking, but it seemed to be almost a satisfied look. Could that be a smirk? Or was there something else? Was it concern?

"This one tells me that she has some experience with you, Ralun."

"Why have you brought her here?"

"Careful how you speak to the Master of Records."

"I'm always careful with how I speak. I understand quite well the position you have placed me in."

"She tells me that you have someone she cares about. A brother."

Ralun glanced at Sam, and he fixed her with a hard-eyed glare. "I have only reclaimed what is mine."

"Yes. About that. How is it that this *brother* of hers is yours?"

Ralun turned to Irina. "It is of little matter."

"I believe that it matters quite a bit, especially if this one has come here thinking to rescue him. Should I not be concerned about the presence of a Verdholm Kaver appearing within our borders?"

"Why must you be concerned? It seems you have captured her without any difficulty."

"Captured? Is that the way it appears? The chamyn brought her to us."

Ralun frowned. "How is it that this is the first I'm hearing of it?"

"Because my house guards are the ones who found her. Now. Tell me about this brother of hers."

Ralun glanced from Irina to Sam.

She worried he might not say anything, and worried even more that something might have happened to Tray, not knowing whether Ralun would have harmed him. Tray was his son, but then again, Lyasanna had been his mother, and that hadn't stopped her from attempting to murder Tray.

"Come inside," Ralun said.

Irina nodded to Sam to follow, and she had no choice but to do so.

Sam followed Ralun, a growing trepidation making her uncomfortable. What would happen inside this room? Ralun had already attempted to kill her more than once, and she had the sense that he would not hesitate to try it again. His expression when he looked at her had been filled with anger and hatred, and it was not undeserved. She had nearly killed him once, and wouldn't have hesitated to do so again, though now that she knew who he was and what he was to Tray, Sam wasn't sure she would carry that out. How could she do that to her brother?

The room they entered appeared to be a sitting room and was every bit as sparse as Sam expected based on the rest of the building. The black and white floor tiles stopped at the entrance to the room, and inside they were a flat gray, as were the walls. The only furniture were two uncomfortable-looking chairs and a wardrobe set against one wall. What surprised her was the bookshelf. It was an enormous bookshelf, spanning the entirety of one wall, and books filled every last bit of it. What types of books must exist here? She could only imagine the way Alec would react at the chance to take a look at some of the Theln books.

Ralun motioned for them to take a seat in the only two chairs, and Sam did so hesitantly, unsure if it was a command or a form of politeness. Completely bewildered by everything happening around her, she complied. After all, she was in his room, in his lands. For now, she would watch and listen. It seemed as if Ralun had concealed something from Irina, and maybe she could use that to her advantage, but it was just as possible that she could not.

Irina took a seat across from Sam, and Ralun remained standing. Sam twisted in her chair, looking around, but saw nothing that gave her any insight as to whether or not he would harm her. At least, there were no weapons visible. Irina had shown no indication up to now that Sam was in actual danger, and from the interaction between Irina and Ralun, it seemed that Ralun deferred to the woman.

"Where is he, Ralun?" Irina asked. She didn't have to raise her voice, and she didn't speak particularly forcefully, yet there was still an expectation in the question, almost a command. If Sam didn't know better, she would have thought her augmented, though perhaps that wasn't it. Irina hadn't seemed augmented at all while Sam had been around her. She had a particular grace about her, but

254 | D.K. HOLMBERG

that was it. Certainly nothing supernatural, not the way the augmentations made a Kaver seem.

"He is safe."

"And who is he?"

Ralun paused, and Sam had to twist in her chair so that she could see both Ralun and Irina. He looked at the woman and clenched his jaw. "He is my son."

Irina's eyes shifted only a little. "Your son? How is it that none of us have heard of this?"

"Because I kept it from the Hall of Records until I was able to recover him."

"Recover?"

"Yes. Recover. He was lost to me for the first part of his life. His mother thought to keep him from me."

"His mother thought to kill him," Sam said.

Ralun frowned. "Kill him?"

"You didn't know? Tray didn't share that with you?"

"He has not shared anything with me. He has been sick ever since reaching our lands."

"What do you mean?"

Ralun looked over at her, and she wasn't confident whether he would answer. It wasn't as if he needed to answer her.

"I mean what I said. Trayson has been sick ever since we returned."

"But he was the one who brought you here. I was there that day."

Ralun glared at her. "I am well aware that you were there that day, Kaver."

"You can be angry with me, but I did nothing other than care for him."

Irina stood and turned her attention to Ralun. "Where is he?"

"He is where he can be cared for."

"I doubt that. If you have kept him from the records, then he is not where he needs to be to receive the necessary attention."

"I will not have this decision challenged."

"You have already forced my hand once. Do not force it again."

Ralun glared at her for a moment. Sam had the sense that there was an old disagreement between them, and for some reason, she felt partial to Irina, though she didn't know the woman at all. But then, Ralun had tried to kill her, so that could be influencing her thoughts.

"Come with me," he said.

He guided them through a door at the back of his room that led into a secondary room, and from there, he opened yet another door. Once they were through here, he lit a lantern. As it started to glow with a soft light, Sam could smell a sickly odor in the air. She recognized the stench of rot. She had encountered it before and had experienced it when the princess had been sick. It was the stink of wasting.

When the lantern began to glow with a steady light, Sam's breath caught. "Tray?"

24

THE EFFECTS OF THE BOOK

S am ran over to the bed and grabbed Tray's hand. It was clammy, coated with sweat, and there was no tone to it. Tray lay motionless, his eyes closed and the strength that she had known in his arms and chest gone. He still breathed, and she was thankful for that, but he didn't even stir when she said his name.

"What happened?" she asked, not looking over at Ralun. If this was his fault, if he was the reason that Tray was lying here like this, not moving, barely breathing, she…

"He has been like that since we returned. When we reached the forest, he fell. The chamyn helped me get him here."

"You were the one injured that day in the swamp. Tray carried you in his arms to get you safely away. He sought to save the father he'd never known. But here you are, fine, and he lies there awaiting death. Why did you ever come to the city?" Sam was almost shaking with anger.

"You know the reason why. He is my son."

"If you cared, why wait until now?"

"I thought he was dead. I thought that she took him from me. I thought that… It doesn't matter. I've lost everything because of *her*."

He looked at Irina as he said it, but Sam had the sense that he wasn't saying it to her, or even about her.

"What happened?" Sam said.

"It doesn't matter."

"I've seen something like this before," Sam said, looking at Ralun. "It's the same thing that happened to Lyasanna."

"Until you saved her, Kaver."

"I didn't know any better at the time. I still don't know."

"She is the one?" Irina asked.

"She is the reason that Lyasanna Anders still lives."

Irina turned to Sam. The calm, polite expression she'd worn was gone. She now glared at Sam, and there was darkness in her expression. Anger. "Lyasanna Anders is the reason that much difficulty has come to our people."

"I don't know what Lyasanna did. All I know is that she tried to kill her own son. I know that she betrayed her family. I know—"

"Her family? Her family was here. Did you know that?"

"No," Sam said, throwing her hands up in the air. "I don't know any of this. I've told you that I don't understand what you're getting at, just as I don't understand why any of this happened. I only came here to help my brother."

"Help." Irina looked down at Tray. "Lyasanna used the Book of Maladies on him," she said.

Sam breathed out heavily. That's what she was afraid of. Given the way Tray smelled, and the rot, she was not surprised that somehow, he had been poisoned by the Book of Maladies. But how?

"Where is it?" Sam asked Ralun. "Where are you keeping the Book that's poisoning him? If you care about him at all, you will use what you know to save him."

"How can I save him? I'm not the one responsible for this," Ralun said.

"How can you not be? You have the Book of Maladies."

Ralun frowned at her. "Whatever made you think that I would have the Book?"

"Because the Thelns have it. You're the reason the Book exists. You're the reason the Book is used in the way that it is. It's your fault that this has happened to Tray."

Irina touched her on the arm. "What is it that you believe?" she asked.

"I already told you what I believe. I know what has happened. Ralun has done something with the Book, and it's his fault that Tray is like this. He's dying because Ralun—"

"He's dying because the Anders have used the knowledge in ways they should not."

"That's not true. The Thelns have the Book of Maladies. They keep it. *You* keep it. You use it and sell your services, working as assassins, killing anyone who…" Sam sank to her knees. What did it matter? Tray was gone. There would be no saving him, not without the

Book of Maladies, and if Ralun had any way of helping, he would've done so by now, wouldn't he? The fact that he hadn't, after going to such lengths to recover him and bring him back to the Theln lands, must mean that he truly has no way of doing so.

And now she would lose Tray. Her brother would die. She had reached him, somehow managing to make it to the Theln lands, but she was too late.

After everything she had been through, that hurt the most.

She released his hand and touched his hair, smoothing it back. In illness, Tray looked so different than he did when he was healthy. Gone was the strength and maturity that he had begun to show. Gone was the irritation, the uncertainty of not knowing where he belonged. Now, he looked so youthful. He looked helpless.

This was the boy—now the man—that she had done everything for. For her entire life, everything she had done—at least everything she remembered—had been done on behalf of Tray. She had taken jobs from Bastan and then Marin so she could better their station and ultimately buy their way into a nicer section. She had willingly risked herself to try and reach him when he was imprisoned. She had continued to push herself, wanting to understand what it meant for her to be a Kaver, so that she could help Tray. And when he had been lost with Ralun to the Theln lands, she had searched for answers about how she could help him and been willing to sacrifice everything so that she could reach him.

And now that she had, Sam felt helpless.

Tears welled in her eyes, and she didn't fight them as they streamed down her cheeks. She sobbed, holding his hand, feeling the pain of losing her brother. He had been the only person she'd had for so long. Even after learning they weren't genuinely related and even that he was part Theln, she still cared for him. It had done nothing to change her feelings toward him.

She felt a hand on her shoulder and shook it off. "I just want a moment with my brother. Is that so hard?"

"Even knowing that he's not your brother?"

This was from Ralun, and Sam looked up. He had a broad face, a strong jaw, and his eyes were deeper set than those of most people in Verdholm. Beneath his black jacket and gray pants, his muscles bulged, making him an imposing figure. One of his legs probably weighed as much as her entire body.

Somehow, Ralun managed to look at her with something bordering on compassion.

"He's my brother," she said. "Everything I've done has been for him."

"I don't understand."

Sam turned back to Tray. "You don't need to understand. I'm not sure that I even need to understand. All I know is that when Marin saved him, she used me, but I think… I think she saved me at the same time. Had I not known Tray, had I not been raised the way I was, I don't know what would've become of me."

Would she have been brought up in the palace, discovering what it meant to be a Kaver, and trained to attack the Thelns much like Kavers who trained in the palace did? Would she have never met Alec? That was likely, since her exposure to sections outside the palace would have been limited. Would he have ever learned he was a Scribe? Had Sam not staggered into his apothecary with that scrap of easar paper in her pocket, his world would never have turned upside down as it is now. Would he have even attended the university?

She continued to sob and didn't bother wiping the tears away. Tray deserved better. He had always had a good heart, and he had always been protective of her, even when she believed there was nothing he could do to help her.

"Where is the Book?" Sam asked.

"In Verdholm," Irina said. Sam looked up, blinking away tears. "Do you understand why the Anders have the power that they do?" Irina asked.

"I don't understand anything about the city. I didn't understand that I was a Kaver or what it meant to have a Scribe. I didn't understand any of it. All I wanted was to help Tray." She was feeling overwhelmed, and her words spilled out from her, tumbling faster and faster.

"They were exiled," Irina said. "Over a hundred years ago, those who now rule in Verdholm were exiled for using knowledge that should not. They took what should have been peaceful and twisted it, turning it into something dark."

"But they didn't. There is the university and—"

"The university has been a way for them to conceal what they do. How else do you think they were able to practice? How else do you think they were able to acquire knowledge and find ways to perfect the maladies they document within their book?"

"What are you saying?"

"I'm saying that the Anders are the ones responsible for the Book of Maladies."

"What?"

Irina glanced from Sam over to Ralun. "Is it possible that she doesn't know?"

"She attacked me in Verdholm. She knows."

"I attacked you because you are the one who tried to kill me."

"Only because you had recovered the Book."

"That you used on Lyasanna."

Irina rounded on Ralun. "Did you used the Book of Maladies?"

Ralun took a step back. Irina was much shorter than he was, and quite a bit smaller, but there was something about the force with which she said it and the intensity in her gaze that seemed to have almost pushed him back.

"She took him from me."

"You said you didn't know about him," Irina said.

"I didn't, not until I went after the paper they'd stolen. When I was there, when I saw her, she told me what had happened."

Sam frowned. All of it began to make a different sort of sense. Ralun had gone to Verdholm because he had wanted revenge for what Lyasanna had done. He had poisoned her, and likely Marin, because they had taken Tray from him. But he hadn't known that Tray lived, not before then.

"When did you learn about him?" Sam asked.

"I learned then. I didn't know about him before then."

Sam struggled to understand what they were telling her, though it made a certain sort of sense. "What do you mean when you say they were exiled?" she asked Irina.

"It is a long story. Those who you know as the Anders once lived in our lands. They began to use the knowledge we acquired in a way that runs contrary to everything we believe. They began to twist it and apply it on others and charged for restoration."

"They claim that you created the Book and still have it. They blame you for it." And yet, hadn't Sam seen a copy of the Book in Helen's home? Could that be the same book? "How many volumes of this were there?"

"By now, there probably are many. Especially given what has come through your university over the years. The Book—or books—are their way of maintaining power," Irina said.

And if Helen had one, maybe it was the same volume that had poisoned Tray.

"I think I know how to help him."

"Without the Book, there is no help," Ralun said. "That is something we have long ago learned. Even the Recorders have failed to restore those who were lost to the Book." He looked down at Tray. "Regardless, he can't be moved. If he is, he will suffer."

Sam sighed. She couldn't take him with her, but there might be something she could do for him. If she could find a way to destroy the page in the Book, it might be possible for her to help him. But, to do so, she needed to better understand exactly what Helen might be after.

"Why would a Scribe need Kaver blood?"

"You are a Kaver. You understand the purpose of the bond," Irina said.

"No. This is different. Why would a Scribe need Kaver blood without a living Kaver?"

Irina frowned. "Where have you seen this?"

"It happened to me. She nearly killed me. There is a woman in the city, a master physicker—a Scribe—who has begun to drain Kavers of blood. We haven't been able to figure out why, or what she intends, only that whatever it is—"

"There are few reasons such a thing would be useful," Irina said, staring at Sam with a strange expression. "None of which she should have known."

"Such as what?"

"With the right amount of Kaver blood—what we call the Spark—she would be able to do much damage."

"Even if the Kaver was gone? Even with the Kaver dead?"

"Their death would be captured in the blood. That would be the point of it, especially if it were done in such a way that the blood was not tainted. It would grant power, and possibly enough power to cause incredible destruction."

Sam frowned. "What kind of destruction?"

"The kind that would destroy everything we have here."

Sam stood, looking down at Tray. Seeing him like this pained her, but she felt a measure of hope that she hadn't in some time. "What if I told you that I might know of some way to help him?" she asked Ralun.

"If you know where the Book is, you should help him,

especially if you care about him the way you claim you do."

Sam nodded. "I do, and I'm willing to, which is why I'm asking you for help."

Ralun stared at her for a moment. "What do you have in mind?"

25

A DANGEROUS PLAN

The inside of the tavern felt dreary. There was a heaviness in the air, and a palpable sense of sorrow, one that struck Alec as his fault. Bastan sat at a table in the tavern, slowly sipping from a mug of tea, his eyes reddened.

"Have you found anything at all?" Alec asked.

Bastan looked away. "No. Whatever Helen plans, it is not active now. Perhaps you thwarted her by saving Samara."

"I doubt it. She plans something, and Lyasanna—"

Bastan turned his head to look at Alec. "Does it matter?"

"You care about the city, Bastan. Whatever else you say, you care about it. You have told me over and over again that you care only about your section, but I know that's not true. You care about all of the city, and I have seen that you will do anything to protect it. Help me now."

"What is there to help?" Bastan asked. "We don't know what Helen intends, and there has been no activity, nothing that would tell us that she threatens in any way. For all we know, she will not attack."

Alec had a hard time believing that she wouldn't attack, especially since it seemed she had spent so much time and effort demonstrating exactly what she would do.

"Sam would want us to help," Alec said.

Bastan rested his hands on the table. "Samara would have wanted to save her brother, and she failed at that. I think... I think it's time that I return my attention to my section, my business, and focus only on that. Anything more... Well, anything more is a waste of my time. All it does is distract me from the people I care about. Had I not gotten involved, had I not allowed Samara to get involved—"

Alec leaned forward and smacked his fist on the tabletop.

Bastan blinked and looked over at him.

"Do you really think you could have stopped Sam from getting involved? You know Sam as well as I do, possibly better. She would have gotten involved regardless of what anyone said to her. That is the way she is. And now that she's gone—*maybe* gone—we need to figure out what Helen is after, stop Lyasanna, and..."

And then what?

He knew what Sam wanted. Though related, it wasn't the same as what truly needed to be done. She wanted to find Tray and was willing to sacrifice everything to do so, which in the end, maybe she had.

This was something else.

"And protect the city," he finished. He *had* to believe Sam would have done that too. She would have done it if only for Bastan.

"If you have any way of starting, I would like to hear it," Bastan said. "Otherwise, I think we need to allow Jalen to rule. Continue to let the city run as it has. And we can let everything get back to being the way it once was."

"Neither of us wants the city to return to the way it once was," Alec said.

He stood and tapped the table.

"I'm going to see what I can find Helen. I'm going to see if there's anything in the Book we found that will provide us some answers. And I'm going to stop her, with or without you, Bastan."

"And when you do, Physicker Stross, what then? Will you go after Samara? Will you traipse across the swamp, risk yourself in the forest, and dare to go into the Theln lands?" When Alec didn't say anything, Bastan shook his head. "I didn't think so. No. What you will do is return to the university. You will settle into your studies. And you will begin to forget Sam. In time, she will become but a memory for you. But for me, the memory of her will never go away. I will never forget about her. She will always be something more to me than someone that I could just allow to disappear."

"Bastan," Kevin said, approaching the table. He wiped his hands on his pants. "You know better than that. You know how Sam felt about Alec, the same way I can see he feels about her. The boy feels bad enough about what happened. Don't make it worse."

Bastan glared at Kevin. "I know he cares about her,

and he knows I care about her, but what does it matter when we keep finding these dead Kavers? Even if Sam were here, I'm not sure I would want her roaming the city."

"What you mean? What dead Kavers?" Alec asked.

Bastan shrugged. "While you were gone, I came across three more like the others. All with wrists slit, and all drained of blood. There wasn't anything that could be done for them."

Alec frowned, leaning forward and resting his chin on his hand. There had to be some purpose for the bloodletting, but what would Helen use it for? What purpose would she have in draining Kavers of blood? He couldn't think of anything that would make sense, not with the traditional relationship of Kaver and Scribe, which meant there was some other way to use Kavers than what he knew.

And it was *using* the Kavers. It wasn't as if they were working together, not the same way as Alec and Sam worked together, blending the two components of their magic. This was just using blood.

And Alec had seen something like that before.

"Would Mags be able to help us with this?"

Bastan glanced over. "Be careful saying her name."

"At this point, I don't know that it matters if I'm careful or not. We're looking for answers, and she's the only person we've seen who uses blood like that. If there's anything she knows that would be able to help, don't you think we should use it?"

"She's an artist, Alec, and that's it."

Alec frowned. He'd met her once, but there had been a

sense about her, a power that came from something more than simply artistry. He might not know what she was, but it was more than a mere artist. "She's not only an artist. No one in these outer sections is quite what they seem."

Bastan watched him for a moment. "You should be careful, Physicker Stross."

"Bastan, I know you want to help Sam. And we both know there is more to the city than what it seems. And if Mags can help, why shouldn't we take advantage of that?"

Bastan took a sip of his tea. He sat quietly, considering Alec for a long moment. "You know that it's dangerous to go back there."

"I know that it's dangerous in any of these outer sections. That's why the central canal separates the outer sections from the inner sections."

"You mean lowborns from the highborns."

Alec leaned forward. "No. I do not."

Bastan took a long sip. When he was done, he set the mug down and pushed it away. "Let's go."

Alec blinked. "Now?"

"If you intend to help Samara, we should go."

Alec looked around the tavern. There were a few other men here that he recognized, all Bastan's, and he turned his attention back to Bastan. "How many men are you going to bring with us?"

Bastan shook his head. "No other men. Not there. Not to see Mags. If we brought anyone else, they likely wouldn't return."

Bastan tipped his head in a nod to Kevin and guided Alec out of the tavern. Once out on the street, Alec felt a chill in the air. This close to the steam fields, feeling the chill was surprising, though maybe it was imagined more than real. He didn't like the idea of returning to Mags. The last time he'd gone there had been a necessity so that he could help Sam, though wasn't that why he was going now? Wasn't it a necessity now?

He believed it was. Anything he could do that would help Sam needed to be done, and that meant he needed to understand what it was Helen was after. Without knowing that, they would be left floundering, struggling to figure out what the next step would be, and then the next, and then the next.

Bastan glanced over at him as they crossed between sections. "She's not expecting me."

"Does that matter?"

Bastan nodded. "It matters. If she were expecting me, I wouldn't be quite as nervous, but…"

"*You're* nervous?"

Bastan fixed him with a hard gaze. "If you were smart, you would be nervous too."

When they crossed into the next section, Bastan unsheathed. It made Alec wish he had a weapon, even if he had no knowledge about how to use one. Even a belt knife, something better than what he had. His was a short blade, meant for cutting up leaves and roots and other medicines. It wasn't intended for attacking or protection.

Bastan looked over again as he pulled a long-bladed dagger from a hidden sheath and handed it to Alec. "You can't be coming here with empty hands. Doing that is a death sentence."

"I have you here."

"It might not be enough."

"It was enough last time."

"That was last time."

As they hurried through the streets, Alec had the sense people were trailing after them. Every so often, he would look back, the memory of what Sam had told him about avoiding detection ringing in his mind. She had advised that they take a meandering path when heading some-place to prevent others trailing them, but Bastan was heading directly through the city.

"We're being followed," Bastan said.

"And that doesn't bother you?"

"It bothers me, but there's damn little I can do about it."

They reached a bridge crossing over to the next section. Three men stood guard on the bridge, though none of them wore the colors of the palace. Each man was armed with a long sword, and one of them held out a crossbow. Alec shivered.

Bastan paused for the first time, clenching his jaw. "Be ready," he said. "These aren't my men."

"Ready for what?"

Bastan didn't answer and started across the bridge. The man with the crossbow brought it up and aimed it at Bastan.

Bastan glared at him. "You intend to prevent my crossing?"

"I know who you are," the man said. He was balding, and there were wrinkles around the corners of his eyes, but he was still solid and muscular. He was not the kind of man that Alec would trifle with.

Bastan, on the other hand?

"If you know who I am, then you know what I'm willing to do."

"What you're willing to do? Are you threatening me?"

"Only if you decide to prevent my crossing."

The other two men raised their swords.

"There are three of us, and I see only one of you with any sort of weapon."

"You don't know who this man is? This is the deadly Davis. I'm sure you've heard of his skill with daggers." Bastan glanced over, and Alec held up the dagger. He probably should have been more threatening with it, or maybe held it more confidently, but as it was, the other two men with swords simply smirked, looking over to Bastan.

Bastan tipped his head in a nod. "If that's what this will be."

He jumped.

It was a cloudy gray sky, but daylight. The last time Alec had been with Bastan, and the last time he had seen the man fight, it had been night. Sam suspected Bastan was a djohn but knew very little about what that meant other than that he had some natural abilities. They were skills that made him dangerous and skills that had given him a certain reputation.

His jump carried him toward the two men with swords. Bastan didn't jump with the same speed or fluidity as Sam with an augmentation, but there was a brutal sort of strength to it. When he came down, he slashed his sword down, cutting the arm off one of the men. He turned quickly to the other man and slashed his blade across his chest. The man fell, and Bastan stepped back to avoid the spray of blood.

It left only the man with the crossbow. That man stared at Bastan for a moment too long before his finger found the trigger. By that time, Bastan had already sunk his blade into the man's belly, twisting it as he pulled it free.

He wiped his hand and blade on the man's jacket before standing and motioning Alec to follow. "Now we had really better hurry."

"Now?"

"This will draw attention."

They hurried across the bridge, and Alec noted commotion behind them. He glanced back to see several other men on the bridge, but they paused, not chasing Bastan. They seemed to regard him warily.

"They will send for others," Bastan said.

"I thought you controlled all of the crossings throughout the city?"

"I control *many* of the crossings throughout the city. There are pockets where my control does not—and cannot—reach."

"Are these the Shuver's men?"

"No."

"Then whose are they?"

"Someone whose attention I try to avoid."

They moved quickly through the street, and Alec followed Bastan, keeping pace, not wanting to let him get too far ahead of him. There were others in the street, and whenever they encountered them, they veered off, disappearing into the shadows. At first, Alec thought that was good, but the more often it happened, the more he realized they were likely going off to get reinforcements.

"Tell me again why you didn't want to bring more people?"

"More doesn't mean better. More doesn't mean faster. Right now, we need speed."

"I'm not particularly fast."

"So I have seen. It doesn't matter. What does matter is—"

Bastan grabbed his arm and jerked him down an alleyway. Alec nearly stumbled but managed to stay on his feet, and they raced along the alley, emerging on another street. This one was empty, though that didn't make Alec feel any more comfortable.

"Are we close to Mags?"

"We're close, but not nearly as close as we need to be. Not nearly as close as I would like us to be, especially with that," he said, motioning toward the end of the street.

There had to be a dozen men approaching. All were armed, though most of them only with swords. None, thankfully, carried a crossbow that could kill from a distance. When they saw Bastan and Alec, they surged forward.

Bastan swore softly under his breath, using a word that Alec didn't recognize, and pulled him the opposite direction along the street. They ran, twisting through the street, turning along alleys, and when they reached the canal, Bastan turned them up and ran along the canal, heading toward a bridge.

Five men reached it before they did.

Alec thought for a moment that Bastan might turn and

head in a different direction, but he threw himself forward and spun with his sword, twisting in a violent explosion of power. Alec could feel it. The sense of it practically hummed in his veins, though he didn't know why that should be.

Bastan made quick work of cutting down the men. He left them dead or dying, bleeding out on the street, and it took a great force of will for Alec to resist the urge to try and help them. Bastan had to grab his sleeve and pull him along with him, forcing him across the bridge.

"Right now, you're not a master physicker. Right now, you're Sam's Scribe. Right now, you're Sam's friend."

Alec took a deep breath before letting it out. Bastan was right. He had to resist the urge to do anything, especially as these were men who intended to stop them. He needed to go with Bastan, get to Mags, and see if there were anything she could do that would help Sam.

They crossed the bridge.

On the other side, two more men waited. Bastan barreled into them, kicking and slashing until they fell.

"We're close," Bastan said. He was breathing heavily, and blood dripped from one arm.

"You're cut."

"It doesn't matter, not yet. We need to get to Mags."

They hurried along the street. Alec remembered this from the last time he'd been here, though then, it had been darker, and he had been in a different place. Then, he had wanted nothing more than easar paper so that he could restore Sam after she fell from a roof, and continue to learn about their abilities.

Now... now there was a much different motivation for him.

Bastan paused, swearing under his breath.

"I don't suppose you remember how to find Mags," Bastan said.

There was a tightness in his voice, and he stared along the roofline, forcing Alec to turn his attention upward. A dozen men, maybe more, watched from the rooftops. Several of them seemed to be armed with crossbows. One stood watching with a longbow, and Alec shivered at the sight.

Against weapons like those, there would be nothing that they could do.

"I remember how to find her from here, but—"

Bastan shook his head. "It doesn't matter. Get to Mags. I will get you enough time."

"Bastan—"

"Go," he said softly.

He shoved Alec along an alley, pushing him out of the way, and Alec staggered, twisting so that he could see Bastan. A crossbow bolt streaked toward him, but Bastan managed to swipe it out of the air, slashing at it with his sword. Another streaked toward him, and once again Bastan managed to deflect it. Alec allowed himself to begin to think that perhaps he might survive, when one of the crossbow bolts sank into Bastan's arm.

"Go," he said.

Alec turned away, hating that he did.

26

REACHING THE ARTIST

The street was empty here, and Alec hurried along it, staying close to the edge of the building and trying to remain in the shadows. It was a technique Sam had taught him, making him harder to see while allowing him to watch his attackers' movements.

The street was familiar, though he wasn't entirely sure that he could find Mags, not from here. But he was determined to try. If Bastan had sacrificed himself for him, he needed to find Mags.

And if Bastan was lost, this had better be worth it.

He saw no other men. Maybe all of them had attacked Bastan, but Alec feared that wasn't the case. More likely, he wasn't able to detect other attackers who might be waiting for him. Could they be on rooftops as they had been before? As he scanned the roofline, he saw none watching. He was careful to observe the windows, looking to see if shadows were moving inside, but he saw nothing.

And then he came across a building he'd seen before. It

was a small, unremarkable building with a sign hanging out front that looked to be two people dancing, though the paint was faded.

Alec looked up and down the street, searching for signs of movement, and saw nothing.

He started across the street.

When he did, doors along the street opened.

People poured out.

Kyza. What was this?

Alec froze. He stood in the middle of the street, looking around. Terror ate a knot in his stomach, and he held the dagger uselessly in his hand. There was nothing he could do against an onslaught of people like this.

Had Bastan known he would get here only to be confronted like this?

Or, more likely, Bastan had intended to draw them away.

He had warned that reaching Mags would be dangerous, especially uninvited, but Alec hadn't known quite *how* dangerous it would be.

One of the men raised a crossbow, aimed at Alec.

"Wait!"

The man stared at him.

"I'm trying to reach Mags. I helped her with her son, Nashon."

The man cocked his head to the side, and two others scurried off, disappearing.

"Please. Go find Mags. She would vouch for me. I need—"

"Quiet." The man's voice was a harsh command, and Alec could do nothing but obey. He didn't dare say anything or do anything, fearing that if he did, they would attack.

Alec stood perfectly still, the dagger gripped in his hand, though he didn't dare raise it, not wanting to give the man with the crossbow any reason to fire at him.

Moments passed before one of the men returned. He leaned toward the one with the crossbow, whispered something softly, and then, thankfully, the crossbow was lowered.

The people in the street began to retreat, disappearing back into buildings.

"Come. She will see you."

Alec looked around. Amazingly, the street was already empty. It was almost as if no one had been there, as if what he thought he had just seen was nothing more than imagined. And he had thought Bastan had command of his section. Bastan didn't have an army quite like this, ready to attack at a moment's notice. Bastan didn't have this level of control, able to wave people away. Bastan was powerful in the Caster section, but Mags was terrifying.

The man with the crossbow guided Alec into her home and studio. An older man sat in the outer room, and he watched Alec with distrust. Was it the same older man he had seen when he'd come before? Was there another?

They headed upstairs, and Alec walked into the studio where he had seen Mags the first time. The old woman appeared from behind a curtain. Her hands were stained red—blood—and her eyes had a hollowed appearance. When she saw Alec, they widened slightly, and her mouth pressed together in a tight line.

"You may go, Helas."

The man glanced over at Alec before nodding and disappearing back down the stairs.

Mags began a slow circle of Alec from a distance, walking around him and forcing him to turn in place so that he could keep his eyes on her. He was hesitant to lose focus of her. He didn't know what she was capable of, only that she seemed to have some connection to blood.

"Where is Bastan?"

"Bastan tried to come with me, but he was caught in the street."

"That fool. He knows better than to come unannounced."

"It's my fault." He swallowed. And because of him, Bastan would be lost. Sam had wanted to rescue Bastan, and now Alec would be the one to have put him in danger, and it would be because of him that Bastan would die.

"Then you will be the one to take the blame for the lives that will be lost today. I will make sure that Bastan knows you are the one who owes that price."

Alec shivered. What kind of payment would Mags require? Would it even be one he would be willing or able to pay?

"I think Bastan is lost," he said.

Mags paused, still several paces from him, and she tipped her head, smiling. "Is that right? Do you believe the people of this section skilled enough to take down *Bastan*?"

"But I saw…"

She sniffed. "If it were that easy to take Bastan down, why do you think I would need so many people here? No,

282 | D.K. HOLMBERG

Bastan is far more formidable than that. They would slow him, nothing more."

"Why would you want to slow him? I thought you worked with Bastan."

"I must ensure my safety, especially in this place."

Alec swallowed again.

Mags leaned toward him and inhaled deeply. "Eshandar."

"What?"

"I smell eshander on you."

Alec shook his head. He didn't know that herb, though maybe he wouldn't. He didn't know much about Mags, but he did suspect she had an arcane sort of knowledge that was quite a bit different from his own. "I don't know what you mean."

Could it be the eel meat? Could she smell it from several paces away even though it was in a closed jar? Maybe she had a different term for it.

Mags inhaled again, leaning in, but keeping her distance. "It's in you. Interesting."

"What is eshander?"

Mag started to circle him again, and when she completed her circuit, she stopped and faced him. "Why are you here, physicker?"

"A question I thought you might be able to answer."

"You have a question you think Mags could answer that a physicker could not?"

"This one has to do with blood."

She started to walk around him again, and as she did, Alec realized she had a trail of blood forming on the floor. It seemed to come from her feet. It was a spiral forming, one that started out much wider and began to narrow as she came closer to him. Seeing the spiral unsettled him, and he worried that perhaps she was using some magic on him. Could she be forming some sort of augmentation using blood?

If he didn't get the answer he needed before she finished, he thought he would have to step outside of the circle. He didn't want to stay too close to Mags, not if she was doing some magic on him.

"And what does a physicker need with blood?"

Alec stared at the floor. With each full circle, she continued to close in on him. Again, she stopped and faced him. He hoped that her pausing would give him time to ask. Maybe this was her way of giving him a countdown, some sort of timer.

All he knew was that he doubted he wanted her to get all the way over to him.

"I have encountered several people in the city who have been drained of blood. Do you know anything about that?"

Mags pressed her lips together and began to circle again, continuing a slow path around Alec. "Those who come to me do so willingly. I would never take from someone without their permission. That destroys the art."

"I don't know what it does to art, but I have seen several people who have had their wrists cut, and their blood drained, and—"

Mags stopped again. She was close, and now she was near enough to Alec that he could smell her. She had a musty odor, and it was mixed with the familiar coppery scent of blood. Alec was all too well acquainted with that,

284 | D.K. HOLMBERG

but his mind washed with the memory of the massive blood loss Sam suffered. The buckets of blood.

"Where have you seen this?"

"Several places."

Instead of continuing her circling, Mags bent and sat down on the floor. She dipped her hand into her pocket, and when she withdrew it, she began to trace a pattern on the floor. Alec noticed that this, too, was done with blood. It was almost as if she were a Scribe, documenting on easar paper, but the way that Mags worked was different.

She was drawing the city.

The detail in her art was outstanding. Alec didn't think he'd ever seen anything quite as well drawn, and she showed each of the sections, with the canals running through them. How was she able to manage such fine detail with only her finger?

"Where did you see this?"

Alec used his dagger and pointed to the sections. So far, the places where they had encountered the Kavers drained of blood were along the merchant sections. He tapped, tracing the dagger from one place to the next, and realized that they trailed the great canal, that which separated the outer sections from those of the inner part of the city.

He hadn't noticed that before, and now that he did, he wasn't certain it was significant, but it *was* troubling.

"Why would they only be happening along the great canal?" He asked it mostly to himself, but Mags looked up.

"Water can do many things. It can be curative. I'm sure that as a physicker, you have much experience with that."

Alec nodded. There were many times when water was part of the medicinal treatment needed to restore people. Many of the combinations his father mixed used water in them as a sort of base. Others used oils, though many of the cleansing mixtures had water.

"Water is life. Without water, man cannot survive."

The canals were a source for the city's water, though it was a process to purify it.

"I don't understand. What do you think they're using the canals for?"

"Water is not only life, but it is used to cleanse."

"Why would they need blood for a cleansing?"

"It is an interesting question. Why would blood be necessary for a cleansing? And yet, are not blood and water related in some ways? Are they not both necessary for life? You cannot have life without blood, and you cannot have life without water. Together…"

"How do you think that idea is relevant to the bloodletting of Kavers?"

"I'm not saying that it would make a difference," Mags said. "You asked what purpose blood might have. It is possible that they have found a grand canvas, and they have decided to create a work that has never been seen."

"A canvas?"

Mags nodded. "You have not asked about the power of blood which tells me that you are familiar with it." She leaned close to him, and she took another deep breath. She sat on the floor, still not moving, and Alec was thankful for that, not sure whether she had given him a reprieve from whatever countdown she had before.

"I'm familiar with the power of blood."

He wasn't sure whether admitting that to Mags was dangerous or not, but he thought that she knew either way and denying it would only create difficulty with her when he needed her help.

"I can smell that you are. Look around you, physicker. What do you see?"

Alec looked around the room. The spiral of blood drew his attention, but when he tore his eyes away and looked at the walls, he saw that they were painted as well, though it was difficult to tell. The walls were a deep maroon, and at first, he thought they were almost black, but the more that he studied them, the more he realized they were painted with blood. She had coated the entirety of this room in it.

He shivered.

"This is my canvas. This is where I work. This is where I create power. Others have a different canvas. And if there are those who know the power of blood, they can use it on their own canvas. It is powerful in the right hands."

"What about the wrong hands?"

Mags stood and clasped her hands in front of her. "In the wrong hands, it is even more powerful. For them, there is not the same reticence to abuse power."

Alec shivered again. Could that be what Helen was after? Had she figured out some way of using the Kaver blood, blood that already had power within it, to become even more powerful?

"You mentioned the power of blood," Alec said.

Mags tipped her head in a nod.

"What if someone who had a natural ability was used in such a way?"

"Such as Bastan?"

Alec hadn't considered Bastan, but that was a possibility. "Bastan, or someone else."

Mags studied him for a moment. "Someone like that would have a great power to them. You add that to the canvas, and it increases what is possible." She stepped toward him, no longer forming the spiral, now creating a line that led straight to Alec. "Whose blood do you know that has such power?"

Alec shook his head. "I can't tell you that."

"Then I can't tell you how to prevent the canvas from succeeding."

Alec took a deep breath. He wasn't sure whether sharing with Mags mattered or not. It was possible that she might know the information already, but it was just as possible that she didn't know. The Kavers had remained hidden in the city for years. He didn't want to be the reason that suddenly changed.

"There are individuals with power. When they come together, when their blood comes together, they have great strength and are able to do even more."

Mags sucked in a breath. "Asalar."

"What?"

"You would be wise not to challenge Asalar. Such a thing is dangerous."

"I'm not challenging anyone. The person I spoke of is using people within the city. They are people who have a natural ability, and she is taking it from them. If she uses it against the canals, if she destroys the canals, everyone in the city will be affected."

"Not in the city."

"What you mean?"

"If she is using the blood of Asalar, it's not those in the city who will be affected. It is Asalar."

Alec frowned. "I don't even know what that place is."

"And yet you do," Mags said, leaning forward and taking a deep breath. "I was mistaken when I said you had the smell of eshander upon you. That's not it at all." She leaned back, and a deep frown crossed her face. "I was mistaken when you first came. I did not realize you had the scent of Asalar. You must be careful, child of Asalar, if this woman succeeds in this."

"Why? What would happen?"

"It's time for you to go," Mags said, turning away from Alec. "I do not want to be a part of this."

"I don't know what this is. Help me, Mags."

"Not this. I would not place myself against someone who would think to risk such power. If she is willing to do so, it means that she has access to even greater power. I am sorry, physicker."

"I helped you once. All I'm asking is for you to help me."

"That debt was paid at the time."

"The debt of your son's life?" Alec wasn't certain if Nashon had survived, and Bastan had never said anything, but the fact that Mags had welcomed him the way that she had and that she had said nothing else suggested that he had. "Was his life worth only a few sheets of paper?"

Mags turned back to him. She stared at him for a long moment, almost as if trying to decide how she would answer. After a while, she breathed out. "There may be nothing that I can do, but Mags will try. For the physicker who saved Nashon, Mags will try."

27

THE SANGR ARTIST

A lec hadn't expected Mags to come with him and be willing to assist, and he still didn't know exactly what it meant that she was willing to help. She led him out of the building, and as soon as they appeared on the street, doors began to open, and Alec had the unsettled feeling that the people inside might attack him much as they had before. Mags looked along the street, and those doors closed once more.

"How many people do you have watching you?"

She glanced over at him. "Everyone."

"Why?"

"The city is unsafe."

"The city is mostly safe."

"Perhaps your section, physicker, but the rest of us don't find the same safety in the city as you do. Anything outside of the central canal is dangerous and is guarded by those who live there." She turned and stared down the street. "And now, we will wait."

"For what?"

"For Bastan to return."

"Bastan's not going to return. Not after what happened. Your people—"

Mags glanced over at him, smiling. "My people? As I've said, my people will only slow Bastan."

"There were more than Bastan could handle."

"Physicker, I realize you don't know the city quite as well as you thought you did, but even you must realize Bastan can manage far more than what it appears."

Alec was going to argue, but he saw movement far down the street, and it took him a moment to realize that it was Bastan.

Alec hurried over to him. The man was injured. He had several cuts on his arm, and where the crossbow had pierced his shoulder were remnants of the bolt, but he was alive.

"You need help."

"Later." Bastan glanced over at Mags. "You convinced her."

"She thinks Helen intends to use the canals to attack Asalar."

Bastan glanced over at him. "She said that?"

Alec nodded. "What is it? Where is Asalar?"

"The people you know as Thelns come from there. It took me a long time and not an insignificant amount of funds to discover that, but it is true."

"I'm not sure that it matters then."

"It matters. If she attacks Asalar, not only will Tray be injured but if by any chance Sam still lives, she will be lost as well." Bastan reached Mags and looked over at her. "You can interrupt what they planned?"

"I am curious, Bastan, how it is that you have found not only a physicker but a child of Asalar."

"They found me, not the other way around."

"The djohn do not typically associate with those of Asalar."

Bastan clenched his jaw. "Perhaps not, but this one does."

"Interesting. You realize what this means?"

"It only means something if word gets out," Bastan said.

"And I imagine you would pay dearly to ensure that word does not get out," Mags said.

Bastan glared at her. "Do not push this, Mags."

"Oh, I think we will have much to discuss when all is said and done."

"Fine. When this is over, you and I can discuss anything you want, but for now, you will help."

"For now."

"She's using the canals," Alec said. "I hadn't seen it before, but when she drew a map of the city, I realized what it was Helen was doing."

"A map?" Bastan looked back toward Mags' building, before turning his attention over to Alec. "You saw a map?"

"Mags drew a map."

Bastan glanced over at Mags. "Perhaps I'm not the only one who has done more than they should," he said.

Mags glanced at Alec, frowning. "Perhaps not," she said.

"I need to gather support," Bastan said. "Allow me to pass through your section unimpeded."

"You have my blessing."

Bastan arched a brow. "You're blessing? Are you sure you want to go quite that far?"

"Only for now. When this is over..."

Bastan smiled. "When this is over, I think there will be quite a bit you and I need to discuss."

"When this is over," Mags agreed.

Bastan glanced at Alec, and then he headed off on his own, at first limping, but gradually, the limp began to fade, and he moved with more strength, almost as if his injuries were healing.

"What sorts of powers do the djohn possess?" Alec asked Mags.

"They are powerful. They do not have any overt magic, not as some do, but they draw strength from chaos."

"How?"

"Ah, that is not something that is well known. All I have been able to determine is that the djohn have power. They feed on violence."

"Bastan doesn't seem to feed on violence."

"No, Bastan is an anomaly. He has never been nearly as violent as some djohn, though I imagine he can be more violent than you realize."

"Why is that?" Having seen the way Bastan was able to fight, Alec believed it, but it didn't fit with what he knew of Bastan. He always seemed so calm and in control. He always seemed to manage to keep everything together.

"There are times when Bastan searches for violence. I imagine you saw him as he came toward this section?"

Mags watched him for a moment, and then she nodded. "I can see from your face that you did. Bastan has had many episodes similar to that. Most go unseen. Most of the time, Bastan will operate at night, because he is a part of the night, and a part of the violence in these sections, but there are times when he allows himself to be seen. Then it is truly a sight to behold."

Alec shivered. If Bastan *did* feed on violence and chaos, how was he able to hide it as well as he did? Unless, as Mags suggested, Bastan didn't hide it. Maybe he allowed it to come out, but only at certain times.

"If you intend to prevent this canvas from being completed and used, then perhaps we should see what we can do," Mags said.

Mags allowed Alec to lead, and they headed toward the central canal, the vast body of water that separated the outer sections from the merchants and the rest of the highborns. It was troubling to him that Helen had chosen there to attack.

If she mixed blood into the canal, what would it do?

When they reached the bridge leading over the central canal, Mags grabbed his arm and prevented him from crossing. "Let me focus here for a bit."

"Focus on what?"

"Focus on what they intend."

Mags smelled the air. She began to walk along the edge of the canal, breathing deeply. Alec noticed that the canal barges typically situated in front of this section were missing. Had Helen moved them? Or was there something else responsible for that?

"It is more than simply a canvas," Mags whispered.

"What do you mean?"

Mags glanced over. "This will be more than a canvas. Whatever is taking place here involves power I do not fully understand."

"And that surprises you?"

"I am a sangr artist. There is not much that is beyond me when it comes to understanding the powers burned within blood, but this, I do not recognize."

She continued to make her way along the street, and she paused every so often, typically to take a deep breath and smell the air. The first few times she did it, Alec just watched, but he began to sniff with her, at first unintentionally, and then he did so because he was curious whether he could smell whatever she was smelling.

There didn't seem to be anything.

But the more he continued to do it, the more he was convinced that maybe he *could* pick up on something.

Mags glanced over at him. She watched for a moment, and she nodded. "You should have the ability to detect the occurrence here. Breathe it in. Taste it. Know that what you think you smell is real."

Alec stared at her for a moment, and then turned his attention back to the canal, breathing deeply again. Each time he did, with each breath he took, he became increasingly convinced he was picking up on something, but what was it? Was it only his imagination, or was there something real?

It was the sense that something was not quite right.

He didn't know why he felt that way, but the more he breathed it in, the more he was certain of it.

It was like an illness. Alec had been raised around

illness, and he knew sickness as well as he knew anything. If there was sickness in the canals, what did it mean that he was able to detect it?

Maybe nothing. Maybe all it meant was that he could smell the strangeness to it. The canals always had a strange odor to them, and it shouldn't be all that surprising he would be able to pick up on it somewhat.

Then again, there had never been any attempt to poison the canals, had there? Other than what Marin had done, and he wasn't even sure whether that would have made a difference.

"It is happening," Mags said.

"What is happening?"

"The canvas. Breathe it in, physicker. Notice what you can detect. It is there."

Alec took a deep breath, and he could smell sickness, but why? "Does it mean she is nearby? Would she have to be here to do... whatever it is she's doing?" he said.

Mags took a deep breath once more. She began to walk in a circle, and her eyes fluttered. "Whatever she is doing is coming out from some central place. It is coming out evenly, as if she is pushing it from a source."

A source? Where would there be a source that would push out to all of the canals?

But he thought he knew.

"Gods! They're beneath the palace."

Mags glanced over at him. "Beneath the palace? Yes, I suppose that would work. There are rumors that the source of the canals pools there. Such a place would be difficult to reach."

"Not if there's already a tunnel there."

And Alec knew there was. That was how Lyasanna had escaped. That had to be what Helen was doing.

"I need to find Bastan."

"I don't know that you have time to find Bastan. Whatever is taking place is happening soon."

"Can you do anything to stop it?"

Mags looked at the canal, her eyes wide. "On a canvas this size? I had thought that perhaps I might be able to influence it, but there is tremendous power here. I had not anticipated anything quite like this. You can smell it, can't you?"

Alec nodded. "I can smell something. It's like a sickness within the canals."

"And if you can smell it, then you should be able to tell that it is powerful. Maintaining such power for any significant amount of time is difficult. Whatever she intends is happening soon."

"Go find Bastan. Have him send as many men as he can to the palace."

"And what of you, physicker? What is it that you intend?"

Alec looked at Mags. What choice did he have? There was only one thing he could do; he had to find a way to stop Helen.

And he didn't think he could do it alone.

"I'm going to see if there's anything I can do to intervene."

"Be careful, physicker. This power is tremendous, and you may be powerful"—she took a deep breath, leaning toward him as she inhaled—"I can smell it on you, but anyone willing to dabble in power like this is incredibly powerful and dangerous. I will see if I can delay it, but I doubt I will be able to buy you much time, if any."

Alec nodded. "Thank you."

"There is no thanks needed, as I have done nothing."

Alec hesitated, thinking that he needed to say something else, something more, but what was there for him to say to Mags? He hurried off, racing across the central canal and through the sections, heading straight toward Arrend.

He needed his father. He needed the poisoner.

If he were able to figure out what was happening, his father would need to be the one to help him.

When he reached his section, the wave of nostalgia that washed over him nearly slowed him too much. Alec ignored it and headed toward his father's shop, glancing over at Mrs. Rubbles' shop for a moment before reaching the apothecary. Would his father be here? If he weren't, Alec would have no choice but to continue on to the palace alone.

When he opened the door, he found someone he wasn't expecting.

"Master Eckerd?" Alec said.

Eckerd glanced over at Alec. "Physicker Stross. I mean, Master Stross. Where have you been? I came here looking for you, thinking that perhaps your father might know..."

Alec looked around. Where was his father? "There's no time. Helen is attacking the canals. She's beneath the palace in the tunnels that they dug to break the princess out."

"You found her?" Eckerd asked.

"I didn't find her, but I think I know where to find her."

"Why do you think she's attacking the canals?" Eckerd asked.

"She intends to destroy the Thelns."

Eckerd's eyes widened. "Could she succeed?"

"I don't think she should be allowed to succeed."

"Alec, you haven't been a Scribe for long. You don't understand the Thelns."

"I understand the people I care about. I understand that Helen has attacked Kavers. I understand what is right and what is not."

"What if she is doing this on behalf of the city?"

"I can't say I understand the Thelns, but I've seen what she's done," Alec said. "She has attacked someone I care about. The Kavers—"

"The Kavers are a means to an end, Alec. The power is within the Scribe. It has always been that way. If you could only see that, if you could only come to understand that the Council of Scribes is designed to protect the city. That is all we have ever done."

"I thought you didn't know anything about the council."

Eckerd watched Alec for a moment. "I found documentation."

"What do you mean you *found* it?"

"It appeared in my room. At first, I wasn't sure what to make of it, but the more I read, the more it became clear to me that the purpose of the Council of Scribes, those of us who understand the power in the city and those of us who understand the dynamics between the Kavers and

Scribes, is to protect the city." Eckerd turned to Alec, and he saw something in his mentor's hand, but he couldn't tell what it was. "The Kavers are a tool, and nothing more than that. They have never been anything more than that. And if Helen has discovered some way of destroying the Thelns so that we no longer need to fear them, and so we can find the information that remains hidden from us… The Thelns stole it, preventing us from knowing what we rightfully should."

"Eckerd, you can't believe that the Kavers are nothing more than a tool."

"Can't I? They are soldiers, nothing more."

Alec could only stare. How could Eckerd actually believe that?

"Where is my father?"

"Aelus? I'm not certain. I came here looking for him, thinking that perhaps he might know where you had gone off to, but the fact that you have returned is fortuitous."

"I need to go. I'm going to find Helen, and I'm going to stop her."

"I'm sorry, Master Stross," Eckerd said.

Alec turned back to Eckerd, and too late, he noticed that something flashed toward him. He twisted, trying to get out of the way, but a needle pierced his hand.

He saw a flash of color, and he could feel the sedative taking hold. With that, he passed out.

28

BENEATH THE CITY

A lec awoke to a horrible stink. It burned in his nose and reminded him of charred flesh, a stench he had experienced while working with Master Eckerd while training in surgery, learning to cauterize wounds. This was similar, but at the same time, it wasn't entirely the same.

He looked around him. Where was he? The last he remembered was that Master Eckerd had attacked him, piercing him with a needle, and Alec had felt the sedative as it had taken hold, recognizing his father's work, and knowing there would be nothing he could do to avoid it. Had it worn off?

Alec knew the various components that his father had been using, and if it had worn off, then it meant he'd been out for quite a while already.

He looked around. He was in a massive underground chamber. Nearby, there was the sound of movement, but he couldn't see where it came from or what it meant. He rolled off to the side and nearly fell into a pool of water.

He rolled back, jerking away from the pool. Surprisingly, the water was warm, and it took him a moment to realize it must be heated by steam vents, much the way the steam burbled outside the city. The canals weren't warm, but maybe they cooled as they flowed from here.

Was this what he smelled? It was an awful odor, but it didn't have the same sulfuric stench that the steam vents had.

Eckerd had brought him here.

It crushed him that Eckerd could have decided to side with Helen. How many of the master physickers had they lost? How many more would they lose before it was all said and done? Would any physickers remain?

That was a concern for another time. Right now, he had to focus on what he could do. He had to concentrate on trying to prevent Helen from poisoning the canals, and from there, poisoning the Thelns.

And yet he paused, hesitating as he thought about what Helen planned. He couldn't deny the fact there might be some good that would come out of her attacking the Thelns. If they were destroyed, if the threat of the Thelns were no more, they wouldn't have to fear them, and perhaps the Scribes could learn from those who remained in the Theln lands.

How many Kavers would suffer?

He wasn't certain, but if what Mags said was true, then the Thelns and the Kavers were related. If she did this—if Helen succeeded—it was possible Sam and any remaining Kavers would die along with the Thelns.

That was not an outcome that Alec could allow.

He crawled back, looking throughout the cavern, searching for signs of Helen. She had to be here somewhere, which meant the others would have to be here too.

In the distance was a faint greenish light.

Alec crawled toward it. He moved carefully, not wanting to make any sound, focused on the way he placed each step, trying to be careful so he could be as silent as possible. Alec wasn't sure that he succeeded, but with each step, he came closer to the greenish light.

What was it?

A shadow hung near it.

Was it a part of the cave?

He looked around and saw no other shadows, nothing else that gave him the same sort of pause, and he hurried forward, scrambling along the rock until he reached the shadow and almost gasped.

A small figure hung suspended from the ceiling. Blood dripped from its arms, collecting on the stones around it.

It would be a Kaver. Alec knew that with sudden certainty, but why here? The others had been done in the merchant sections along the central canal, so why would Helen have used this place this way?

He reached for his knife to cut the man down, but it wasn't there. Nor was Bastan's dagger. Eckerd must have taken them. So even if he could reach the rope, he had no way to cut the man down, but he had to do something. The physicker part of him refused to allow him to leave this person suspended like this.

But how?

He stood on his toes, and he could just barely reach the rope binding the man's wrists.

To pull them free, he had to remove some of the slack in the rope.

He stooped under the hanging figure and moved the man's legs onto his shoulders and pressed up, allowing some slack in the rope. He reached up, working at the binding with one hand. He managed to loosen it enough that he could slip a hand out, and he did the same on the other side.

Alec sagged, lowering the Kaver carefully to the ground. There was nothing he could do here to help him, but he thought he could slow the bleeding by placing a tourniquet, wrapping a strip of cloth around his wrists.

He worked quickly, tearing free a section of cloth from his own jacket, trying to do so as quietly as possible, but in the cavern, any sound seemed magnified. He quickly tied off a strip around each arm and hoped that would be enough. He needed to get him out of here, and then to the university.

Who else was here?

He moved toward the greenish light.

What he saw as light was not that at all. It was a flame that flickered, burning out of the ground. No one was in sight, so he attempted to approach, but he couldn't get too close to it, the flame was too scalding hot.

It was a naturally occurring flame, which surprised him. On top of the flame, there was a pot, and within it boiled some concoction that stank.

Alec pulled down the sleeve of his jacket to protect his

hand and pulled the pot free. He tipped it over onto the stones, not wanting whatever Helen was mixing to contaminate anything else.

Alec looked up, scanning the rest of the cavern. There had to be someone here. Eckerd brought him, which meant that somehow, he could find Helen, if only he could figure out where she was.

Up ahead, he saw another shadowed figure, along with another green light.

Alec raced forward, expecting to find another Kaver, and was not surprised when he did. This time, it was a woman. He did the same thing as before, and propped her up, getting underneath her so that he could loosen the ropes around the Kaver's wrists, and lower her to the ground. She moaned, and Alec placed a hand over her mouth and whispered into her ear, "Shh."

He made quick work of tearing off strips of cloth and tying them on her arms to stem the bleeding, and once again, he found another pot boiling over an open flame. He pulled it off the flame poured it out, dumping the mixture onto the stones. This time, he worried that perhaps that was a mistake.

What if that was what Master Helen wanted? Maybe she wanted to contaminate the stones.

No. He didn't think that likely. There would be water somewhere else, someplace other than where he had awoken, and she would be using that to taint the canals and somehow poison the Thelns.

He looked around and saw another figure. And then another. By the time he reached the fifth person, and was

lowering him to the ground, he heard the sound of footsteps behind him.

Alec stepped back, trying to hide, and slipped.

He made too much noise.

Before he could even stand, two large men dressed in
thick robes were there. They lifted him, jerking him
forward. They dragged him through the cavern until a
brighter light appeared in the distance. Lanterns, dozens
of them, ringed a massive pool at the center of the cavern.
All around the pool, more figures dangled from the
ceiling like the five people he'd saved. He suspected there
would be pots boiling near them, much like the others.

One person appeared out of the darkness.

Helen.

She glared at him. "Physicker Stross. Or should I say,
Master Stross?"

"You're not going to succeed," Alec said.

"I'm not? Do you have any idea what I'm doing?"

"You intend to poison the central canal so that you can
attack Asalar."

She shot him a quizzical look. "Interesting. Perhaps we
would have been better off to have brought you in sooner.
I had thought that by forcing you along, we might be able
to expel you, but you have proven far more capable than I
ever would have expected. It's a shame this will be the end
for you, Stross."

"You won't succeed. I've already prevented—"

Helen stepped forward. She smelled of heat and sweat
and dried blood. "You have prevented nothing. It's
amazing you have survived as long as you have, but
considering everything else, you have prevented nothing."

"Why are you sacrificing Kavers?"

"I am not sacrificing Kavers at all. Most of them willingly offered themselves, especially when they realized what it was I was doing."

"Do you really believe that you can destroy the Thelns?"

"I believe the power of this augmentation is enough to destroy them. When it's complete, we will finally be able to return."

"Return to where?"

"To Asalar, of course."

"Why would you want to return?"

She glanced behind her, looking at something for a long moment, before turning her attention back to Alec. "We were exiled. Exiled for searching for a greater sort of power. Exiled for reaching for more. And now? Now we will return."

"Exiled from Asalar?" Alec couldn't hide the confusion that he felt, and it probably didn't matter if he tried.

"I have lived in this stinking city for nearly a hundred years. It has taken a long time to re-accumulate enough power for this to succeed. Now there will be no one who can stop me. Not even someone like yourself, an apothecary who thinks himself something more."

Alec stared at her, and his heart raced. "You were responsible for the Book of Maladies."

Helen grinned at him. "We let the rumor out that the Thelns were responsible for it. It was effective, especially as crossing the swamp and then the forest is nearly impossible."

"But Lyasanna went."

"Lyasanna was allowed to go. There was an attempt at a reconciliation, but…"

"A reconciliation? Is that why she went?"

"The Anders were summoned, but I ensured Lyasanna was the one who went. Who better to go and recognize the potential that remained there than Lyasanna, the only one of the Anders who has ever been a Scribe?"

"Did you know about Tray?" When her mouth twisted in a frown, Alec smiled. "You didn't. You didn't know that she almost stayed."

"Yes, she almost stayed, and she would have sacrificed everything we had been working for. It took some persuading for Lyasanna to remember everything that had been done to her family."

"But it wasn't done to her family. It was done to the Scribes? That's why the Scribes can't return from the Theln lands, but the Kavers can."

And if the Kavers could, that meant that Sam shouldn't be in any danger. That idea gave Alec a measure of hope. Maybe Sam wouldn't be in danger going to the Theln lands. Maybe she would be safe there, and he didn't have to fear anything happening to her.

As long as he was able to prevent Helen from attacking. If he couldn't, if he couldn't find some way of preventing that, it might not matter.

There was a strange, almost bitter odor that he recognized.

"You're not going to succeed with this," Alec said again.

"I've already succeeded. You preventing a few Kavers from participating will do nothing. This war will be over, and there's very little that you can do to stop it. We will return to our homeland, and—"

Alec laughed, cutting her off. "You won't. You won't even make it out of this cavern."

"And why is that?"

Alec looked over. "You've been so concerned about the world beyond the city, that you have neglected the dangers within it."

"There are no dangers to me inside the city."

"Ah, but that's where you're wrong. The city itself has become home to others, many others. They come here thinking the university is something real, and they can be offered the opportunity for healing, but that has never been the case, has it?" He started to understand. If he were to need to create a Book of Maladies, how better to do it than to have people coming to him with symptoms that could be documented? Alec had participated in it. He likely had contributed to the making of the Book, at least a volume of it. "And yet, the university has become more than what you ever expected."

"The university has served its purpose."

"And that purpose has been to destroy others? You haven't wanted to truly help them at all, but some of the physickers have. And those physickers are responsible for all of that accumulated knowledge. And the university drew powers you never expected. Drew attention to the city you never could have anticipated."

What Bastan had told him began to make sense. But Alec understood it even differently. There was danger in the city, but that danger was self-inflicted. It had been drawn by the promise of the city itself. It was drawn by the promise of help and healing, regardless of what the Scribes who had founded it had intended.

"Enough," Helen said. "You can sit back and watch as this plan comes to fruition, or you can be incorporated into it."

"I don't have the necessary blood for what you intend." He laughed again. "Tell me, *Helen*, what will you do with them?" He pointed to the far end of the cavern where many people were congregating. "You need Kavers, but you've used them all for your plan."

Dozens upon dozens of people had converged, and Alec smiled. He knew even without them being close enough that it was Bastan and an army of others from the outer sections. Maybe Mags would have come. Perhaps the Shuver. Maybe countless others who had abilities that were kept on the periphery of the city. All of them approached.

"Without your Kavers, what are you going to do?"

Helen glanced at Alec. "Do you think I need Kavers to be augmented?"

"I think you need their help. I think you need your soldiers, as Master Eckerd said."

Helen turned away, and she jumped. She moved quickly, and with an augmentation that carried her. Alec could only watch, and he listened to the sounds of battle as sword hit sword, fighting that took place all around him. He wanted to help, to do anything, but found he didn't need to.

Bastan reached him. "Are you harmed?" he asked.

Alec shook his head. "I'm not, but did you stop her? Did you defeat Helen?"

Bastan glanced back. "I don't know who we have, but we'll bring them out of here, and you can help us determine who all have been involved."

Alec smiled, feeling relief at their success.

And then the ground exploded.

29

A RETURN AND THE PLAN

The boat carving through the swamp was different from the canal barges. Rather than the flat bottom of the canal barges, this had a sharp keel, and it managed to move much more quickly than the barges had been able to do. Ralun rowed, using a set of oars fixed on either side and swept them through the water with a powerful stroke. Each time the oars pierced the water, they propelled forward faster and faster.

A dozen boats were around them. Thelns occupied each one.

Marin looked over at Sam. "This makes me uncomfortable," Marin said.

"Because you don't think it's right?"

Marin glanced from the Thelns over to Sam. "I've been raised my entire life to fear the Thelns."

"And yet you have helped Tray."

"Because he was a child who deserved more. Because he was not a complete Theln."

"No, he is part Theln and part Scribe."

She still didn't know whether that would matter, and didn't know whether there would be any way they could restore Tray, saving him from the poisoning that he suffered from, but first, they had to reach the Book, and then they had to stop Helen.

"I didn't know that we were exiles," Marin said.

"Not you, the Scribes were exiles. You served the exiles," Ralun said.

"And because of that, we all deserve to suffer?" Sam asked.

"You are all descended from the Anders. They have done nothing but create pain and violence wherever they have gone. The Anders are responsible for great destruction."

"We might be descended from the Anders, but none of us knew what they had done. It would've been easier had you shared."

"It would have been easier had Verdholm been interested in peace," Ralun said.

Sam looked out over the swamp. That was the hardest for her to come to terms with. Kavers had attacked, and it seemed as if it would be an easy thing for them to have ended, to have come to terms with the fact that they were not the enemy of the Thelns and the rest of Asalar, but how, especially when there were those within the city, particularly high-ranking Scribes, who had a vested interest in maintaining that distinction?

"They have used the university to gain power and wealth," Ralun said.

"And they have used it for some good," Sam said. She

thought of Alec and everything he had learned, everything his father had taught him. Would that have been possible were it not for the university? Even if the university had been created as a way to hide what they did, many others would have suffered had Alec not receive the training that he had.

No answers came to her as the city loomed in the distance.

As they approached, Sam couldn't help but feel somewhat traitorous. She was returning to the city with Thelns, and if she were wrong, if she had been deceived, she would be putting the city in danger.

Sam glanced over to Marin. "How have the eels prevented the Thelns from reaching here before?"

"They mask the presence of the city."

"And when you attempted to unmask it?"

"I was angry," Marin said. "I thought only of getting Tray out of the city and helping him reach his father."

"But you would have sacrificed the safety of the entire city."

Marin glanced up to Ralun. "They were never going to attack the entire city. That has never been their intention."

Sam breathed out heavily. It was a lot to take in. A lot to understand. But right now, her only focus was to get to the Book for Tray.

But would they be in time?

Marin guided the boats as they cruised through the canals. They reached the central canal, and it was wide enough for them to proceed several boats across.

Marin frowned and signaled for Ralun to slow.

"What is it?" Sam asked.

"There's something amiss." She stood at the railing of the boat and stared down at the water. Marin frowned as she did, looking into it for a long time before Sam joined her. "Does it appear reddish to you?"

Sam nodded. It *did* appear reddish, which was strange. Normally, the canals were a dirty brown color. They were never clear, and that dirty water concealed the presence of the eels. This water had taken on a hint of color that almost looked like...

"Blood," Sam whispered. She looked over at Marin. "That's what this has to be."

"Helen wouldn't waste the blood like this."

Sam looked around. "What if there is some strange augmentation she thinks to place?"

Marin frowned. They reached one of the merchant docks, and she motioned for Ralun to guide them up to it. The dock itself was empty, the barge missing, and Sam and Marin climbed out. The Thelns on the boat with them joined them on the shore.

Sam had found the Thelns to be practically pleasant, certainly not what she had once imagined them to be. They were not the horrible beings she had thought them. They were not violent, and they had done nothing to harm her. And, considering what she had seen in Asalar, there was a beauty to the people.

"What now, Kaver?" Ralun still had an edge of resentment in his tone, and Sam couldn't blame him. How could he not, after they had been battling for as long as they had?

"I don't know," she said. "I'm not sure—"

Ralun sank to his knees. He looked up at Sam, his eyes wide. "What is this? What have you done?"

Sam looked at Marin. "Kyza. What happened?"

She looked out over the other boats on the canal, and the Thelns were writhing. All of them had dropped, and they moaned, as if unable to move.

"This is Helen," Marin said.

"Kaver!" Ralun said, trying to reach for her, but he couldn't. He stretched up, as if to grab her, but he contorted again in pain and dropped to the ground.

"Is this the Book?" Sam asked.

"I don't know. I don't see how it could affect so many people."

Sam looked over to the canal. The reddish hue to it was more evident from the shore.

"It's whatever she's doing. However she's using the canals, she's somehow targeting the Thelns."

Sam crouched down next to Ralun. His eyes were closed, and he moaned. "I don't know what's happening, but I will help you. I will figure out what Helen has—"

Marin moaned and dropped to the ground.

"Marin?"

"It burns, Samara."

"What is it?"

Marin shook her head. "I don't know. It's almost as if my body is burning from inside."

Sam looked at the Thelns and then over to Marin. How was it affecting Marin too?

More significant, why wasn't it affecting Sam?

"Find the Book, Samara," Marin said.

"I can't leave you."

"You *need* to leave me. You need to find the Book. Otherwise, I'm going to die here the same as all of these Thelns."

Sam looked up, trying to figure out where they were in the city. She hadn't been to this section—not that she knew—but it was a merchant section. From here, she thought she could find Arrend, and there, she hoped that Alec's father still had the Book.

She patted Marin on the shoulder. "I will go as quickly as I can."

She ran off, assembling her canal staff. As she ran, she noticed warmth working through her, almost the same sort of warmth that she had felt when eating eel, but this was different. This seemed to radiate out from her. It was uncomfortable, and she could feel it becoming more painful.

Was this what was happening to Marin? Was this what was happening to the Thelns?

Why had it not affected her before now? Why did it not incapacitate her?

The only thing she could think of was that Alec had given her some of his blood. Maybe it protected her.

She jumped across a canal, racing toward the apothecary. She reached a section familiar to her and tore through it, and then she was in Arrend. Sam reached the apothecary and hurried inside. There was no sign of Aelus.

Why was the apothecary unlocked?

Sam looked around, searching for signs of him. She found him on the floor, lying near the back of his shop, sleeping soundly. A pot boiled on his hearth.

Sam shook him but to no avail. He did not come around.

Kyza!

She looked through his stack of books, but the Book they had taken from Helen's home was not here.

Could Alec have returned and taken it?

If so, it could be anywhere. She had no idea where Alec was.

She needed easar paper.

With easar paper, she might be able to counteract the effect of this, at least long enough for her to recuperate. She thought she might be able to delay what was happening to Marin and the Thelns.

Where could she get easar paper?

She thought about going to the university and thought about the supply that Alec had, but that was unreliable, especially if she didn't know how much he might have created.

There was one place she could go, but how much paper was there?

Sam raced toward the palace. Her body burned, her insides starting to feel as if a flame raced through her. If she didn't get there quickly, how much worse would this get?

As she ran, she focused on an augmentation. Healing. She focused on it, wanting it to tamp down the burning within her. The cold sensation came slowly, but it came, pushing back the pain.

Could she hold on to it?

She had to. Somehow, she had to.

Sam reached the canal separating the rest of the city

from the palace. She launched herself over, pushing off with her canal staff, and when she landed on the palace side, she hurried for the building. Already, her strength began to wane. She doubted she would be able to hold on to the augmentation much longer,. And if she couldn't, would she end up incapacitated the same way as Marin and the Thelns?

Sam staggered into the palace. She looked around. Where was everyone?

Upstairs. That's where she needed to go. There would be a supply of easar paper there if she could reach it.

Sam dragged herself up the stairs. Each step was difficult, but she pulled herself along until she reached the top and sprawled out on the landing. Sam got to her knees. She focused for a moment, thinking of an augmentation. Strength. If she could add strength, she should be able to reach the room she needed.

As before, when the augmentation rolled through her, it did so slowly.

Strength seeped back into her. Sam got to her feet and staggered along the hall. At the end of the hall, almost dropped to her knees, the augmentation fading, not nearly enough to counteract whatever was happening to her.

She focused on one step and then the next. She reached the room. They had been using Elaine's room to store the easar paper they had recovered. Where was it? Could there be enough left for her to counteract whatever it was that was happening?

She found the drawer in the desk. She pulled on it, but it was locked.

Sam blinked, trying to clear her head. Not only was weakness overtaking her, but pain tore through her.

She reached for her lock-pick set and pulled out of her cloak, thankful Irina hadn't stolen it from her. Everything had been in her cloak when it was returned to her, for which Sam was thankful.

She jammed the pick into the lock on the drawer. She had a key somewhere, she was certain of it, but right now, it didn't matter. All that mattered was somehow finding a way to get the drawer open and get to the easar paper.

Somehow, she managed to pick the lock.

Sam slipped but pulled the drawer open as she did. She reached inside, grabbing the stack of easar paper. When she pulled it out, she flipped through the pages, trying to figure out how much they had, and realized that there was a marking on each page.

She hadn't noticed that before. Had they taken the time to even look at the papers?

Marking meant that it had been used. The marking meant that it was part of the Book.

Sam didn't even know whether the paper could be reused.

She sank to the floor, holding the pages in her hands. She had failed. The Thelns would die from this. Sam and Marin would die. And Helen would succeed.

30

THE SCRIBE'S INTENT

The ground thundered, and it startled Sam awake. She had been sinking into nothingness, beginning to lose consciousness, and losing track of everything that was happening around her when the explosion struck.

It was nearby.

The walls of the palace shook, trembling with the force of the explosion.

What was it? What was it that she detected?

Sam dragged herself to her feet, still clutching the pages from the Book. She staggered out into the hallway and saw people running.

Where had they been before?

Sam reached the top of the stairs and slipped, tumbling down them. Miraculously, she managed to maintain her grip on the pages, so that when she landed, she fell and nearly struck her head.

She looked over. The door to the cells beneath the palace was open, and smoke drifted out of it.

Could the explosion have come from there?

Sam pushed off with her canal staff, climbing to her feet, and staggered down the hallway. She focused on augmentations, trying to draw out something, using whatever strength she had left. She was tired and didn't have much remaining, but there was enough for her to do this. The augmentation washed over her, and she took a deep breath, drawing in the strength from it.

Kyza, help me.

Sam reached the door and saw an opening where the wall had been, the same opening Helen had used to extract Lyasanna. The smoke was coming from there.

Sam climbed through the hole, and it quickly became dark—far too dark for her to see. The smell of smoke and another stink, one that she had noticed before, but only at the university, filled her nostrils.

The ground sloped downward, and Sam staggered, following the slope, slipping and beginning to tumble. She tried to catch herself and couldn't. She held tight to the pages of easar paper but lost track of her canal staff.

When she finally stopped rolling, she saw light.

It was a greenish sort of light in the distance and people moved around. Someone screamed. Other people moaned.

Sam got to her feet and started forward. Bodies were bent over, and she recognized a few of them as Bastan's men.

What would Bastan's men be doing here?

"Bastan?"

She coughed, and her voice didn't seem to carry very far.

There was movement near her. She turned and fell forward, and someone caught her. She looked over and saw a familiar face. "Kevin. What happened here?"

Kevin looked down at her. "Sam? I heard you were taken."

"I'm back. What happened?"

"The woman you've been searching for was doing something here. Bastan brought us here, and we were trying to stop her when there was an explosion."

An explosion.

"We think we stopped her—"

Sam shook her head. "You didn't stop her."

"How do you know? She didn't get to do anything before the explosion happened. Alec managed to stop—"

"Alec is here?"

"Alec is the one who brought us here. He figured out where this was taking place, and he stopped her. Whatever she was doing is over."

"It still happening. I feel it. Whatever she's doing is happening to *me*."

Kevin slipped an arm around her shoulders. "Oh gods, Sam."

"Where's Bastan? Where's Alec?"

Kevin started her forward, and they reached Bastan. He was crouching over someone lying on the ground, and it took her a moment to realize that it was Alec. Blood poured down the side of his face. Something must've struck him. But he was awake. Alive.

As Bastan sat Alec up, both of them turned to her, and they threw their arms around her at the same time.

"How are you—"

Sam cut Alec off. "Helen. I don't know what she's doing, but it's killing the Thelns. It's killing Kavers."

Alec and Bastan shared a look. "We stopped her."

"You didn't stop her. Whatever she was doing…" Sam swallowed. "I thought I could bring easar paper, but it's been used."

"What do you mean it's been used?" Alec asked.

"The easar paper. It was already used. I think she used it to create the Book—"

"Do you have it with you?" Alec asked.

Sam pulled the pages out, and Alec flipped through them. "We need to destroy these."

"Destroy? Alec, we need to use them to figure out a way to stop whatever she's done to us."

"I think whatever she's done is tied to the Book. She's using Kaver blood to augment it but drawing on a much more epic scale." Alec turned, taking the pages, and crawled over to one of the bluish-green flames erupting from the ground. He held one of the pages overtop the fire and looked at Sam as he did. The flame consumed it, but not quickly.

"Fire doesn't burn easar paper like this," Sam said. "Nothing does." They had been lucky when they had tried to counter the Book before and had destroyed the page, but that had taken considerable effort. If this was using multiple Kavers and their blood, it was possible that there would be no counter for it.

"There is something," Alec said. When Sam frowned at him, he shook his head. "I came across it by accident. When I was trying to make easar paper, we had been using different things, trying the different eel venoms until we realized that it was the svethwuud. But the venom counteracts the paper."

"Which venom?" Sam asked. She fell, unable to support herself anymore. Bastan grabbed for her, and she shook him off. It was easier to remain on the ground.

"The neutral venom."

"How does it work?"

"I don't know," Alec said. "All I know is that when it's mixed, both the tail venom and the oral venom, it seems to counteract the easar paper. It was an accidental discovery."

"We need that mix," Sam said.

"I... I don't have any. Gathering eels would take too much time." He turned to Bastan. "Might you have any of your supply left?"

"I might have some," Bastan said.

"It's not the eel meat that we need. It's the venom."

"I've stored the entire eel."

Pain surged through her. "If you're going to do it, it needs to be quick."

31

THE END OF THE BOOK

A lec stood at the edge of the central canal holding a vial of mixed eel venom. It had taken a while to harvest, but with the help of several of the junior and higher-level physickers, they had managed to acquire a significant quantity.

When he had smeared it on the easar paper, it had done nothing other than make the paper easier to burn. With the paper destroyed, he had hoped that Sam and the others would recover, but they hadn't. It meant the augmentation still held. It meant that the canvas was greater than easar paper.

Then again, he knew the canvas was the canal.

He'd hoped it would be more straightforward, and that Helen's stockpiling of paper meant she had used it for this purpose, but that hadn't been the key at all. And if not the paper...

That left only one possibility; he would have to try

pouring it into the water, though he had no idea if it would work.

What choice did they have?

And now, they stood at the edge of the canal, preparing to pour it into the water.

Sam moaned, no longer awake. Whatever augmentation and poisoning Helen attempted was killing her. Bastan had found Marin and the Thelns, and his people had gathered them up, moving them to a warehouse for safekeeping. If this failed, if they all died, what would happen then?

Alec motioned to the physickers on either side of him. They followed him to the water's edge and began to pour the eel venom into it.

Would this be enough to disrupt the augmentation? Would this be enough to change the canvas, as Mags would say?

The water had taken on a pinkish color. How much blood had Helen poured into it? How much had she used to poison the canals?

If everything went right, physickers all around the city would be pouring in a similar mixture into the water.

Now they had to wait.

Alec looked over, watching Sam.

The water began to slowly lose its pinkish color. Gradually, it started to become a dirty brown color, and then, even that faded. It became clearer, no longer dark, and he could see to the bottom.

He'd never been able to see to the bottom of the canal, and though he knew the water wasn't that deep, seeing it as clear as it was now was striking.

Someone coughed behind him, and he spun.

Sam sat up, rubbing her head. "Alec?"

"Kyza, Sam," he breathed, hurrying over to her. "How do you feel?"

"Tired. Beat up. But the fire is gone."

Alec sighed and looked around the canal. The physickers had succeeded. They had helped the Thelns. Most didn't even know them, but when he had explained that the entire city would be poisoned, they had been willing to listen and had been willing to attempt his treatment. It had surprised him how quickly they had responded. Then again, hadn't Alec proved himself time and again? He shouldn't have been surprised that they followed him so willingly.

"You should rest."

Sam stood and looked around. "I can't rest. Not yet. Tray needs me."

"You found him?"

"I did. Helen used the Book on him. We need to find it. I thought it might be at your father's apothecary. That's where I went first, thinking Helen was using the Book to do this, but I didn't find it there. And your father was out, collapsed."

"He's been testing sedatives, trying to find some way to prevent Helen from harming us."

"Where is the Book, if it's not at your father's apothecary?"

"I hid it at the university," Alec said.

"We need to go."

"Sam... you're not in any shape."

"I don't know how long Tray has. He was in rough

shape when I left, and it took the better part of two days to get here. Every delay means Tray is closer to dying. I can't lose my brother."

Alec helped Sam up. "Then I guess we have to go to the university."

They weaved through the streets. The city was quiet, and no guards prevented them from crossing between sections. By the time they reached the university, Alec was half expecting to find people congregated on the university or the palace section, but there was no one.

Had Helen's attack done more than he realized?

They hurried inside, with Alec guiding Sam, barely keeping her propped up. He did everything he could to support her, but he couldn't hold her much longer. He didn't have to. They had only a little farther to go. He supported Sam as he guided her up the steps to his room and paused when he entered.

He chided himself. This wasn't where he'd left the Book.

Before leaving, Alec grabbed a jar on his desk. It would have eel flesh, and maybe he would need it. Maybe Sam would need it.

When they turned around and left the room, Sam looked over at him. "Where are we going?"

"I forgot that I had moved it. I put it somewhere I thought it would be useful and less likely to be found and confiscated."

"Where?"

"In the library. In the masters' section."

They hurried along the hallway, and when they

reached the end, nearing the door to the library, Alec saw it was ajar.

Someone was here.

Who would have come with all the activity taking place in the city? Who would have been here when all of the physickers, including many of the students, had been taken out to support the canals?

"Sam, I don't think—"

The door opened, and Master Helen, Eckerd, and Lyasanna appeared.

"We stopped your plan," Alec said. "I don't know—"

Helen jumped forward, somehow still augmented. She grabbed him and threw him forward, where he hit the wall, almost collapsing.

"It's not over. Other things can be done. Once we solidify our control over the city again, there will be—"

Sam lunged at her.

Helen moved out of the way easily, and Sam stumbled, collapsing.

"Ah… It seems as if your Kaver has suffered."

"Leave her alone," Alec said, regaining his footing.

"A Kaver would be useful for what I have planned. If there are any remaining, I will see to it that they all participate in what we have in mind."

Alec reached into his pocket, curling his fingers around the jar of eel. All he wanted was a piece, maybe two so that he could get one to Sam.

"Alec?"

He turned to see Jalen standing at the end of the hall. "Jalen. It's…"

Lyasanna darted down the hall.

Alec pulled the jar out of his pocket and opened it, his heart sinking. It wasn't eel at all, but his father's sedative.

Helen stalked toward him. "I have had enough interference from you. I think that perhaps we will drain you the same as we have drained the others. I'm sure I can find a use for it."

As she reached for him, Alec did the only thing he could. He tossed the sedative at her face.

She jerked back, but not quickly enough.

Helen spat, glaring at him. "What is this? What have you…"

She sank to her knees.

The sedative was fast acting, and a significant amount went into her mouth when he tossed it at her. Even with an augmentation, she wouldn't be able to fight it for long.

Alec pushed himself off the wall and looked over at Eckerd. "You can decide. If you're going to continue to fight with Helen, I will see you face justice. If you would choose to heal, and if you would choose to serve the people of the city, I won't prevent that."

"The Thelns—"

"The Thelns were never the enemy. The enemy has always been Helen and the others like her. They are the reason the Thelns have attacked. It's a long story, but I will explain if you stand down."

Eckerd looked down at Helen lying motionless. She still breathed, but she was out.

"I was only trying to do what I thought necessary for the university."

"I'm well aware of what you were trying to do."

Eckerd went to his knees and bent his head. "Do what you must."

Alec ignored him and looked down the hall. Jalen was making his way toward him, dragging his sister by the arm. She was limp, and Alec frowned. "What did you do?"

"It seems that all of my training to pretend to be a Kaver has paid off. My dear sister always thought that I was a lazy Kaver, and I decided I needed to prove I was not lazy."

"Keep an eye on these two," he said to Jalen, pointing to Helen and Eckerd.

"What do you need to do?"

"The Book. I need to retrieve the Book."

Alec reached for Sam and helped her to her feet. She looked over at Helen and then Lyasanna. A satisfied smile came to her face.

He hurried into the library and into the masters' section. Alec moved a few books out of the way and reached for the hidden book. When he pulled it out, he set it on the large table in the center of the room.

"Now we have to destroy it," Alec said.

"Only the page that made Tray sick," Sam said from behind him.

"Not only that page. We need to destroy the whole Book. And any other volumes. These cannot exist."

Sam nodded. "How?"

"With the eel venom. And then with fire. And then, you and I will see if we can place an augmentation that will heal your brother."

EPILOGUE

"Are you sure it's safe?" Alec asked as they approached the forest.

"I don't know that it's safe, but the chamyn won't attack, not since we are coming with the Thelns."

Alec looked over and saw the line of Thelns in their boats. When they all reached the forest, the Thelns led the way through. Ralun had been silent, and for that, Alec was thankful. He wasn't sure what he would say to the man, not sure whether there was anything to say. Ralun had tried to kill them, and now, they were supposed to work together? Now, he was supposed to believe that Ralun was not a threat?

Were it not for Sam, he didn't know that he would.

With the city safe—and Bastan in control of keeping an eye on Helen and Lyasanna—they had ventured out of the city, planning to be gone only a short time. Sam didn't want to be gone long, but she had wanted to come to see whether their augmentation had helped Tray. From the way she described his condition, he could already have been lost.

"I never thought I would come this far," his father said behind him.

Alec looked back. "You don't have to."

"I owe it to your mother to visit."

"Do you think she knew?"

"I don't know what she knew. I know she was sent to gather information, and I know she missed her homeland, but she never spoke of it. She had been willing to stay for me. There is so much I wish I could've done differently, and I wish I could have helped her, saved her…"

"I know, Father."

As they made their way through the forest, Alec had a sense of the strange creatures watching them from the treetops, but they weren't attacked the way they had been before. They were allowed to pass directly through, and in little more than a day, they reached the edge of the forest, and from there, a sweeping plain spread out in front of them. It took two more days to reach the outskirts of the Theln territory, and when Asalar came into view, Alec could hardly believe it.

The city was beautiful. Sunlight glittered off the buildings, catching the amazing tile work placed along the sides of towers, creating a dazzling, almost sparkling effect. The entirety of the city amazed him. It was enormous, all made of a similar gleaming stone inset with colorful tiles, catching the sunlight in ways that even the palace in Verdholm did not. Ralun guided them down a side street on the outskirts of the city before heading toward what appeared to be a palace.

At the palace, Ralun separated from the rest of the Thelns. They disappeared, leaving the party from Verdholm with Ralun. Alec's father clapped him on the shoulder and turned to him. "I will leave you here."

"You will come, apothecary," Ralun said. "As will you, Kaver," he said looking at Marin.

Aelus and Marin both looked over at Ralun and then nodded.

They headed into a strange building with black and white tiles, and he guided them to the second story and into one room and then another.

Inside this room, the smell of sickness wafted out. Alec recognized it as the same stench as had emanated from the princess. It might have been a wasting, or it was something similar, either way, the malady used on Tray was awful.

Alec hurried over to Tray's bed. He was thinner than he'd last seen him, and his face had a slight sheen to it. He checked his pulse, finding it regular, and when he listened to his breathing, it was regular.

"He will recover."

Alec turned to see a dark-haired woman standing in the doorway. She was slightly taller than Sam, and her dark hair was pulled back behind her head, tied with a purple ribbon.

"You must have found the Book?"

Aelus stared at her. "Who are you?"

"Why?"

"You... You look so much like my wife."

The woman frowned. "Wife? What was her name?"

"Tesiya."

The woman's eyes widened slightly. "She was my sister."

"Sister? That would make you Irina."

The woman frowned and looked from Alec to his father. Could it be possible? Could Alec have found an aunt after all of this?

"Sam?"

Alec turned his attention over to Tray. He had opened his eyes, and Sam smoothed back his hair while he lay there, squeezing his hand. "I'm here, Tray."

Marin rushed over to his side and looked down at him. In that moment, Alec realized that though Tray's real mother had no interest in him, he had always had a mother. It was much the same way that Sam had always had a brother and father.

"How?"

"How? You big idiot, you know I was never going to give up on you."

Tray breathed out heavily. "Sam, you won't believe what I've been through."

She threw herself on him, hugging him, and Alec rested his hand on her shoulder while she sobbed, tears of relief for her brother pouring from her.

"Why don't we leave them for a moment," Irina said. "It seems this will be a family reunion for many of us."

Sam looked up at him. "It's okay. Go. Learn about your family. I'm going to stay here with mine for a little while longer."

"I don't like being apart from you."

"And I don't like being apart from you, and we won't have to be, not anymore."

He leaned in and kissed her on the mouth. Sam kissed him back, and he felt a cold washing through him, the same as he felt when they placed an augmentation.

He stepped back, smiling, and looked over to see his father watching him, uncertain what expression burned behind his eyes. Maybe it was irritation, maybe it was sadness at thinking about what they'd lost. Maybe it was uncertainty.

As they stepped out into the hall, his father clapped him on the shoulder. The expression had changed, replaced by a smile. "I'm proud of you, Alec. You are much more than I ever hoped you could become."

"I'm sorry I won't be the apothecary you wanted."

"No. Not an apothecary. You have forged your own path. You have become something more—much more." He glanced back to the door. "And you have found someone who makes you happy. That's all a father can hope for."

Alec looked back and saw Sam and Tray murmuring to each other. Marin watched them both, a satisfied smile on her face. It was the same one Alec's father had.

Their families were back together. After everything that had happened, their families had been reunited.

Alec smiled as he made his way down the strangely checkered hall after his father and his aunt. And now that everything had ended, he and Sam could finally learn what it meant for them to be something more than Kaver and Scribe.

They could be Alec and Sam.

With the thought, warmth washed over him, like when she'd kissed him, similar to an augmentation, though different. Energy surged through him, and for a moment, he thought that he imagined it. But it was too strong to ignore. Power surged through him.

Alec hesitated for a moment. Maybe there were a few things they still had to learn. And perhaps they weren't entirely done being Kaver and Scribe. But they still were Alec and Sam, and together, they could determine what that meant for them.

***

Looking for more great fantasy? Grab Dragon Bones: Book 1 of The Dragonwalker. The series is great for fantasy fans and I know you'll love it!

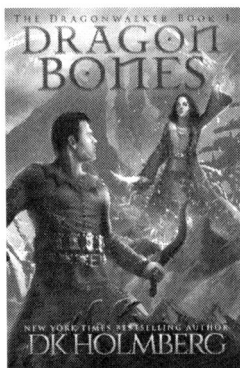

Dragons have been gone from the world for centuries, though their power remains.

A war fought a thousand years ago removed the destructive threat of dragons, allowing fire mages to use the magic stored within their bones to protect the empire for millennia. The empire has known a fragile peace, held together by that ancient magic.

Fes has always longed for stability. Raised within the slums of the empire, taught to steal and hurt others to make his way, when he's discovered by the emperor's chief fire mage, he's given a chance to use his particular gift for gathering lost dragon relics to become something more.

An encounter with a priest in possession of a dragon bone reveals the existence of a new power that threatens to return the long dead dragons to the world. Chased by the dangerous enemies, Fes travels into the bleak lands of the Dragon Plains before others can reach it. If he survives, what he discovers means the continued safety of the empire and a promise of wealth and freedom. If he fails, the deadly power of the dragons might return.

Yet, with a growing and unexplainable magic within him, it's the promise of understanding who he truly is that might be the most valuable, only it's the same power that leaves him with questions some within the empire don't want answered.

Dragon Bones is the exciting first book in an epic new fantasy series.

ALSO BY D.K. HOLMBERG

The Book of Maladies

Wasting

Broken

Poisoned

Tormina

Comatose

Amnesia

Exsanguinated

The Collector Chronicles

Shadow Hunted

Shadow Games

Shadow Trapped

The Shadow Accords

Shadow Blessed

Shadow Cursed

Shadow Born

Shadow Lost

Shadow Cross

Shadow Found

The Dark Ability

The Dark Ability

The Heartstone Blade

The Tower of Venass

Blood of the Watcher

The Shadowsteel Forge

The Guild Secret

Rise of the Elder

The Sighted Assassin

The Binders Game

The Forgotten

Assassin's End

The Teralin Sword

Soldier Son

Soldier Sword

Soldier Sworn

Soldier Saved

Soldier Scarred

Printed in Great Britain
by Amazon